Young Goonz

WELCOME TO FARROCK

A Novel By

Reality Way

Good2Go Publishing

CHAPTER ONE

It was July 2, 2010, in the middle of Hammels Projects located in the FarRockaway section of Queens. One of the Young Goonz who went by the name of D-Block was in the horseshoe, standing in the front of building 84-16. This particular area in the projects was called the horseshoe due to the shape of the parking lot that was in the dead center of the three buildings that surrounded it on Beach 84th Street. The three buildings were 84-12, 84-16, and 84-18.

Although it was damn near 90 degrees on a hot summer day, D-Block was going to the head with a fifth of Hennessey. If you could call chain smoking Newport's a chaser, then that's the only thing he had to cut the harsh taste of the cognac. D-Block was a little tipsy, but he was definitely on point, especially when he saw the unfamiliar hooptie come speeding through the horseshoe with windows too tinted to see inside the car. In one smooth motion, D-Block sat the bottle of Yak on the black gate with one hand while sliding the 45 P-90 Ruger off his hip with the other. The hooptie came to a complete stop right in the front of 84-16.

D-Block made a quick assessment of the area. There were numerous kids running around playing, and a few old nosey motherfuckers sitting around waiting to be an eyewitness to some shit. D-Block took the safety off using his right thumb, then shielded the gun behind his back, picked up his bottle, and took a swig, never taking his eyes off the car. The window rolled down slow and D-Block heard the familiar voice scream out, "Click Clack Boom." D-Block smiled, tucked his gun away, took another swig, and then walked to the car.

"Foe, what the fuck is you driving my nigga."

Without responding to D-Block's question, Foe replied, "Hurry up and get in. It's hotter than a motherfucker out in this bitch. All type of D's riding around the hood."

Foe was 27 years old compared to D-Block's 18 years of terrorism. D-Block's love for Foe was unconditional. Foe treated him as his equal, never like a little nigga or a soldier, and he trusted the young boy with his life. Foe had been through hell and back. He was young and wild until a few years back. He never felt it would be wise to try to dictate how the young boys go about things. He felt like that would just make them rebellious, like when older niggas tried to tell him shit. It wouldn't just go in one ear and out of the other; in fact, Foe would do the total opposite of what they would say on purpose, just to show motherfucker's that he had his own mind. What Foe would do when he wanted to school one of the Young Goonz, was dug into his past altercations, and tell one of the stories that coincided with the present situation, then pretty much let them make their own decisions. Foe dealt with D-Block a little differently because D-Block was much more level headed then the rest of the Young Goonz that was in his age bracket. The admiration he had for Foe allowed his young mind to be receptive to Foe's educated stories of street wisdom that he would be able to utilize in the future.

Foe pulled off smooth as soon as D-Block closed the passenger side door. The car bent to the right out of the horseshoe and headed down the beach. They got about twenty blocks away from Hammels Projects when Foe pulled the hooptie over. With his foot still on the brake, he put the car in reverse, clicked on the hazard lights, and took the steering wheel off.

"Give me the blicky," D-Block snatched the Ruger off his hip in a hurry then passed it to Foe. Foe placed the gun in the stash box, put the steering wheel back on, turned off the hazards, put the car back in drive, and then pulled off into traffic.

D-Block always studied Foe's calmness. It seemed as if he always had his thinking cap on even when he wasn't thinking; and he was always calm, never hyped up, not even when he was mad. Foe then poured the remainder of D-Block's Hennessey in the McDonald's cup that was in the middle console, looked through the rear-view mirror, and then tossed the empty bottle out of the window. That's when Foe decided to tell D-Block one his many true stories, "Years ago, I was in Baltimore City, I had just got finished grinding on Boarman and Granada, off of Garrison Blvd. I was on my way to my little low crib I had on Clifton and Fulton when the Narc's got behind me and pulled me over. I wasn't dirty and my bogus driving license held me down on many occasions so I was like fuck it. Long story short, I had some hoes in the car the night before and one of them bitches left an empty Corona bottle in the back seat. That gave them dick heads probable caused to search my shit because the bottle was in what they called, "In plain view." They searched me and found the forty two hundred dollars I had in my pockets, and straight violated. These dirty motherfuckers pulled out an ounce of weed that they had in their own stash and gave me a fucking ultimatum. 'We could take you downtown for possession of marijuana, pocket all this money, except let's say about a hundred dollars and let you spend the night in lock up, or we could just take half of it and let you enjoy the rest of your night.' I chose the latter."

D-Block was about to say something when Foe cut him off, "Oh did I mention that I was on the run for a body at the time." This was the third time D-Block heard this story, but he listened as if it was his first, knowing that each of Foe's stories had several different meanings and it was left up to him to figure out how applied to the present.

D-Block looked through his side-view mirror, saw that there wasn't a car behind them, grabbed the McDonald's cup, and tossed it out of the window.

Foe looked at D-Block with a confused look on his face and said, "I was gonna drink that."

Meanwhile, back in Hammels Projects, three of the Young Goonz was in 84-12 apt.1H, smoking grade A haze and drinking Ciroc. They had six prepaid cell phones sitting on the table that rang nonstop from the minute they were turned on. There was a dope phone, a weed phone, and a crack phone. Those three phones were for customers only. The other three phones were for the three different apartments that held the work. Two runners would sit on the bag (as they called it) at all times.

Whenever they got a call from apt.1H letting them know who wanted what and how much they wanted, one of the runners would stay and hold the spot down while the other one would go and make the sale, or, "Bust the head," as they called it. On this particular day, G-Pac, Thuggy Thug, and Gunz were in apartment 1H. G-Pac was dark skin, stocky, about five feet six inches tall, with one of them tough looking faces. He had, "Young Goonz" tatted on his back, with a slew of other tats that covered 60 percent of his body.

The thing that set G-Pac apart from the rest of the Young Goonz was his demeanor. You wouldn't even know that he existed until somebody violated his team. He had a reputation for walking straight up on a nigga and shooting him in broad daylight, with no regard for human life or the law. Reckless, but most definitely effective. Now Gunz, on the other hand, was the total opposite of G-Pac.

Gunz was a straight loud mouth, brown skin, slim, with dread locks. He stood about six feet tall and no matter what he was doing, he just had to pop shit about it. He popped shit when he rolled dice. He popped shit when he played basketball. He popped shit to the cops and anybody else that would piss him off. Bottom line was this... Gunz loved to pop shit.

Nobody really knew why his name was Gunz because one thing was for sure and two things were for certain; Gunz wasn't shooting nobody. He never even owned a gun. Not to say that the boy wasn't official because that was far from the truth. Don't get it twisted; he was quick to beat the breaks off a nigga in a heartbeat. He put a few so-called tough niggas on their back pockets. They would have to hold that ass whooping down, because not too many dudes wanted to take shit to another level with the Young Goonz.

Thuggy Thug...The name speaks for itself, straight fucking live wire. Thuggy Thug was five ten, brown skin, with a nice build for his size, but what stood out of the most about his physical complexion were his eyes. It's hard to explain the color of the nigga's eyes, but they were a hazel light brownish, greenish color. Everywhere he would go; some bullshit would pop off, which would result in him letting his hammer off. He did a three-year bid for a gun charge. The day he was released, he shot two dudes in two altercations. From that day on, everybody in the team knew son wasn't playing with a full deck. One night, Thuggy Thug relaxed his hair and put on a black trench coat. With a shotgun and a Mac 11 under the trench, he walked through the projects a few times then went back to the crib leaving niggas puzzled. He didn't have beef; he just got a rush out of the fact that niggas couldn't figure him out. Thuggy Thug would move around FarRock gripped up just waiting on a stupid nigga to act as if he didn't know how to act. Even though he was militant and quick to off a nigga on switch, he thought everything was funny... even tragic situations.

Gunz was getting tired of answering the phones, "Yo where the fuck Loc at. I already told this nigga about leaving me stuck in this hot ass crib on his shift."

"Be easy my G, I'm bout to hit his phone right now." G-Pac stated to Gunz as he dialed Loc's number. After letting the phone ring several times, Loc's voice mail picked up. G-Pac hung up because real niggas never leave messages. Well at least that what they were taught.

"His shit went to voice mail."

Thuggy Thug busted out laughing. "That nigga know why you calling...you should have blocked the number. That nigga probably somewhere drunk chasing pussy."

"He need to leave that bottle alone. Son don't function right when he gets tipsy. The runners in the stash crib was complaining that Loc be sending them to bust the wrong heads. Last night, this nigga sent one of the runners to make a dope sale to a crack head," stated Gunz.

Thuggy Thug thought that shit was hilarious and fell on the floor laughing, holding his stomach. He laughed so hard that G-Pac and Gunz started laughing too. Nobody could stay mad at Loc for too long.

He was family and his loyalty to his Young Goonz was impeccable...with his drunken ass.

Little did they know, Loc was far from drunk, and he had a good reason for not answering his phone. Loc was in the passenger seat of the rented Mazda with Jersey plates. He had on all black, and he was focused.

The driver of the Mazda was the one and only, P-Killa. They were parked across the street from the notorious

Edgemere Projects in FarRockaway, Queens. The sun had already fallen, and with July 4 only two days away, there were many fireworks going off in the area, which was perfect for P-Killa.

"Loc you ever heard of the term 'shock and awe'." Loc looked at P-Killa as if he were crazy and said, "Nah."

"Follow me on this my nigga...shock and awe were a military tactic used to catch the enemy off guard, which was the shock value of the shit. The level of violence used by these motherfuckers left people all over the world in awe."

Loc didn't give a fuck about no shock or no goddamn awe. All he wanted to do was blow the nigga Bless's head smooth off so he could have a drink or two...or three.

CHAPTER TWO

oe and D-Block were on their way back from Mott Avenue when Foe spotted the Mazda with the Jersey plates. He made a quick right turn on beach 54th Street. D-Block's alertness caused him to sit up in his seat and ask Foe. "Where you going?"

Foe replied as calm as a killa. "Crazy...you coming?"

D-Block laughed at Foe's joke, but he still wanted to know why the fuck were they in Edgemere Projects.

"It's like this my nigga, remember that shit that popped off in Sing Sing when Crazy Mone got stabbed."

"Yeah, that was like a year ago, right." D-Block asked. "Yeah, something like that...well check it, the nigga that poked son came home yesterday. His name is Bless; you wouldn't know him. You were like ten years old when that nigga went to jail."

"Why he hit Crazy Mone...some jail shit."

"Nail, Crazy Mone was in the yard biggin up the Young Goonz, you know repping his team like any real nigga would do, not knowing that the nigga Bless was holding a personal vendetta against me, and the rest of the Young Goonz.

"For what?"

"When Bless was home, his right-hand man was the nigga Leeky. I heard Leeky was taking care of Bless while he was up north too." It all started to make sense now to D-Block.

Reality Way

There was a rumor in FarRock that Foe was the one who laid Leeky down over a childhood beef that started when they were in public school.

As crazy as that shit sound, but that's what the rumor was. Nobody knew whether the shit was true or not, not even D-Block. D-Block thought about asking Foe did he slump the nigga, but he knew Foe would start telling him a story that didn't have shit to do with his question. So instead, he pulled his baseball gloves out his pocket and asked, "So where the nigga Bless at?"

"Be easy." As he parked the hooptie behind the building that was numbered 54-49 on Almeda Street. Foe leaned his seat back to stretch his long legs out in the crammed up hoop ride.

"We had the line on this lame ever since he came home yesterday, so now we just gonna sit here and lay on him...your dig."

Foe dug the half of blunt of Cush out of the ashtray and sparked it. He thought that it would be a good time to school D-Block on how to move in the pen. Midway through the conversation, Bless walked out of the building talking on a cell phone.

Foe wanted to jump out and leave the nigga right there but sticking to the script always guaranteed success. So instead, he reached under his seat and pulled out of the pre-paid Boost Mobile.

"General I salute you...I put a hole in any nigga tryna shoot you...it ain't nothing cause loyalty is what I'm used to... and what I won't do, I have one of my troops do...niggas uh kill you."

P-Killa was singing along to his G-Unit, Beg For Mercy classic C.D. "Yo Loc. This shit right here is straight fucking murder music. Every time I gotta slump a nigga; I listen to this C.D.

Loc knew that P-Killa was crazy as fuck, so he just nodded his head as if he agreed with what P-Killa just said. That's when they heard the phone chirp. P-Killa turned the music down and told Loc, "Get ready."

P-Killa answered the phone, putting it on speaker without saying a word.

The familiar voice on the other end only gave a description, "White fitted cap, white Tiblack shorts, black and white Jordans, coming your way."

Loc reached in the back seat and grabbed the Mossberg pump that P-Killa loaded with deer slugs earlier that day.

Loc saw Bless approaching the Mazda, at first he was going to jump out and blow the nigga head off his shoulders, face to face, but changed his mind quick when saw that Bless had his head down looking at his phone or sending somebody a text message. Loc thought it would be better to let Bless pass the Mazda, then creep up on him from behind, the same way the lame did Crazy Mone.

"When I get out, pull off, make the right on the next block, I'll meet you over there...oh yeah, keep the car running."

Foe took the Sim card out of the Boost Mobile, melted it with a lighter, tossed it out of the window then pulled off, "Put your seat belt on my nigga."

They made it around the corner just in time to see the masked man with the hoodie on, gripping the pump shotgun.

Foe tapped D-Block, pointed at Loc, and said, "Watch this."

Loc jogged right up behind Bless. Once he was a good two feet behind him, he raised the pump, using both hands. Loc took about five steps without Bless even knowing that the shadow of death was on his heels. "BOOOM," Loc squeezed the trigger and Bless head exploded like something out of a video game.

It took the bystanders a few seconds to realize that the BOOM they heard wasn't fireworks.

D-Block didn't know exactly who the mask man was, but he knew that he was one of the Young Goonz.

"That shit looked crazy...whoever did that is bout that mess."

Foe smiled knowing that D-Block was fishing, he didn't say a word, and Foe just kept driving.

Loc jumped in the Mazda and P-Killa pulled off smoother than a baby's ass. They rode in silence all the way to the liquor store on Beach 25th Street. When they walked inside, Loc came alive, he grabbed the biggest bottle of Hennessy in the store and kissed it.

This nigga was a certified alcoholic at sixteen years old. When they walked out of the liquor store, Loc's heart skipped a beat. The Mazda with the Jersey plates was gone with the mask, glove, and the shotty still in it. Right before Loc got to say a word, P-Killa asked him, "Why you looking like you lost your best friend?" P-Killa hit a button on his key chain and a brand new 745I chirped, with the lights blinking off and on.

That was P-Killa at his best. He was always a step ahead of his own self. He always told people that the P in his name stood for, "Proper planning prevents piss poor performance."

They got in the spotless BMW, cracked the bottle, poured themselves a nice shot of Yak and held the cups up as P-Killa spoke with his eyes closed.

"Rest in poop to all my dead enemies...whether I did it or not...y'all just memories."

P-Killa opened his eyes to catch Loc pouring his second cup of Yak. Loc smiled and said, "What." P-Killa shook his head, threw back his cup of Yak, and pulled off thinking, "This nigga really need some help."

The buzz about Bless cold-blooded murder died down less than two months later. C-Dollars was in a recording studio in St. Alban Queens, finishing up on his mix tape.

"FarRock stand the fuck up. It's your boy C-Dollars...shout it out to all my Young Goonz... West drop that beat...yo yo, yo, yo...I ride in my Benz. I stride in my Prada's. The chain got these lame ass dames screaming, "Holla." C-Dollars wasn't the best rapper in the team, but his swag was always on a million. He had an aura of confidence and anybody who was somebody knew he had much potential just by being in his presence for five minutes or more.

C-Dollars was always thinking about the bigger picture. He had six brothers and two sisters; He was the oldest at 25 years old. He wanted to move them out of the mean streets of FarRockaway before it was too late. Whenever he was out of town or vacationing somewhere, if somebody was to ask him what FarRockaway was as if he would always say the same thing, "It's the only place in the world where opportunity never knocks."

He was a networking genius. He would never leave the house without his two phones, his iPad, and his BlackBerry. Some people use the term, "Communication is a must." Well to him, it was the key to success.

After laying down his vocals, C-Dollars stepped out of the soundproof booth, checking his phones for any missed calls. Just as he began to scroll down, one of the phones started to ring with one of his songs as the ring tone, "My neck glow. My wrist glow. I like to welcome y'all to the light show."

When he saw that it was Whitey calling, he knew it was

time to 'talk sports'.

Whitey was the dope connect that Foe met up north in Clinton Correctional Facility. Foe introduced Whitey to the team a few years back and he'd been nothing but loyal and consistent from day one.

The Feds were so good at deciphering phone conversations that anybody that was still fucking with them hot ass phones had to come up with his own unique way to do business over the phone. Whitey once told Foe, "The Feds had been tapping phones ever since Malcolm X went to the Holy City of Mecca." Whitey was a sports fanatic, so what he and C-Dollars came up with was official.

The day of the re-up, they would watch an hour of sports center on ESPN, when it was time to phone bang, they would actually be talking sports and highlights that occurred a day before.

The conversation itself was a smoke screen. It was the unspoken words that meant business. It went like this. Since Whitey was calling at exactly five o'clock, he was letting C-Dollars know that the half of key of dope was ready. Five o'clock was equivalent to 500 grams.

The location of the drop off was determined by how long the conversation lasted as they talked sports. It was five different drop off locations and each minute had its own location. On this day, the conversation lasted exactly three minutes, which meant the dope would be dropped off in Brooklyn.

After the call ended, C-Dollars kicked it with West for a few minutes, paid for the studio time, then left.

As C-Dollars was walking toward his car, an old white lady who was walking her sharpei looked at the young boy draped in diamonds, getting inside the Mercedes Benz with a look of disgust and disbelief.

C-Dollars rolled the window down, stuck his head out of the window, and said to the old bitch, "Yeah...I dropped out of school, but I went to my E-Class. Then he pulled off fast in his brand new E-Coupe laughing his ass off.

It was late August; the summer was ending so Jiggy Jack decided to throw a big barbecue in Hammels projects big park for the Young Goonz. Everything Jiggy Jack did; he made an event out of it. There was a basketball tournament going on with eight different teams from all over FarRock. Each team had its own color jersey, which for some strange reason always made dudes in the hood play harder.

D.J. Slimey was playing all the hottest tracks that were out, plus he played all off the Young Goonz music off their multiple mix tapes. The song that got the whole park pumped up was the hood anthem called, "GO HAMMELS." They had six big grills blazing with all types of food; they had a grill for the no meat eaters, a grill for the no pork eaters, and a grill for other alternatives. There were beverages and snacks for the kids. Alcohol and weed for the adults. It was enough food to feed a village. Jiggy Jack had a good heart and loved to see everybody enjoying themselves. Money was never an issue, so he paid for everything himself. He had a thousand Young Goonz T-shirts made up in a variety of colors and sizes, which was being handed to everybody that entered the park. The hood loved free shit so some people were doubling up.

females from Hammels were out there in abundance. Half dressed with their hair done, and their nails did. They knew it would be much competition with chicks coming from all the other projects in FarRock, so they had to represent for their hood. Hammels' chicks were real territorial and would cut a bitch quick for trying to fuck the Young Goon that they were fucking. The only problem with that was the majority of FarRock chicks were tough and if they wanted to fuck a nigga, they would fuck the nigga. Jiggy Jack was more worried about the chicks acting up then anything. He knew that niggas knew better then to disrespect his function. He wasn't worried about that at all.

On the other side of the park was where the gambling was going down. They had a poker table, a black jack table, and a huge circle rolling dice. At the dice game, one of the Young Goonz name Young Bash had the bank and he was talking his shit.

"All down is a bizzet, everything good, fifty and better you broke ass niggas, you super fly bum ass niggas...oh, and if you play with my cash, Thuggy Thug gon shoot yo ass."

Everybody bursted out laughing. Young Bash was a funny motherfucker; the boy had jokes for days. He got his money up, then moved out of Hammels where he was born and raised. He didn't move to the suburbs though, this nigga move from one hood to another. It was ten times better than FarRock, but it was still the hood. He moved to Sheepshead Bay Projects in Brooklyn, which turned out to be less violent, and way more money than FarRock. I mean way more money!

Young Bash was a flashy motherfucker, too. He had a custom-made chain that was filled with diamonds. The pendant was a horseshoe with 84th side in the middle of it, repping his hood all the way out in Brooklyn.

Young Bash shook the three dice in his palm and started talking to the dice, "Daddy don't need no shoes. I got a hundred pair of them...Daddy don't need no car. I just copped a Benz. Daddy don't need shit. Daddy just wanna win...get em' bitches."

All three dice landed on four as soon as they hit the ground. Young Bash screamed, "Trips...nobody move, nobody get murked...I done killed for less."

Back on the other side of the park, Jiggy Jack saw Foe, P-Killa, Slimo, Looch and Nitty engaged in what appeared to be a deep conversation. He walked over and joined in.

"All I'm saying is this. We need to start investing some of this money into our music. We created a nice little buzz online and through the DVD's, but we need to start doing shows.

Young Goonz

"Not like we would be doing it for the bread, we just need more exposure. I'm telling y'all niggas is feeling our shit, and not just in FarRock. Everywhere I go; they screaming Young Goonz is hot," said C-Dollars.

Looch was one of the major money funders in the Young Goonz camp, so niggas listened when he talked.

"Man fuck that music shit, it's not lucrative anymore. The internet and the major labels fucked that whole game up. Besides, we got more money and assets then the average rapper. Next thing you know, the Feds will be all in our business.

Looch was one of them fly, yellow niggas that was hood but presented himself with a touch of class...and he used to be a shooter, so he was respected in FarRock.

"It's deeper than music and money. We need to create a brand, something that could withstand the next 20 years of ups and downs.

a failing economy, something our kids could eat off of so they don't have to come up the way we did," said Slimo, who was already retired from the street life? He was one of the smart ones that actually got in and got out before it was too late.

Nitty jumped right in, "Whatever it is I wanna be in charge of the management. I got my associates degree for that shit. I'll come with the same approach that I come within these streets. Y'all know I'm on my Block Bully shit. Matter of fact, that's what we gonna call it, Block Bully Management." Nitty was one of the Young Goonz, who everybody had love for; he even made the fiends love him when he was a street hustler.

The conversation was interrupted by a commotion at the dice game. Jiggy jack ran across the park to find Gunz beefing with some niggas from Redfern. Jiggy Jack pulled Gunz to the side and said, "Don't start no dumb shit out here with all these kids running around."

"I don't start shit. I finish shit."

"Listen to me my nigga, don't make me look bad for trying

to do good...aight." Gunz didn't respond to Jiggy Jack's last comment. He just span off, and walked back to the dice game.

Luxury cars were lined up and down Rockaway Beach Blvd. so the only thing that made the LS460 stand out was the fact that it jumped the curb and was riding through the park real slow. Nobody was familiar with the Lexus, so everything came to an abrupt stop. D.J. Slimey cut the music off. Two of the Young Goonz Scooby and Messhall walked toward the Lex without pulling out of the guns they had concealed under their shirts.

Just as they reached the Lexus, all four doors popped open. Three bitches that looked like they just came from a "Straight Stuntin" photo shoot stepped out of the car accompanied by the pimp of the hood, Shake Don.

Scooby and Messhall made a quick u-turn and headed back to the dice game. D.J. Slimey put on GO HAMMELS and the whole park went crazy.

"GO-GO-GO-GO HAMMELS...WE ABOUT TO TAKE THE HOOD BACK TO 88 SUMMER. WHERE NIGGAS GOT STOMPED EVEN IF THEY AIN'T FRONTIN."

Foe was standing on the top of a bench doing his two-step with a bottle of Hennessey in one hand, while waving a Young Goonz T-shirt in his other hand.

Shake the Don pointed to Foe in acknowledgement. Foe popped his collar and gave Shake the Don the thumbs up for his spectacular entrance. Foe favorite part of the GO HAMMELS song came up and he sang with it, "EVERYBODY IN HAMMELS. EVERY LAST CREW. WE HAD HOLES IN OUR SOULS-WE WERE RAISED IN THE SHOE."

Jiggy Jack hired a camera crew to catch all the festivities of the day. Knowing that one day, it would play a small part in his marketing scheme.

Later that night, the sun went down and all the kids were out of the park by then. The neighbors started calling the cops complaining about the music and the noise that the rowdy crowd was making. The pigs from the 100-precinct came and shut shit down...you know, typical hood shit!

CHAPTER THREE

The biggest most ruthless crew that dominated and regulated the Rockaway area was the, "Young Black Mafia," otherwise known as the YBM crew. The YBM crew had a real strong following throughout the whole FarRock. There were four O.G's that each ran their own separate crew of YBM soldiers.

O.G. Shorty-D ran the YBM soldiers in Hammels Projects. O.G. Sunny ran the YBM soldiers in the Sixties (side blocks) and 71-15. O.G. Death Row ran all the YBM soldiers in Edgemere Projects, Ocean Village Houses, and the 40 Projects (the one in FarRock) While O.G. Duke ran his YBM soldiers in Redfern Projects, and the whole Mott Avenue area.

The O.G.'s tried to keep their crews in order as best as they could, but when you got hundreds of different dudes all down with one movement, you're always going to have thousands of different personalities to deal with.

The O.G's never expected that their movement would spread like wild fire, but when you got so many fatherless sons and motherless daughters running around the hood, it's not shocking when they're flock to the closest social group in their immediate circumference and call them family. The YBM crew was ringing bells all throughout the five boroughs in New

York City, especially in the prison system. The YBM crew was so violent and out of control that the police had to start parking, the big N.Y.P.D. buses in every projects and side block in FarRock, not necessarily to prevent crimes from happening, but to be the first responders when a crime did happen.

The cops these days were a little smarter than back in the days. They knew that this new generation of young niggas wer straight fucking crazy. Freeze meant run, and drop the gun meant shoot. Plus, they were to under paid to be out there risking their lives. The super cop days were over.

FarRockaway was a section in Queens that was considered, "The worst part of Queens." Back in the early eighties, the city shut down the only good thing that FarRock had to offer, which was Rockaway Playland Amusement Park. To make matters worse, somewhere in the early nineties, Surfside Movie Theater was also closed down, which was the only movie theater in FarRock.

That left the youth in the middle of the projects in the crack era. The school system was battered and their parents were addicts. The only thing left was the magnificent beach. "Not." The beach was horrific in the hood. From Beach 90th Street all the way down to about Beach 15th Street was fucked up. Broken bottles in the sand, dope needles in the water, and big ass holes in the Boardwalk. Now from Beach 90th Street to about Beach 120th Street where the white people lived was beautiful. It was blatant that nobody gave a fuck about the conditions of the hood.

The O.G's were having a sit down at the Chinese buffet on Crossbay Blvd. Death Row called the meeting to address some of the issues that were going on within each of the YBM camps.

"We all know why we're here so let's cut to the chase fellas. Duke, your re-up dropped to an all-time low this quarter. Sunny, you doing good on them side blocks, but you spending more money on bail and lawyer fees then a motherfucker. Shorty-D, you sit on your work so long that you're always two re-ups behind. So let's figure this shit out quick, so we could get back to our wonderful lives...oh, and don't pardon the sarcasm.

Death Row was the brains behind the YBM finances and there was no better way to describe his physical appearance then he looked exactly like Tony Yayo from G-Unit.

Duke was the first to speak up, "Motherfuckers complaining about the product. The local fiends are copping but all the outside love is gone. Whatever they got on Gateway and Central Ave is killing my whole flow...you heard." Duke was one of them tall pretty boy niggas with 360 waves, but had the attitude of an ugly nigga. "We need to holla at my man Chico from the Bronx and get some better work. He's a little expensive, but I'll pay for quality and consistency anytime...I need my Sedahurst and Long Beach customers back, then shit can get back to normal."

Sunny was the next one to speak, "My youngens is off the fucking meat rack. When they're on the block grinding everything is good, but soon as their shifts are over...it's like they black out on some wild shit. I can't leave em' in the pen to teach them a lesson, because that'll hurt the block...feel what I'm saying." Sunny was a fat black crazy nigga and violence was his middle name. So his followers were just a reflection of him.

Shorty-D was aggravated and it came out when he spoke, "Y'all niggas already know. I ain't really with all that slaughtering the block shit. I'mma stick up kid and my crew follows my lead. Plus, the Young Goon niggas got that shit on lockdown on my end. They're taking everything from Beach 81st Street, all the way down to 125th Street. The fiends don't even walk through the hood.

Them niggas make home deliveries...Death Row, you told me you had some shit lined up, so I've been waiting on that shit."

Shorty-D was about five foot three, a hundred and twenty pounds soaking wet, light skin with long cornbraids. He was half-Spanish, so he had that good hair that bitches loved to braid.

"We ain't the only ones with issues. I'm still trying to figure out how Bless got smoked right on the five four and ain't nobody see or know shit. That makes us look bad as a whole." Duke said in way to piss Death Row off.

"Listen, whoever killed my nigga will be dealt with. The streets talk, and I'm always listening." Death row responded without losing his cool. "Did Bless have drama with anybody you could think of?" Sunny questioned.

Death Row looked up to the left side of his brain and shook his head. "Son was only home one day after doing eight years, so I don't know if that was an old beef he had or what, we didn't even get a chance to kick it."

"Yo Shorty-D, let me find out them Young Goon niggas got you and your team down there starving in Hammels." Sunny said antagonizing Shorty-D.

"Shorty-D never starves...that's for one, for two, I keep my skat in a nigga face when it's feeding time."

"Well, rob one of them Young Goon niggas to come up with your portion of the re-up." Duke joked, causing everybody to laugh, even Shorty-D.

"Nah...I fucks with a few of them niggas, that's why I don't violate the ones I don't like. Plus, we all know the saying; never fuck with the nigga that don't fuck with nobody."

Death Row was getting tired of the sap rap, "Aight, this what we gonna do. First, we gonna holla at Duke's man Chico to see if we could get some better twerk. Sunny, send some of them knuckle heads to Central Ave and Gateway to make it hot, at least the bail money and lawyer fees could be spent for the cause." "With all due respect, the niggas on Gateway and Central ain't no lames, they laying shit down hard body." Duke warned. "Just make it hot enough to slow down their cash flow so Duke could get the rest of his work off...yeah there might be casualties, but the end will justify the means." Death Row stated to Sunny.

Death Row turned to Shorty-D, "I got the scoop on three gambling spots in Binghamton, New York. I got people on the inside. They gonna holla at me on the next big night so be ready to roll when I holla...and just for the record, FUCK THE YOUNG GOONZ, nobody stops the YOUNG BLACK MAFIA from eating."

About a week after the YBM sit down, Sunny was on his block in the Sixties giving orders to two of his young shooters,

"Look alive my niggas, cause its going down tonight. Remember, I want this shit done Cali style. Do not get out that motherfucking car. When ya'll pull up on Gateway more than likely they're gonna run up on the car thinking ya'll fiends. Ya'll gonna have to get up out that bitch with the quickness, cause if them niggas box ya'll in the middle of that block...it's a wrap, understand."

Both young shooters nodded their heads and smiled. "Oh yeah, don't forget to put these on." Sunny tossed each of them a black hooded sweatshirt that had Young Goonz imprinted on the front in bold letters. Right before Sunny walked off, he told them, rather warned them; "Don't fuck this up."

Sunny figured that If he could start a war between the Young Goonz and the Gateway crew, not only would Duke get off his work, but Maybe Shorty-D could catch up to the re-up while them niggas would be preoccupied with the beef.

Young Goonz

Sunny had to keep his little scheme to himself, knowing that if he told the rest of the O.G's what his intentions were, shit would get all political and probably get vetoed.

Sunny hated the politics; he was in love with violence and deception. He honestly felt that it was the American way. In fact, that's how he got his position of power with the Young Black Mafia. So he felt there was no need to deter from what was so successful in the past.

Gateway was run by an official nigga that went by the name of Blue Guns; everybody called him B.G. for short. B.G. did a ten-year bid for a body when he was sixteen years old. The prison life made him militant and direct. At times, he appeared to be a little stern. Some people considered him burnt out, which was far from the truth. B.G. just lived inside his head. The one thing that nobody could deny was the fact that he was a hustler.

B.G. didn't have family or a girlfriend to do his bid with him. He quickly learned in the pen that anything that held value could be turned into money. When his ten-year stint was up, he was introduced to the dope game and exceeded all expectations. He put together a team of the most loyal, toughest, young heartless motherfuckers he could find in Gateway, and he never looked back every since.

He ran a smooth operation and instilled in his grinders that the customers were to be treated like family, not fiends.

"Fuck the world...Love the customer," was his slogan.

It was a regular night like any other night. The money was pouring in as usual. B.G. just so happened to be on the block this night, just over seeing things. Cars were coming in and out of the block at a rapid speed, fiends were walking up from every direction, copping and keeping it moving.

B.G. was talking to one of his people and paid no mine to the silver 1995 Acura Legend that drove pass him real slow and came to a stop in the middle of the block. Two little niggas from the Gateway crew ran up to the car to see what they were trying to cop. That's when all hell broke loose. Automatic gunfire erupted on the block. B.G. first reaction was to get low because the shots sounded too close, he didn't know if somebody was shooting at him or what. He looked up to see flashes coming from the silver Acura, as he tried to get behind a parked car.

By the time, the Gateway boys could respond, it was too late. The silver Acura sped off and turned the corner fast. B.G. and a few of his soldiers ran to the street where the two young boys laid. B.G. noticed that the first little nigga was already dead. Shorty had a black hole in his forehead that didn't even start to bleed yet, and his chest was spilling blood on the concrete. It hurt his heart to see shorty laid out like that in the middle of the street. He was only fourteen years old, but he looked even younger now that he was lifeless.

B.G. ran over to the other little nigga who was still alive. Shorty was hit in his chest and shoulder, but he was fighting death to the death.

"Hold on lil' man. The ambulance is on the way." B.G. said as he placed his hand over the young boy's hand.

"I'm good...I'mma...kill them...niggas." He said in between taking sips of air. Who was it? Who shot you?"

"Young...Goonz from...Ham...mels."

"Aight stop talking lil' man, just try to breathe." B.G said as the cops came swarming the block with their sirens blaring.

B.G. watched Gateway turn into a crime scene in a matter of minutes. He summoned his closest comrades inside one of their cribs on the block. Everybody in the crib was in frenzy mode, asking all types of unanswered questions. B.G. told everybody to sit down and shut the fuck up.

"I know who did it." His comment caused a murmur in the room, followed by a bunch of who's. "It was them Young Goon boys."

"Where? From Hammels?" Asked one of the Gateway niggas. "No from fucking Mars, what other Young Goonz you know nigga." B.G. spazzed. The room went silent; everybody there had the same look of confusion on their faces. "Can anybody tell me why the fuck them bitch ass niggas came down here and aired my fucking block out." Everybody shook their heads no. "So nobody in this room had a run-in with any of them clowns." After getting the same response, somebody banged on the door, startling a few of them out of their deep thoughts.

B.G. walked to the door snatching it open with so much force that the door almost came off the hedges. He could be a little intimidating when he was mad. B.G. was six two, two hundred and twenty pounds all muscle, blue black, with a bid head. When B.G. saw that it was his right-hand man Jah at the door he relaxed and embraced him with a dap and a homeboy hug.

Jah whispered in B.G.'s ear, "Lil' man gonna make it. The bullets went in and out." Jah was B.G.'s other half. If B.G. was only playing with a half of deck, then Jah was playing with the other half. Jah grew up in six hundred schools and group homes, nothing or nobody ever loved him except B.G, so it was loyalty over royalty until his casket closed.

Listen, it's on sight with all of them bitches, straight fucking like that." B.G. said to the room full of warriors.

"On sight with who." Jah asked.

"Them Young Goon niggas from Hammels. They the ones who did that bird shit.'

Jah was crazy, but he wasn't no dummy. He had a funny look on his face when he asked B.G. "Young Goonz...you sure?"

B.G. didn't answer Jah's question. He just continued to talk to his shooters. Jah sat down and started brainstorming. Even though his first reaction mentally was something didn't sound right, he said, "That nigga Looch fuck with that skinny bitch wit' the fat ass right up the block on six Gibson Street. That CLS500 be parked over there all the time...And you know what else I was thinking, the nigga P-Killa be outta town lying niggas down, taking over their blocks. It ain't no secret that we getting crazy paper down here, maybe them niggas want our block."

"Well I ain't no motherfucking outta town nigga and this ain't no motherfucking outta town blocks. We gonna show these bitches who they fucking wit." B.G. said, so pumped up that spit was flying out of his mouth.

CHAPTER FOUR

Everything was going smooth in Hammels Projects so there was no need for some of the Young Goonz to be in the hood. Some niggas were stuck in FarRock for the rest of their lives, while others were shakers and movers, no matter where they went, they had enough know how to adapt to their environment and still get money without offending the local natives.

Foe was down stairs into a basement on the Eastside of Detroit city, learning how to grow grade A Haze. Foe had nothing but love for the city of Detroit. He felt that it was the only city he had ever been to that wasn't governed by the police. Detroit was nothing like New York with its heavy police presence.

Foe had his chocolate girl wonder Babe with him. Babe was bad as hell, five eight, a hundred and fifty pounds solid, with the dreamiest eyes Foe ever stared into. Babe didn't have a fat ass, but them titties were crazy, and the way she rode the dick had Foe a little fucked up.

Babe drove a white H2 Hummer and demanded attention no matter where she went. She played a few major dudes out of their paper but when it came to Foe, she couldn't control nothing with him, which was a major turn on to her. She was tired of walking over weak men her whole life. Babe needed a real man, like Foe.

The fact that Foe was from New York was one thing, but Babe was feeling hisself in the crib aura, that was something else. Every time she lay up with him. She felt like this is what living was supposed to feel like. One night, they went to the

Zoo Bar together to see Young Jeezy perform. To Babe, it felt like every bitch in the club was all in Foe's face. His swag made him so god damn approachable that even the sexy bartender slipped him her number on a napkin.

Babe had never been a hater, coming from the land of the players. She knew exactly how niggas gave it up, but Foe had her off her game and she loved it. That same night she decided that Foe was cut from a different cloth, and he deserved to be treated like it.

Babe was sitting on Foe's lap talking to her bestie Peaches on the phone.

"Bitch I ain't going to no fuck ass club...my Daddy is in town. I'm sitting on top of the world right now, hoe."

Whatever Peaches said caused Babe to respond, "If you knew what it was hitting fo yo ass wouldn't be talking jive." A few seconds passed and Babe said, "I don't know, let me ask him...Daddy, Peaches said, "Do you wanna find out why they call her Peaches and cream."

"Tell her I said, "Do she wanna find out why they call me Mr. Minaj." Babe put her hand in her Vicky secrets and started talking nasty as fuck to Peaches in the sexiest voice.

"You hungry bitch...hum? You want something to eat and drink...hum? Thirty minutes later Peaches was ringing the doorbell. "Goddamn," was all Foe could say when he opened the door and saw Peaches standing there wearing a peach-colored body suit with open toe shoes on.

Peaches body was un-fuckin-believable. She was five four, a hundred and thirty five pounds, all ass and titties, caramel complexion, with that look that oozed of good sex.

What's in the bag?" Foe asked. "Oh these, these are the peaches." "Okay, so where the cream at?"

Peaches walked up to Foe, grabbed his dick through his Roca Wear sweat pants and said, "The cream is in here, and I'm gon' get it baby."

"You a nasty lil' bitch, ain't you?"

Babe stepped out of the bathroom wrapped in a towel, fresh out of the bathtub and said, "You ain't see nothing yet, Daddy. Wait till she warm them peaches up." Foe grabbed the Hennessey out of the cabinet, two six-packs of Coronas out of the fridge and said, "It's gonna be a long night." Peaches walked over to the stove to warm up the can of peaches, looked at Babe, winked her eye, and said, "I hope so."

While Foe was in The D, Jiggy Jack, P-Killa, and Dot was in Toledo, Ohio sitting in a trap house having a deep conversation about wars and politics. P-Killa was convinced that the government's only concern was gold and land.

Jiggy Jack felt it was all about power and control, while Dot felt it was a secret society and we would never know the half. Barack Obama had these niggas trying to understand what the fuck been going on in America for the past nine years with the Bush administration.

Once a nigga in the hood thought he figured some shit out, he couldn't wait to break it down to anybody that'll listen. Jiggy Jack excused himself from the conversation to check on some of the Young Goonz. First, he called C-Dollars, Looch, and Slimo, who at the time was down in Richmond Virginia having drinks in an after hour spot.

"What's really good my nigga?" Jiggy Jack asked Slimo.

"Everything...we down here in VA., lamping, what's good with you?"

"Who me, you already know. I'm Gucci. Where Looch and C-Dollars at?"

"Them niggas got a bitch sandwiched on the dance floor right now." "Aight, just checking in on the home team." "As long as Whitey keep us smiling, feel me."

"Okay okay, ya'll niggas keep ya'll heads up and eyes open."

"You know we on point like freak bitch nipples." Slimo replied. Jiggy Jack ended the call with Slimo, next he called D-Blocks phone. "What the hell is all that noise in the background?" Jiggy Jack asked.

"Young Bash and Loc wrestling in the lobby, you know when them nigga get to drinking, they start fucking buggin."

Jiggy Jack heard one of them scream out, "ARRRRRR," and all he could say was, "Unbelievable."

"Did you speak to Thuggy today?" D-Block asked.

"Nah...I was gonna holla at him when I got off with you, why wussup?"

"I been hitting the nigga phone for the past hour and he ain't picking up. I spoke to Rah and Chillz, they're in the Horseshoe, and they said they ain't see niggas all day."

"So. where y'all at?"

"We out here in Brooklyn fucking with Young Bash crazy ass." Jiggy Jack heard a loud bang, "What the fuck was that?"

"Them niggas just slammed into the mail box."

"Aight my nigga, them niggas probably somewhere fucking with some hoes. I'mma see if I could catch em...one."

Thuggy Thug, G-Pac, and Gunz were nowhere to be found, because they were at a hot ass house party in Redfern Projects that some shorties invited them to. The party was packed from wall to wall and it was a straight sweat box.

It was something about them project living room parties that made the youngens feel like they were in the hottest club in town. Maybe it was the fact that everybody in there were too young to go to the club, or maybe it was all the dry humping and sweaty walls mixed with intoxicated adolescents who set the roof on fire.

Everywhere the Young Goonz would go; they would stand

out from the rest of the crowd. When you were that young rocking all that bling, it never went unnoticed.

All three of the Young Goonz was dripped up and draped out. The attention they were getting from the Redfern chicks were crazy, but it was like that in every hood. When dudes come from one projects to another...the chicks start flocking.

G-Pac had a 21 shot 9mm star on him with an extra clip in his back pocket, that one of the females from Redfern that was feeling him snuck in for him because if you weren't from Redfern, they were searching at the door. G-Pac wasn't drinking heavy; he'd been sipping the same half of cup of Hennessey since they had arrived at the party.

Thuggy Thug and Gunz were already twisted, as usual. Gunz had two little hot in the twat shorties in the middle of the dance floor, while Thuggy Thug had a thick little red bone in the corner with his finger deep in her cooch.

Niggas from Redfern hated on the Young Goonz hard, especially the young boy who Gunz was beefing with at the barbeque in Hammels. The young boy was a YBM soldier by the name of Flip and he was always looking for a way to get his name known.

The party ended at three forty-five in the morning. Everybody was hanging out in the front of the building when Thuggy Thug, G-Pac, and Gunz came out of the building with three cuties from Redfern that they were about to take back to the Horseshoe.

That's when things got a little out of control. Flip bumped the shit out of Gunz, causing him to spill his liquor all over his gear,

"Watch where the fuck you walking stupid," said Gunz as he attempted to shake the liquor off his shirt.

"What...nigga you in my hood, YBM motherfucka."

"Word...and I guess that shit supposed to mean something to me." Anybody from the streets knew it would be a good time to get out of harm's way if you didn't have nothing to do with what was about to pop off. A few of the YBM boys heard the riff and stopped what they were doing and walked to the commotion, but so did Bart, Chillz, and Smokey, who jumped out of the parked car that they were laying low in. They blended in with the rest of the crowd without letting their presence be known.

G-Pac caught eye contact with Smokey and winked at him on the low. Gunz wasn't about to back down in the front of the bitches.

"I'm saying, wussup you got something you wanna get off your bird chest."

One of the girls from Redfern screamed out, "Goddamn...can't we have a good time without motherfuckas fighting and shooting for once."

Nobody paid home girl no mine and shit was about to go down when O.G. Duke rushed through the crowd, "Fellaz...what the problem is, oh shit, nobody told me that the infamous Young Goonz was in the building, doing it big, shining and shit."

Duke wasn't no dummy. He didn't like none of them motherfuckers from Hammels Projects, but he had to keep his cool in front of the onlookers. "Thuggy Thug, what's good boy?"

Everything...except your lil' man over here talking out of the side of his face."

I could back my shit up too, and my name is Flip nigga. I'm nobody lil' man."

"I never heard of you." Gunz taunted.

Duke wanted to test the heart of his young soldier. "Look it ain't no need to get crazy and disrespectful out here. If ya'll got issues, do it how grown men do it and shoot the five wit' the hands. Gunz took off his chain and watch, both his cell phones and passed it to G-Pac. G-Pac passed it to Thuggy Thug. He didn't want nothing in his hands, just in case he had to reach. G-Pac gave Gunz a hard look and said, "Make this shit quick, so we could get the fuck outta here."

Gunz and Flip were both drinking all night so the fistfight turned out pretty even. It ended how the majority of hood fights end, on the ground with niggas wrestling around until other niggas break it up.

"Duke, grab your boy. I got mine. This shit is a wrap," said Thuggy Thug." When they were pulled apart, Gunz and Flip gave each other dap out of respect on some old school shit, and it was over just as quick as it started. Shit like this don't happen often in FarRock, this normally would have ended with crime scene photos.

Duke could have won an Oscar that night for playing the peace maker for the crowd.

"It's FarRock love down this end my niggas. We ain't on no it's all about YBM shit. As long as niggas don't violate we invite all real FarRock niggas with open arms, ya'll wanna chill...we got more drink is, piff, it's whatever."

"Nah...we good, we were on our way out already," said Thuggy Thug. "Aight, let me walk ya'll to ya'll car, I know you fly niggas probably got three Benzes parked over here somewhere."

Thuggy Thug turned to the crowd and said, "Let's move, we out."

Smokey, Bart, and Chillz emerged out of the crowd and linked up with G-Pac, Thuggy Thug, and Gunz. Duke had to admit it to himself...that was some real slick shit. The Young Goonz walked to two black on black matching Tahoe's, jumped in, and pulled off without the cuties from Redfern.

Duke learned something valuable that night, and that was them Young Goonz was militant minded and calculated with their movements.

CHAPTER FIVE

D eath Row and Shorty-D were parked outside of a gambling spot in Binghamton N.Y. They had been sitting stationary for about an hour waiting for all the big money cats to arrive.

On the next block, they had a minivan filled with six of Shorty D's soldiers just waiting on the go. Death Row already schooled them about the ins and outs of the jooks, and any minute now it was about to go down.

"So you still ain't figured out how to get in where you fit in with all that money running around, Hammels.

How many times we gotta have this conversation, the Young Goonz got that smash. It makes no sense to even try to compete with them at this point. I ain't gonna have my team sitting on felonies and can't move the shit."

"Yeah I'm feeling that, but everything that was ever created only started with a thought...and I respect anybody that's focus on getting paper, but when it's to the point where me and my team can't eat, then there's a problem. I know you could understand that, right?"

"I could dig it." Shorty-D said in agreement with Death Row.

"Plus you already said you weren't feeling some of them niggas anyway, so I don't see what the holdup is."

"The hold up on what, I know you not suggesting that we rob them niggas and start an unnecessary war."

"War...I wouldn't actually call that a war, them niggas don't measure up. We too strong for that. There's strength in numbers you know."

"Yeah, but you and your team don't live in Hammels. Me and mine do and I'm not feeling that shit at all."

"Them niggas got lil' niggas driving BMW's right pass you and your team every day. I seen the lil' nigga T-Black driving one of them niggas S550 on Mott Avenue the other day. That lil' nigga like eleven years old, and he was by himself...I mean if that don't got your team already jumping ship, then I bet they thought about it already. They gonna be screaming Young Goonz in a minute."

"Never, my team is loyal."

"Loyal to what...being broke."

Shorty D knew what Death Row was saying was true, but he also felt that, for some reason, Death Row had a personal vendetta against the Young Goonz and was about to find out why.

"Yo what you got against them dudes, cause I can't help but to think that this shit is deeper than the money. My loyalty is to YBM so there's no need to keep me in the dark about shit."

"Death Row sparked the blunt, took a good drag, and said, "I believe the nigga P-Killa bodied my nigga Fiz a few years back. Fiz had violated Jiggy Jack and a couple of other Young Goonz. The hood was talking. I heard about it all the way down on my end. I believe that's why they didn't ride on Fiz because everybody already knew what it was. It was too exposed. It would have been too obvious if something happened to Fiz, then...so about a month later, me and Fiz had a light little fall out over some money in front of too many people, then the next day my nigga got slumped. Now, the hood looking at me like I'm a foul nigga. I know it was the nigga P-Killa cause one of my bitches seen the whip he was in and wasn't nobody in the Rock driving one of them shits but him. So now, it's like I get a bad taste in my mouth whenever I hear any of them niggas names, or see an eleven year old driving a bigger Benz then mine. Shorty-D sat there quietly trying to absorb what Death Row just told him. Shorty-D didn't know Fiz, so he showed no emotion at all, "Was Fiz YBM?"

"No...but like I said that was my nigga."

Shorty-D took the blunt from Death Row, took a pull, and said, "I got my own issues with Jiggy Jack and C-Dollars, but I fucks with G-Pac, D-Block and Foe."

"Foe. Fuck that nigga Foe. He laid Leeky down. He's on the top of the YBM to do list. He better not let Problem get that good ol' drop on em.

"Man that shit is hood politics. Foe my nigga."

"What you trying to say, you riding with your man or your family. You coming at me kinda hostile, too."

"You should be the last nigga in the world to question my loyalty when it comes to this YBM thing."

Death Row laughed as he took the blunt from Shorty-D and said, "You was starting to scare me...plus look it like this, you ain't feeling the nigga Jiggy Jack or C-Dollars. Let's say you violate one of them. What you think Foe gonna do...yeah, all that man shit would go right out of the window. That's why I ain't got no mans, either you my YBM family or you an outsider...bottom line."

Death Row's phone rang. It was his people inside the gambling spot letting him know that it was a full house and everybody was caked up.

Death Row hung up and told Shorty-D to call his soldiers and tell them to roll. The soldiers ran up in the spot, tied everybody up, and made off with more than they expected. Death Row pulled off behind the minivan and started singing one of the late, great Michael Jackson songs. "You been hit by, you been hit by, a smooth criminal."

Y   Z

A month passed since the drive by on Gateway. B.G. and Jah were sitting in the parking lot on Beach 86th Street, across the street from Hammels projects. They sat in the black on black Dodge Charger watching everybody that went in and out of Sam & Eddie's corner store.

They saw a few dudes that they knew who were repping Young Goonz, but they were out there waiting on one of the big fish, not foot soldiers. They could have easily sent a few of their own foot soldiers to Hammels to air shit out, but that's not how B.G. or Jah gave it up. Those two niggas loved putting in that dirty work. Jah lived for moments like this and he was tired of waiting

Jah told B.G. to drive around Hammels projects. After making two laps, Jah said, "Fuck this. Park at the end of the horseshoe. The first one of them niggas I see; I'mma get out and tighten his ass up."

It was cold on this particular night and from the distance that they were scoping things out from made it difficult to see faces. Many dudes were bundled up with wool knitted hats and hoodies on their heads.

Jah was ready to shoot anybody. He made a conscious decision that he wasn't leaving Hammels without shooting somebody and he was sticking to it.

G-Pac, Chillz, and Scooby walked out of 84-12, heading to the bang out building in the back of Hammels projects on Beach 81st Street. The bang out was a building that many of the dudes from the back of the projects hung out with all the little hot chicks.

G-Pac was laughing at Chillz. Technically, Chillz was

legally blind without his glasses on, but he would never wear those shits. That made life a little hectic for him when it came to seeing shit. Whenever Chillz phone rang, he would have to put the phone damn near on the tip of his nose just to see the number of whoever was calling.

That's what caused G-Pac to laugh. No matter how many times you see Chillz put that phone to his face, the shit looked funny as hell.

"Fuck you laughing at, bitch." Chillz asked knowing G-Pac was about to start his bullshit.

"You and your blind ass. You gonna need a see and eye dog in a minute if you don't put themmotherfucking glasses on."

Scooby smiled and shook his head. Scooby never said much of anything. He was only sixteen years old and it was strange how he rarely used words to express himself. They were walking passed the horseshoe when D-Block stuck his head out of 84-18.

"Where ya'll going."

"To the bang out." G-Pac replied.

"Aight, I'll be back there in a minute...I sent Connie to the liquor store for me."

Jah was squinting his eyes when he saw them walking passed the horseshoe.

"There them niggas go right there." Jah put one in the chamber, put his hood over his head, and jumped out of the Charger.

Jah ran right up behind the Young Goonz and squeezed...Boom Boom Boom. After the third shot, Jah's gun jammed. One shot hit Chillz in the back of his upper thigh, while the other two shots whistled passed G-Pac's head.

D-Block thought he was bugging when he saw the dude with the hoodie run out of the horseshoe in a crouched position. Once he heard the three shots, his suspicions were confirmed. Without thought, D-Block bolted out of the lobby with his 45 P-90 in hand. When he turned the corner, he saw the dude with the hoodie bent over smacking his gun and trying to jack it back.

Still not sure exactly what was going on, D-Block looked through the path that ran through the projects and saw Scooby helping Chillz off the ground. G-Pac jumped from behind a tree when he saw D-Block and frantically pointed at the dude with the hoodie on. D-Block put it all together in a tenth of a second and started letting the four-pound roar. Boom Boom. Boom Boom Boom...Boom.

The nigga in the hoodie got low and crawled behind a tree. D-Block was just about to run down on the nigga when he heard car tires screeching. His first thought was the cops, so he ran back toward the entrance of 84-18.

D-Block saw the black Charger hop the sidewalk. He got a quick glance at the driver and realized that it wasn't the police. D-Block ran behind the Dodge, but he couldn't get a clean shot with his Young Goonz still running through the path.

Jah jumped in the Charger and B.G. sped right through the projects. He tried to run G-Pac over but G-Pac jumped over the gate and ran through the grass.

B.G. knew he couldn't make it all the way back to Gateway if somebody in Hammels called the cops and gave a description of the car. He figured it would be best if he pulled over in Edgemere projects and called his comrade Stink.

Stink answered his phone on the first ring, "What it do, B.G...long time no hear."

"I'm in a little jam right now."

"What's shaking...I gotta grip up?"

"Nah, it ain't nothing like dat. I just need to come scream atcha for a minute."

"Where you at my nigga?"

"Look out of the window."

"That's you in the Charger...come up."

B.G. and Jah got out of the car and walked in Stink's building. Stink had a small but dangerous team called the Black Cowboys on the other side of Edgemere projects.

Big E, Benzo, and Morg were what he considered his family. They were all in building 51-15 apartment 5A getting their smoke on and listening to music when Jah and B.G. walked in. The first thing Jah noticed was all the guns that were spread out on the table.

"God damn. What the fuck all the guns for?" Quoting a line from the late great Biggie Smalls.

"We warring with them YBM niggas. Me and the boy Problem banged it out last night." Stink said as he bopped his head to the music.

But fuck all that, what kind of jam you in, killa?" Stink asked. B.G. didn't want to tell Stink what just transpired in Hammels, not that Stink loyalty was questionable. B.G. just didn't know the status of the nigga that dropped in Hammels. Nobody was in the business of admitting to a murder, so B.G. lied.

"We can't find no good bud in the whole Rock." Stink was a G and he read B.G.'s elusiveness.

"Fuck it...whatever it was; ya'll good now." Stink winked at B.G. and pulled out a zip lock bag full of that good choke. "Roll up."

Young Goonz

Back in Hammels Projects, the police had the area where Chillz was shot taped off. The Young Goonz was in 84-16 apartment 6E about twenty deep. D-Block, G-Pac, and Scooby were telling the story with more humor then concern. G-Pac was telling the rest of the Young Goonz.

"Yo whoever that stupid ass nigga was should have known better then to try to cook something with that bullshit ass high point." Everybody laughed at G-Pac's comment. D-Block cut in, "This motherfucking four peez got mad kick. I couldn't hit the nigga and I was mad close to the bird. This shit almost broke my arm."

Scooby phone rang. It was Chillz calling from the hospital, "Yo, it's Chillz on the phone. I'mma put it on speaker."

Chillz voice boomed through the distorted sounding speakerphone, "Ya'll bitches better not drink all my Yak. I'll be out of here in a few minutes. I need a drink and my gun...I think I know who pop me."

Everybody in the room stopped laughing and got serious. Thuggy Thug grabbed the phone from Scooby and asked Chillz, "Who was it my nigga?" Chillz took a deep breath, and then said, "My baby moms." The whole crib erupted with laughter.

Gunz shouted out, "Somebody get Shake The Don on the phone, tell son we need ten naked bitches over here ASAP. We throwing a party for Chillz tonight."

About an hour later, the party was on and popping when Chillz limped through the door with a cane in his hand. Chillz grabbed a bottle of Goose out of Loc's hand, guzzled it straight from the bottle, walked to the middle of the floor, dropped the cane, stuck out his wounded leg, and started killing that shit.

Everybody in the crib went crazy and started singing..."Do the stanky leg...do the stanky leg...do the stanky leg."

While the party was jumping in the living room, G-Pac and Thuggy Thug were in the back room brainstorming over a bottle of Remy Martin VSOP. From the outside looking in, one would think that the Young Goonz was wild and reckless. Truth be told, they were, but at the same time, they were as serious as cancer when it comes to war.

"You couldn't see the nigga face at all?" Asked Thuggy Thug.

"Nah. We didn't even hear the nigga creep up, I heard the shots, felt the shits fly by my wig...If the nigga gun didn't jam, it would have been real ugly, cause the nigga got up close and personal."

"So what you saying is son was playing for keeps?"

"Yeah, he definitely tried to park something close to the curb, and for the little glimpse I did get, son wasn't no young nigga. I mean, I couldn't see his whole grill but the little I could see, mixed with the nigga body language, tells me that son wasn't young at all."

Thuggy Thug mind was spinning and the Remy wasn't helping him think any clearer, "We gotta make an example out of somebody quick. We can't have niggas thinking it's something sweet in this horseshoe."

"My dude this shit is deeper than that. Somebody is pissed the fuck off at us and we don't even know who or why...and I keep getting this feeling that this shit is gonna get worst way before it gets better," said G-Pac.

CHAPTER SIX

You know the hood talk, so when word got down to Death Row about what popped off in the Horseshoe, he hit Shorty-D's phone.

"I told you them niggas ain't built like that."

Shorty-D was feeding his pit bull puppy and had to stop after hearing Death Row's comments.

"Tell me you didn't send that missile without giving me the heads up."

"Word to Bless, I had nothing to do with that, but that don't mean that I can't celebrate."

"You ain't the only one celebrating. The nigga Chillz got hit in the leg. Them niggas is over there in that Horseshoe partying hard. They got strippers and all kinds of shit popping over there."

Death Row was tight on the low when he heard the nigga only got hit in the leg, but he didn't let Shorty-D know it.

"Shorty-D let me hit you back; I gotta take care of something, YBM for life."

"You already know." Shorty-D replied right before he hung up.

Death Row hit Sunny's phone and let him know that one of the Young Goonz was popped in the leg in the Horseshoe. Sunny had no way of knowing if it was the Gateway crew that put that work in, but he was disappointed with whoever did it. "Uh fucking leg shot," is what Sunny thought to himself as Death Row talked.

"Fuck them lames though. Duke man Chico is ready. I talked to Duke and he's waitin on us," said Sunny.

Cool...I already got Shorty-D's paper so tell Duke to set it up."

B.G and Jah left Stink's building around three o'clock that morning. When they got back to Gateway, Jah was still mad as fuck that his gun jammed on him. Jah kept asking B.G. "Do he think the nigga that he hit was dead." B.G. kept telling him that he didn't know.

B.G. was tired of hearing Jah's constant rambling. He just wanted to check on his block, then call it a night. B.G. wasn't the type to dwell on shit repeatedly.

The Young Goonz was going to pay for what they did with their lives, and that was that. So to B.G., there was absolutely nothing to talk about.

A few days pasted, Jiggy Jack was in a recording studio in Brooklyn with Dot. He felt that Dot was more marketable and passionate about being a rapper. A few of the other Young Goonz felt like they were better than Dot on the mic and that Jiggy Jack should be focusing more on their mix tapes then his, besides Dot was from Brooklyn. Jiggy Jack didn't give a fuck where Dot was from, he was nice with it and he was a Young Goon. Plus Dot's work ethic was official. Dot wasn't running around trying to kill niggas. He was in that booth. Jiggy Jack knew that it only took one to get the rest of the team in the door. He had a vision and everybody had to fall in line, whether they liked it or not.

Dot was in the booth going crazy, the boy had bars for days and his flow was Hot 97 ready. Dot was real versatile. He could spit bubble gum rap, or hardcore hood shit. It didn't matter, just put the beat on and he would back the fuck out.

Jiggy Jack was online sending invitations to a showcase he

was putting together. He was only inviting FarRock up and coming artist to perform at the showcase. Jiggy felt that FarRockaway was only respected for keeping it gangsta, which to him was stupid when it was so much talented people out there. So he was focused on displaying so that talent so the world could see.

He didn't mind the competition from other FarRock natives, in fact, he encouraged it. Whenever he heard other FarRock niggas going hard, he would put the pressure on the Young Goonz to go even harder. He supported all FarRock rappers; he would spend money on their mix tapes, even if he knew they were whack.

The other thing that was on his mind was the botched attempt on the Young Goonz the other day. He knew that a war right now would be a major setback. Jimmy Jack worked too hard to get out of the hood and now he was trying to get his people productive light. Plus, no matter what would go down in the hood involving the Young Goonz, the police would always make him the foal point of their investigation. Not like Jiggy Jack was the H.N.I.C, he just always assumed that they hated him for slipping through the cracks. When he was out there in them streets getting money, they could never catch him red handed doing shit. To make matters worse his name popped up in a few murders, which they could never get to stick. I mean, how could they stick if he wasn't the shooter.

Now that Jiggy Jack was caked up and didn't hustle in the streets any more he was paranoid, thinking they would one day set him up. All he wanted to do was turn a negative into a positive.

Many of FarRock niggas hated Jiggy Jack too. Some felt he didn't deserve his riches, and to be a fat black gorilla looking nigga. He still out shined most. Every bitch thought he was the cute teddy bear kind of gorilla, so his confidence was that of the sexiest man in America when it came to the ladies.

FarRock niggas felt like if you weren't banging your hammer then you weren't gangsta, and if you weren't gangsta then you didn't deserve to shine. As politically incorrect as that sound, it made a whole lot of sense to broke niggas that'll do anything to eat.

Jiggy Jack had his own logic, which was called P-Killa, g-Pac, Thuggy Thug, Foe, D-Block, and the list goes on. (Act stupid). Plus he had other official niggas outside of the Young Goonz that owed him a hundred favors, and would be offended if he was violated in the smallest way.

Jiggy Jack done helped so many dudes out that were in jams, without looking for anything in return that his ghetto pass stretched throughout the whole FarRock.

He bailed dudes out of jail, paid lawyer fees for criminal cases and appeals. He helped other dudes pay their rent when they were facing eviction. He spent thousands on baby showers. One time, he brought a dude a car that was tired of the street life and needed a good set of wheels to get back and forth to work.

Dot stepped out of the booth and mixed up his favorite drink. Dot would cop a bottle of Absolute and a bottle of Apple Pucker and make his own Apple Martinis.

Dot was so serious about his music that he wouldn't even drink until his vocals were already laid down, just so his voice wouldn't slur when he rapped. He used to hustle cracks hard in Brooklyn, but he fell back after he caught a few cases that good lawyers wiggled him out, thanks to Jiggy Jack.

Dot was listening to the playback of the five songs he just recorded while sipping his Martini, when C-Dollars walked in the studio.

Death Row, Duke, and Chico were in an apartment somewhere in the Bronx.

Death Row brought two of his testers with him to test the quality of the heroin. One was a sniffer, while the other was a shooter.

The sniffer told Death Row that he didn't get a drip after he took a snort. Which meant that the dope wasn't all that.

The shooter said it was all right, pretty much the same as the last shit they had. Death Row was pissed, but leaving the Bronx empty handed was better than being stuck with some garbage. He was trying to calculate how much money that his crew would miss until the drought was over.

They were just making it back to FarRock when one of the dope fiend's phone rang in the back seat. "Yeah...aight I'm on my way." The fiend told Death Row to go to the horseshoe

"Them boys out there giving out testers like it's 88 and motherfuckers saying it's good as shit too."

Death Row pulled in the horseshoe five minutes later and couldn't believe his eyes. There were three dope lines in front of all three buildings and the fiends were in a frenzy, pushing and shoving. Free dope could cause a fucking riot in FarRock...and the shit was good!

Messhall and Scooby were passing out testers in the front of 84-12. Bart and Buda was passing them out in the front of 84-16, while Smokey and Woody were doing the same in the front of 84-18.

The nigga Gunz was standing in the middle of the buildings, popping shit and making sure nobody got off one line and get on the other.

Death Row testers made it back to the car and jumped in like kids at a candy store.

"Let me see that shit." Duke demanded. The stamp on the bag had a Horseshoe on it. Duke shook his head in defeat and handed back to the fiend that almost snatched Duke's finger off to get his junk back.

When they got back to Edgemere Projects the fiends took

their hits right there in the living room in front of Duke and Death Row, they ain't have shit to hide they were trying to get high...and that they did. Those motherfuckers started nodding and scratching like that was the first time they had gotten high in their lives.

"Man I ain't had no shit like this in ten years," said the shooter in between nods. The sniffer was so fucked up that he couldn't even talk.   The higher they looked. The more pissed off Death Row got. "Man... something gotta give them clowns about to steal the Rock with that shit."

Duke couldn't stop staring at the fiends, the sniffer done scratched blood out of his ankle. While the shooter had been trying to light the same cigarette for the pass ten minutes.

It didn't take a rocket scientist to see that them Young Goonz was working with a monster..." Motherfuckas." Duke thought.

Whitey did it again. Fiends were coming all the way from South Side Jamaica Queens to cop that Horseshoe. Everybody in FarRock was feeling the effects of that dope. Nobody was eating but the Young Goonz.

B.G. and Jah were starving down their end, they had just re'd up the day before the Horseshoe took over the world, so the dope they copped went bad on them. They couldn't move the crack they had because Duke had the crack game on lock, down that end. B.G. was more concerned with the dope. That shit was like a smack in the face to the Gateway crew.

"Them bitch made niggas smoked my lil' man, now they're stopping my money. It's time to show these niggas to their graves," said B.G. with fire in his eyes.

"We gotta bring everybody in on this one. We calling on all forces. We ain't getting no money anyway, so fuck it, let's get on our Ignorant shit." Jah replied.

B.G. called Stink and let him know that he needed him and the Black Cowboys to come together and handle something.

Stink didn't want to talk on the phone, so he went to Gateway to holla at his people. How the Young Goonz came on the block, killed one lil' nigga and hit the other one up. How they had went to Hammels Projects and put that work in the day they came to his crib, and now how the Young Goonz got the whole FarRock starving with that damn dope they got.

Stink couldn't believe what was coming out of Jah's mouth, and right off the top, he dismissed the outlandish shit that Jah said. Stink didn't waste no time breaking down how he felt about the situation.

"First and foremost, how do ya'll know that it was the Young Goonz that shot the block up...matter fact get shorty in here that got hit. I wanna holla at him."

Five minutes later the lil' nigga walked in the crib. Stink got straight to the point, "How you know who shot you shorty?"

"Cause they had Young Goonz hoodies on and the nigga screamed out Young Goonz motherfucka, then started shooting."

"Did you see their faces?" Stink asked.

"Nah, they had on mask."

"Okay shorty, be careful out there alright."

"Two shots couldn't stop me, I took em' and smiled."

When lil' man left the crib, Stink looked at B.G and Jah.

"Are ya'll serious. Them niggas don't move like dat. Think about it, all the rumors about dudes they were supposed to have laid down is always speculation, cause nobody could say for certain that it was them...why would they come down here and switch their style, and to shoot to lil' niggas...I'm sorry, but I ain't buying that shit at all. Plus ya'll can't give me one good reason why them niggas would violate. They know ya'll fuck with the Black Cowboys and their love for us would have made them holla at us before they would bust a move like that. Nitty and Big E are cousins so if there were issues we would have got wind of it way before it got violent. Now as far as the dope, they already sent word down to us that if the Horseshoe dope was fucking up our flow, they were willing to do business, so we could get that...that's not a problem. Now I understand why ya'll react the way ya'll did, because when it's time to ride for a violation, everything else don't matter. I believe the situation could be fixed because the nigga Chillz only got hit in the leg but we gotta find out who the fuck pulled that stunt, niggas playing serious games with niggas lives."

Jah and B.G. didn't question Stink's input; in fact, what he said made more sense than the Young Goonz actually shooting up their block.

"Listen...I'mma go to Hammels and probably with them niggas so we could get to the bottom of this sideways shit."

"Hold up, I don't care if you tell them niggas we were responsible for that, just make sure they know exactly what went down on our block," said B.G.

"Trust me my nigga ya'll ain't got shit to worry about," said Stink. Jah laughed and said, "Oh trust me...we ain't worried at all."

Later that night Stink and B.G. jumped in the Tahoe and headed to Hammels. They stopped at the liquor store on Beach 87th Street instead of going straight to the Horseshoe. When they walked inside three hot in the ass chicks from Hammels jumped right on their dicks.

"Yo Stink what it do...can we drink with ya'll...we trying to get bent and bent up, feel what I'm saying."

"Nah sexy, come down here for that...when ya'll coming to the Edge to chill with me and my niggas?"

"Give me your number and we'll holla tomorrow night."

As they were exchanging numbers, Shorty-D and three of his shooters walked in the liquor store. Stink gave the cutie he was talking to his money and told her to pay for the bottle and to bring it to the Horseshoe.

Stink and Big E walked out of the store for one reason only, and that was because the liquor store had cameras in it. The Black Cowboys were far from shook. It wasn't a secret. The Black Cowboys had beef with the YBM crew, and it was on sight no matter where they bumped heads at.

Shorty-D and his boys walked out right behind them, "Yo Stink... what's good with you and my niggas in the Edge baby boy."

"Fuck I owe you an explanation or something...them niggas be down there body bluffing...why wussup," as he unzipped his army jacket, exposing his bullet proof vest and the handles of the two Glock 10s that sat under his arm pits in the double shoulder holster. Big E put his hand in his Carhart coat pocket and wrapped it around the handle of his 357 bulldog."

"Watch your mouth before I wash it out with blood," said one of Shorty-D soldiers as he reached for his gun, but changed his mind quick when he saw the blue and white cop car drive by slow. As soon as the car was out of sight, the guns were drawn.

P-Killa and Nitty pulled up just in the nick of time, cause it was about to go down.

"I know one thing, if one of you niggas shoot my cousin then you better shoot me too," said Nitty.

P-Killa didn't like situations where guns were out and he didn't have one. "Let's all put the guns down before somebody make a mistake and shoot me."

Nobody budged. The owner of the liquor store ran out screaming, "I call police. I call police." He didn't want no bodies drooping in the front of his storefront. Business was already slow enough, so that he didn't need.

The mere mentioning of the police being on their way was enough to disperse the Mexican standoff. Stink and Big E jumped in the truck and followed P-Killa and Nitty to the

Horseshoe.

All the Young Goonz was in 84-16 lobby listening to the Young Goonz mix tape when P-Killa, Nitty, Stink, and Big E walked in the lobby. It was at least twenty-five of them in there and they were all singing along with the chorus. "CLICK CLACK BOOM. WE COULD WAKE THE NEIGHBORS UP. CLICK CLACK BOOM. WE COULD WAKE THE NEIGHBORS UP. CLICK CLACK BOOM. WE COULD WAKE THE NEIGHBORS UP.

Stink and Big E joined in with the chant. Stink loved the way the Young Goonz was always hyped up no matter what the situation was, these niggas energy was crazy. He also could understand why anybody that wasn't affiliated with these niggas would hate their fucking guts, because they were doing their numbers and doing it big.

When Stink saw Chillz, he was reminded of his purpose for being in Hammels Projects. Foe emerged from the crowd, embraced Stink and Big E with daps, and love is love hugs. "What's shaking gangsta?" Asked Foe. "Niggas in their boots when they got beef with us." Stink replied, sharing a laugh with Foe.

Stink wanted to get right to it, so he told Foe he needed to holla at him and P-Killa in private, that it was a matter of importance. Big E stayed in the lobby while Stink, Foe, and P-Killa got in the elevator and rode to the sixth floor.

They entered apartment 6E. Foe walked around the crib to see if was empty. He opened the back room door and Gunz had a little brown-skinned chick bent up on the bed blowing her back out. Home girl looked at Foe then back at Gunz and kept fucking like she like to be watched. Foe closed the door back and checked the other rooms.

When he opened the bathroom door Loc drunk ass was sleep in the bathtub, wrapped up in the shower curtain. Foe noticed the gun sticking out of Loc's jacket pocket, so he slid it out and placed it in his own back pocket, then left the bathroom.

"Come on, we outta here, let's go next door to Rah crib." Foe said to P-Killa and Stink.

Everything was cool in Rah's crib. Rah was on his way back down stairs to the lobby as they walked in. As soon as they all sat down in the living room Stink came right out with it, "I know who shot Chillz that day in the Horseshoe."

That was the last thing they expected to hear, so it kind of caught them off guard. P-Killa adrenalin started pumping, already thinking about revenge. Foe maintained his composure and asked Stink, "Who?" "It was my niggas from Gateway."

"Why the fuck niggas from Gateway come down here shooting at my niggas," asked Foe.

Stink took a swig of his Yak and said, "Somebody rode down on them niggas, right on their own block and aired shit out. One lil' nigga got smoked, while the other one got hit up."

"So...what the fuck that got to do with us." P-Killa asked through clinched teeth.

Stink scratched his head, then said, "Whoever rode on them niggas had Young Goonz hoodies on and they screamed out Young Goonz right before they started blaming."

P-Killa laughed and said, "So let me get this straight. Them niggas from Gateway, that supposed to be sharp and swift mentally came down here and tried to kill my youngens without doing a proper investigation first."

"My G, everybody don't think how we think, they did what they felt justified in doing. We just gotta be thankful that none of our niggas ain't having nightmares in the dirt behind that shit...what's important now is trying to figure out who tried to throw us under the bus like that," said Foe.

After brain storming for about an hour nobody could figure out who, what, or why. Stink broke the silence, "Them niggas wanna holla at ya'll to make sure there ain't no bad blood in the air. It was definitely about to get messy, but I got wind of it, and let my niggas know that if ya'll was gonna cook something it would be for a justified reason, and they definitely wouldn't have known who or what hit them."

Foe and P-Killa respected how Stink read the bullshit somebody tried to pull so they agreed to meet the Gateway boys. Stink hit B.G. on the phone, and they felt a good neutral zone would be on the Boardwalk on Beach 50th Street. Stink assured both parties that nothing was going to pop off, so everybody headed to the location.

CHAPTER SEVEN

Shorty-D had already called Problem in Edgemere and let him know that Stink was in Hammels right after the liquor store run in.

Problem and Craps were parked on BEACH Channel drive, with a clear view of the Horseshoe. They had their eyes on Stink's Tahoe for the past hour and a half when they saw Foe, P-Killa, Stink, and Big E walk out of the building and separate to their vehicles.

They knew they were outnumbered, which was the only reason they didn't jump out dumping clips. Problem and Craps were official gunslingers for the YBM crew. They were smart, dangerous, and most of all they were patient.

When Problem laid eyes on Foe, he forgot all about Stink. The hate that he had for Foe for killing his boy Leeky was extreme. Even though it wasn't a fact, nobody could convince him different. He wanted to jump out and murder the nigga so bad that he started sweating.

Craps knew what his boy was thinking so he tried to break the tension, "Look at these niggas, you could tell their all gripped up. We should pull off before they see us in this car."

Problem knew he was right; he started the car and pulled off slow without turning on the headlights.

"Word to Leeky, I'mma kill that nigga son," said Problem.

"I know my nigga...in due time, in due time."

When everybody made it to the Horseshoe, P-Killa told Foe to let him do all the talking. P-Killa knew how Foe felt about Chillz being shot so he didn't want to risk losing control of the situation. Foe was cool with it. He didn't really want to talk anyway. He was there to listen, or kill if he had to.

It was real dark on the Boardwalk, and the only thing that could be heard was the sound of the waves crashing on the shore. The headlights from the three vehicles lit up the boardwalk on Beach 50th Street.

Stink introduced everybody then P-Killa spoke first. "Either ya'll extremely stupid or ya'll telling the truth, I'm hoping ya'll extremely stupid, because the truth is too complicated for me."

Jah jumped right on the defense, which was what P-Killa wanted. "Listen homeboy, we ain't come out here to help you figure out what you should or should not believe, because when I don't know what to believe I start shooting niggas."

P-Killa smiled, turned to Foe and said, "I guess we know who shot Chillz."

B.G. realized that his boy just made a spectacle of himself, so he took the conversation back down the right road.

"Listen, we understand that ya'll feel violated, so try to understand how we feel, because we lost one of ours, I watched niggas pull up on my block and kill a lil' nigga that was out there hustling for school clothes for him and his sister because their moms is smoked out...and the shooter screamed Young Goonz.

Ya'll should feel good that Stink pointed out a few things that didn't add up because we wouldn't be having this conversation, it would have just been a whole lot of unnecessary funerals."

P-Killa had no choice but to respect what B.G. said, even though he noticed the indirect cockiness of B.G. words.

"It's obvious whoever pulled that stunt wanted us to clash.

We ain't gonna give them lames what they want. I say we come together for the mean time and see who get pissed off. Bet that'll flush the maggots out. That should force their hand to make another move and be exposed themselves, but this time, we'll be ready," said P-Killa in the sincere and humble tone.   B.G. was skeptical about making an alliance with the Young Goonz he didn't want to take on any unnecessary drama.

"Who ya'll beefing with down that end." B.G. asked. P-Killa laughed and said, "Nobody in particular, but we are what you consider a broke nigga's nightmare."

"Yeah that Horseshoe stamp got the whole Queens buzzing." B.G. managed to slip that in. P-Killa knew B.G. through the hook out there so he decided to extend his hand. "On the strength of your lil' man who got sent back to the essence, I'll plug you in with my boy C-Dollars and he'll get that to you at the same price we pay, but only with one condition...ya'll gotta Horseshoe stamp the bags."

B.G. didn't give a fuck what was on the bags. He saw an opportunity to get his block jumping again and feed his team. The only thing he had had to do was let his people know that it wasn't the Young Goonz that shot the block up and the rest would be history.

"All we ask is loyalty over royalty," stated P-Killa as he extended his hand to shake on it.

B.G. shook his hand firmly as he looked P-Killa right in his eyes and said no fucking doubt. Let's show these suckas how to play chess.

Foe and Jah were face fighting each other the whole time B.G. and P-Killa talked. Stink peeped it and hoped that they could put their differences to the side, because if they didn't this whole shit could back fire in his face.

P-Killa assured Stink that he and the Black Cowboys could get the dope too, under the same conditions that he gave the Gateway crew and just like that. The talk ended with admiration for each other.

On the way back to Hammels Projects, Foe and P-Killa thought it would be best not to tell the rest of the Young Goonz what they just found out. Foe and P-Killa had the minds of military generals. During their time of incarceration, they read all the Art of War, 48 Laws of power, 50th Law, George Jackson, and any other books that dealt with revolution and strategies of war.

They both had their own understanding of the things they studied, which caused them to clash mentally but when they were on the same page, everything was perfected with a science, and that night they were on the same page.

A few days later the word was spreading fast that the Horseshoe brand was on Gateway and Edgemere Projects. It was much more convenient for the fiends, now they didn't have to ride all the way down to Hammels just to wait on a long line. B.G. loved the cash flow. He had his shooters on deck and vowed not to let history repeat itself.

Now he had dope fiends running UP to the cars to take the order, then they would run back to one of the soldiers to get the work.

The money was pouring in faster than the speed of light. If B.G. had any doubt before about who shot his block up, he knew for sure now that it wasn't the Young Goonz.

When Duke found out that the Horseshoe dope was on Gateway, he was in disbelief, so he sent a fiend from Redfern Projects to Gateway to cop. The fiend came back and confirmed the rumors. Duke was tight, and he couldn't understand what connection the Gateway crew had with the Young Goonz.

Meanwhile in Edgemere Projects Morg and Benzo from the Black Cowboys were in their dope spot moving more bundles of the Horseshoe then they could count. In any hood in America, you could tell who's getting the dope money by watching which direction the early morning rush was heading to; it's always a stamped to the good shit.

The Black Cowboys had a few young killas posted up around 51-15 watching for cops, stick up kids, and most of all YBM niggas. They had strict orders to shoot first and think later.

Edgemere Projects was buzzing about the Horseshoe dope, and the Black Cowboys made it no secret how it was going down. They had lil' niggas on the corner of Beach 54th Street screaming, "Horseshoe. Horseshoe," like a scene straight out of the Wire.

Death Row was in a flaming fury. He didn't give a shit that the Black Cowboys were eating. He just didn't like the fact that niggas from Hammels had their logo in his hood. Death Row figured that, one way or another, the Young Goonz was getting a nice grip for spreading that good shit around. He was sitting in his Range Rover on Beach 59th Street when his phone rang. It was Duke on the other end, and he was spazzing out.

"Yo these niggas on Gateway got shit clicking with that Horse- shoe shit. How the fuck the whole New York is screaming drought, but the Young Goonz got enough to spread out."

"Death Row was already thinking the same shit, "Hell if I know, but something gotta give...your heard. I'll rather declare war on them niggas and the Gateway crew, plus these Black Cowgirls before I let them stop YBM's money."

"I'm calling a meeting ...eight o' clock," said Duke, and then hung up without getting a response from Death Row.

Death Row, Shorty-D, Sunny, and Duke held the meeting at

IHOP in five towns. Even though they ordered a table full of pancakes, waffles, and turkey sausages, nobody was in the mood to eat. They ordered just so they could occupy that table without drawing attention to themselves.

Duke called the meeting so he was the first one to speak. "It's time to let our nuts hang. The Young Goonz done shut down YBM's income throughout the whole FarRock. The crack money ain't cutting it, so it's time to stir the beach water...any suggestions."

Sunny had an idea, "Let's snatched one of them niggas up and make them come out their pockets on some ransom shit." Sunny is what you would call an extremist, with an exaggerated sense of reality.

Death Row didn't want to shoot his request down directly, so he said, "Yeah that's gangsta but first we need to focus on stopping that money flow they got going on."

Shorty-D shook his head and said, "Ya'll under estimating them niggas...real talk. The money they getting in FarRock don't even scratch the surface compared to what they getting outta town. The only way to stop their flow out here was to get some better dope."

With all due respect Shorty-D, that's not the only way to stop a niggas flow because war is the best solution when it comes to that shit, why you think America hates terrorism. Terrorism fucks up the economy." Duke said trying to sway the rest of the O.G.'s to entertain the thought of bringing it to the Young Goonz.

Sunny was lost in his own thoughts. He felt that the O.G.'s could be a little too political at times. Sunny just wanted to bang on motherfuckers. It didn't matter who or why. He just wanted to ride. "Know what I'm saying Sunny," asked Duke.

"No fucking doubt, my G." Sunny replied without even knowing what the hell Duke was talking about.

Young Goonz

Sunny wanted to tell the rest of the O.G.'s that it was him who sent his knuckle heads to shoot up Gateway, trying to start a war with them and the Young Goonz. But now that his plan backfired, he felt that some things were better off left in the dark. He still couldn't figure out how the Gateway crew and the Young Goonz were fucking with each other after that incident.

"Ya'll know them niggas is having that showcase shit on Mott Avenue tomorrow night, I say we go up there and test the hearts of these chumps." Sunny said as he stabbed a butter knife through a stack of strawberry pancakes with whipped cream on them.

Duke and Death Row were feeling Sunny's idea. The O.G.'s were ready for war, except for one. Shorty-D knew that their plan was forced and borderline stupid because the Showcase was on Mott Ave, not in the projects where all the money was being made. So to pop off anywhere but the hood would defeat the purpose, unless the war wasn't really about the money. Shorty-D felt like he was about to get the short end of the stick, but his loyalty was to YBM, so he said fuck it to himself, raised a glass of orange juice and said ft YBM to the death," then thought, "Literally."

Death Row went over the plan for an hour. Shorty-D was relieved when he found out that none of the O.G.'s would be at the showcase when the shit hits the fan. Not that he was shook of the Young Goonz, he just had firsthand knowledge that if you were going to violate the Young Goonz, you better be ready to kill because they were some sneaky ass, dangerous motherfuckers.

When the O.G.'s went back to their hoods, they gave the orders to their soldiers, except for Shorty-D, he wanted to wait. He thought it would be best not to say shit to his followers until he saw how shit would play out on Friday.

CHAPTER EIGHT

Jiggy Jack was on the stage hyped up screaming into the mic. "Check it out. Each crew can only perform two songs, and then you got to step off the stage. This is not your album release party. Show case your talent then enjoy the rest of the show.

The spot was packed from wall to wall, and you could count on one hand how many females were in the whole spot. With all the weed smoke and low lights, it was hard to see, unless a nigga was close up on you, or on the stage.

A group from Ocean village that called themselves, "Hard White," was on the stage getting it in. They had the crowd in a frenzy. C-Dollars couldn't wait to hit the stage and represent for Hammels Projects. C-Dollars told Dot, Precise, Carty, and Deuce four hundred to hit the stage with him when it was time for him to perform.

Young Bash brought some of his Brooklyn niggas with him to let them hit the stage too. He had them on some Young Brooklyn Goonz shit, so it was all good to Jiggy Jack.

Jiggy Jack peeped the YBM crew. They were about fifteen deep with YBM shirts on. It was crews from every project and *side block throughout the whole FarRock. As the night went on performance after performance, the spot got liver by the minute.

The Jamaicans from 15th Street hit the stage and raised the roof when they started to chat. Jiggy Jack listened to every performance and was in awe with all the talent that was displayed.

He vision was to start a label and letting all these artists come under that umbrella. Jiggy Jack zoned out visioning it all.

Then came the moment Jiggy Jack was waiting on. The Riot Squad was exiting the stage after tearing the shit down and the Young Goonz was hitting the stage. C-Dollars Ice lit up the room and the show was on, "When I say Young, ya'll say Goonz...Young." The crowd screamed Goonz. "When I say click clack, ya'll say Boom...Click Clack." And the crowd screamed Boom. C-Dollars had the crowd going nuts; his aura on stage was artistic. You would swear he was a platinum selling star. When he finished his first song, he took the time to shout out all the crews that came through and represented.

This was the last song of the night and he decided to talk money,

"Where all my dope boys at, if you rettin that paper and you laughing at the haters, then shit is for you... This dope boy fresh/ this dope boy clean and this dope boy shine. This dope boy gleam."

Everybody in the spot was so amped up that nobody peeped the YBM niggas moving through the crowd, getting closer to the stage.

Jiggy Jack and Young Bash were in a zone, pumping their fist when the shit popped off. The YBM crew rushed the stage throwing blows and swinging bottles. C-Dollars was so caught off guard that he didn't even feel it when his diamond chain was yapped off his neck. He was hit in the head with a Moet bottle and he dropped to his knees with a big gash in his head that was pouring out blood.

C-Dollars jumped up, shook off his dizziness, and started rumbling with the rest of the crowd. Jiggy Jack and Young Bash tucked their chains in, ran up on the stage, and joined the action.

The brawl was going on for a good two minutes when the first shot echoed through the room. Blackow, "That's when the fighting stopped and the running started. The whole crowd rushed toward the exit at once. A few dudes were trampled and nobody stopped to help them up.

Problem and Craps were parked across the street when they heard the shot go off. That was their cue, when the crowd bust through the door in a panic, they pulled their ski mask over their faces, hopped out of the car, and moved toward the crowd. They saw the Young Goonz running toward the parking lot and they let their guns do the talking...pop pop pop. Pop...pop pop...pop. Boom...Boom Boom Boom...Boom...Boom.

C-Dollars went down first; he was hit in the leg, and grazed in the back of his head. Precise was hit in his hip, which slammed him into a parked car. Pressure took a slug to the back and lay on the ground unable to move.

Problem and Craps stopped to put in fresh clips when Young Bash and his niggas from Brooklyn started throwing thunder. Craps took a hollow head to the shoulder. An innocent bystander wasn't that lucky when a slug entered his forehead, killing him on impact.

The cops from the 101st precinct were blitzing the block as the shots were still being fired. One car tried to speed up on Problem and it was fired on too. Problem didn't have a problem with letting a few slugs rip through the squad car. That gave him and Craps enough time to hop in their car and peel out. After bending a few corners, Problem shook the cops and drove Craps all the way to Jamaica hospital to get some medical attention.

The Young Goonz got everybody off Mott Ave after the wounded was rushed off in ambulances.

The cops were already asking a thousand questions. They didn't give a fuck about who shot the Young Goonz. They just knew if they found that out they would find out who shot at them.

Jiggy Jack was in St. Johns hospitals waiting room calling the shooters and letting them know that niggas violated and that the shit was on. C-Dollars was getting his wounds cleaned when he noticed his Y.G. chain was missing. C-Dollars laughed aloud, but said to himself under his breath, "They better pawn that shit in for casket money."

Early the next morning the Young Goonz met up in Brooklyn at one of Young Bash cribs. The police was all over Hammels Projects, snatching anybody up looking for information. All they knew at this point was that Jiggy Jack put the showcase together and things got out of control to the point where an innocent bystander lost his life and somebody opened fire at the police.

Jiggy Jack had already phoned his lawyer and informed him on exactly what transpired, just in case they pulled him in for questioning.

The Young Goonz was talking murder from the moment they walked in Young Bash crib.

Foe, P-Kills, C-Dollars, Looch, Jiggy Jack, Nitty, D-Block, G-Pac, Chillz, Loc, Scooby, Messhall, Gunz, Smokey, Scope, Rah, and Buddah attended.

When things finally settled down Foe stood up and said, "Murder, death, Homicide. Kill kill kill...that's all I'm hearing. Alright I get it. Them niggas is gonna die...tell me something that I don't know like the getaway plan, cause killing niggas is easy, but getting away with it takes a skill...them motherfucking crackers don't got a problem with giving a nigga fifty years, so focus on that."

D-Block added on, "Yeah, not only that, I was thinking more on the lines of this, them niggas no they violated so they're gonna be on point. It ain't no need in walking into no hot ones, so a say we go at them niggas from the blind side...some shit they won't be expecting."

"Where them niggas from the sixties right?" Asked P-Killa. "And them niggas YBM...right...so let's do it like this, instead riding on them niggas from the sixties, let's just ride on tihe people...I mean, them niggas is all over the Rock...but like Foe said, "Let's put our brains behind the anger."

"And eventually we gonna catch them niggas from the sixties slipping too. I just can't wrap my mind around the fact that them niggas tried to kill us. that shit was straight planned, because whoever them niggas were with the mask on, they definitely wasn't inside the showcase, because as soon as we came out they were already running down on us," said C-Dollars as he winced from the pain that shot through his leg from the gunshot wound.

It I think everybody should stay off the radar until it's time to bomb. Don't show your face in FarRock, make them niggas think we hiding on some scared shit." Jiggy Jack suggested, which caused a few emotions to flare up. Thuggy Thug jumped up spazzing, "Fuck all dat.

Them niggas gotta die horrible deaths, and I want the whole Rock to know we did it, so this shit could never happen again nobody violates us. Not even the fucking cops, fuck the CODS they could get it too...Ya'll always worried about being discrete about shit, that's why niggas must think we ain't about that mess. We let them motherfuckers know that we put the mash on them, and still get away with it. fuck that, let em' prove in court."

"Click Clack Boom...time4e' wake the neighbors up," said G-Pac. "Let's hit the lil' nigga from Redfern that Gunz knuckled up with the other night when we went to that whack ass party."

We could hit him too, but I got some other shit in mind..."

For the next twenty minutes, Foe drew up the play with the assistance of P-Killa, the plan was more about timing and swiftness, not about the actual violence.

"Aight, but what about the YBM niggas from Hammels?" Chillz asked.

"I say we play that one by ear, if they jump bad...let the fifi kick their ass back down, because we gotta keep that Horseshoe flowing. At the end of the day we might need some getaway money," said C-

Dollars as he sat down propping his foot on Young Bash coffee table.

"All head shots," screamed Thuggy Thug, "All fucking head shots... Head shot Hammels."

"Shock and All," screamed Loc. Which caused everybody to look at him with the what the hell you talking bout look.

P-Killa laughed and said." Shock and Awe my nigga...its Shock and Awe."

After P-Killa and Loc shared their private joke with each other about Bless getting half his head blew off P-Killa said, "As soon as the sun drop, we gonna keep eyes on them niggas until it go down, all the hoopties is clean so whoever's driving, maintain your composure on your way there and back. If we could knock off the big heads that'll be sweet, then we could deal with their lil' crash dummies."

"Now I know everybody in this room wanna personally get their hands dirty, but that's not what the plan is...so we gonna stick to the script and make a good fucking movie...so what part do you wanna Play is the question.

The whole room erupted with why they felt that they should be the one to put in that work.

Jiggy Jack sat there quiet with mixed emotions. Everything he do is for him and his niggas to get out of the hood and live better lives.

War was the last thing he wanted, but now that the blood of his people were shed the gloves had to come off. When morals and principles get in the way of dreams and aspirations, the story never ends well.

As the day went on and it was now getting closer to night, the Young Goonz was getting more amped up by the minute.

G-Pac decided that it was time to call Stink, "Yo what's good. What it look like?"

"I'm parked across the street from these niggas building. I don't see big man but all his little flunkies is over there," said Stink. aight, keep your eyes on them clowns, it's going down in a few." C-Dollars told everybody to quiet down because he had something to say. "Listen, there's no need to be naive about this shit. When the shit hits the fan, FarRock is gonna be so fucking hot behind this, that if not done right and the dick heads get wind that it was us who did this shit they gonna be snatching everybody in the team up, they could get their hands on. They might even put a case on anyone of us hoping that somebody talk. Let's just assume that they put one and one together with what we about to do, what went down at the showcase, and they start snatching us. When you get to that precinct, don't say shit, absolutely nothing. Play a deaf mute for all I care, just don't talk to them pigs about nothing. The lawyers are retained, so trust that he'll be on the way...and if the dick heads start harassing you just be like, "Officer, please don't violate my Miranda rights." C-Dollars grimaced in pain again, then said, "And Jiggy Jack is right about not showing your face in Hammels. They can't catch what they can't see. I mean, if you ain't in the Horseshoe grinding, then it ain't no need to be out there anyway. The fiends want that Horseshoe and ain't nobody stopping that money. We just gonna switch it up a little, instead of making the deliveries ourselves, we gonna start sending the chicks to do it like Young Bash do out here with Reeva the Diva. So all them little pops that ya'll keep in that horseshoe smoking and fucking all day let them know it's time to earn some of that money ya'll be spending on them. Them YBM niggas might be sucka deep, but we over a million dollars strong, so fuck them niggas. Yeah, they got heart but we got brains."

"A human body could still live when brain dead, but when the heart dies...the body dies...your heard," added P-Killa.

Foe put his arm around P-Killa's shoulder and said, "Young Goonz love," and the rest of the fella's replied, "Young Goonz loyalty," and just like that the Young Goonz was on their way to

Young Goonz

FarRock.

CHAPTER NINE

Looch, Thuggy Thug, and Smokey drove around Redfern Projects a couple of times before they parked across the street from the Chinese store.

Looch was driving and it was time for young Smokey to earn his stripes. Thuggy Thug was gonna be his shadow, basically what Thuggy Thug was gonna do was stay behind Smokey, not too far and not to close, just in case the YBM niggas try to return fire after Smokey empty out. He would pretty much be his back up.

Smokey had two sixteen shot nines and he was ready to give the funeral home some business.

YBM boys were about six deep in the front of the Chinese store.

It was a regular night. They were out there selling weed, cracking jokes, and pressing every cutie that walked pass them.

Looch was watching their body language and said, "Look at these niggas, slipping like nobody told them that they should be on point too."

"Just tell me when to go," said Smokey.

"As soon as we get the call," said Thuggy Thug as he put on his leather gloves.

When Nitty pulled up to Edgemere Projects, Stink pulled off. G-Pac and D-Block were in the whip with him.

The YBM boys from Edgemere was official when it came to

playing with them hammers, so this hit had to be done by niggas with a little more experience. Nitty knew that it would be complicated to get close to the YBM building because those dudes stay on point. That's why he decided to drive the black on black Chevy Impala. They were looking like the police in that shit at first glance.

D-Block had the fifty shot Mac 11 and G-Pac had the 50 cal. Desert Eagle. Everybody in the Chevy knew that this was going to be the craziest shit they ever did, but it was no turning back now.

Nitty called Looch and said, "Ready when you are."

"Let's do it right now." Looch replied.

Thuggy Thug and Smokey cocked back their guns and put their hoods on their heads. Smokey got out first and walked toward the Chinese store. He walked right up on the YBM boys and asked, "Where the weed at fellas?"

"We got it right here, what you," homeboy didn't get a chance to finish his sentence. His words were cut short when Smokey backed out of the two Berettas and woke the mother fucking neighbors up.

Two Beretta's going off at the same time echoing off the buildings in Redfern Projects sounding like the war in Iraq. The YBM boys were scattering. A few of them ran a few paces then dropped straight on their faces. One dude was running right toward Thuggy Thug, which really want a good direction to be running in. Thuggy Thug hit dude with two shots, point blank range to the chest with a 44 Bull Dog.

Looch drove right up on them as smooth as a breeze. All Looch could hear was Thuggy Thug laughing as him and Smokey jumped in the whip. "Damn...Ya'll niggas smell like mad gun powder," said Looch as he pulled off. Looch dipped right through Nassu, which was a minute away from Redfern Projects...and the quickest way out of FarRockaway.

As soon as Nitty hung up with Looch, he started the Chevy, jumped the curb, and drove through Edgemere Projects at top speed. When he approached the YBM building, two of the YBM soldiers dipped inside the building when they saw the Impala.

Nitty stopped right in the front of the crowd. The YBM boys were clipping their weed, thinking that the pigs were coming to fuck with them; that's when D-Block and G-Pac jumped out of the car throwing thunder. The Mac 11 was so unkind.

The YBM boys tried running in the building, which gave D-Bock a better target. He just aimed for the entrance and let them niggas run into the hollow heads. After about 30 shots, the Mac jammed up. G-Pac chased them into the lobby. Two dudes were on the floor trying to crawl to the staircase. G-Pac walked up and over one of the YBM boys, head and squeezed. G-Pac turned to other nigga, walked up to him, but was seconds late because the nigga was already dead from one of D-Block slugs. G-Pac kicked the dead nigga in the head then ran out of the building.

The fifty fourth precinct was the old housing police station that niggas named the fifty-fourth precinct because it was on Beach 54th Street.

Nitty was speeding through Edgemere Projects while the CODS were speeding in. The only thing that saved them was that the police thought that they were actually police too. Nitty drove the back street on Beach Channel Drive all the way to the Marine Parkway...15 minutes later. They were back in Brooklyn.

Young Goonz

The Young Goonz was still in Brooklyn when Young Bash got the call to turn on the news. Every nigga in the crib turned his attention to the flat screen plasma inside of the entertainment center. The news reporter voiced boomed through the surround sound system, "We having breakingnews coming out of the FarRockaway section of Queens Detectives here on the crime scenes have confirmed that five people were killed and four others were wounded. Two of the wounded is in critical condition, while the other two young men are in stable condition. We are told that the two men in stable condition is not cooperating with the detectives at this time...The shootings took place in two separate housing developments in the Rockaways, and we don't have any reports as of yet if these incidents are connected."

I am standing here, in the well known for violence Edgemere Projects where you can see that the police have this building taped off. One man lays dead in the front of this building, while another two man lay dead in the lobby of this building.

The crime scene unit is collecting evidence at and around the location. When we obtain more information about these deadly shootings we will report them to you...now I'm sending this over to the second location where Bill Thomas is reporting...Bill."

Thank you April. This is Bill Thomas reporting to you from the Redfern Projects in FarRockaway Queens, where two young men were gunned down and killed and four others were wounded...witness say that two male blacks possibly in their teens wearing dark clothing opened fire on a group of young men in the front of this Chinese restaurant."

The Young Goonz had heard enough and the whole crib exploded with excitement. The celebration was on. The bottles came out and the Young Goonz was behaving like they just won the Championship game. Even though everybody was hyped a few of the Young Goonz was smart enough to know that five premeditated bodies wasn't anything to be taking lightly. Like Jay-Z said, "This ain't a movie dog." Collectively the Young Goonz was be taking lightly. Like Jay-Z said, "This ain't a movie dog." Collectively the Young Goonz was responsible for quite a few murders, but five bodies at one time is considered inhumane, not counting the two dudes in the hospital on critical, cause there's no telling if they would make it through the night.

Foe looked over at P-Killa and broke his grill down. The unspoken facial expression could only mean one thing...they asked for it.

Jiggy Jack was online at www.newsone.com listening to all the details. There was nothing said connecting the incident from the night before at the showcase to tonight's events, and they had no suspects. Jiggy Jack still had a funny feeling that there would be hell to pay and he would be footing the bill.

Jiggy Jack thoughts were interrupted by the oh so familiar chant of...Click Clack Boom/ We could wake the neighbors up.

The Young Goonz wasn't the only ones watching the news. Death Row, Sunny, Duke, and Shorty-D were in Allen Town PA. Staring at the T.V. in total disbelief. Everything was a joke twenty-four hours ago when Problem called them and explained how it went down on Mott Ave.

Nobody was laughing now. Duke and Death Row were already receiving call after call. They already know exactly who on their team was dead or in the hospital.

Sunny checked on his crew and was surprised to find out that nothing didn't go down in the sixties.

Nobody in the room wanted to admit it, but for the first time in a long time, the O.G.'s were somewhat worried.

Duke was sitting there thinking back to the night when Gunz knuckled up with one of his soldiers. He remembered how the Young Goonz was moving that night, like if push came to shove they would have caught niggas off guard with them other three niggas that were laying in the cut...then he thought...nah, them lil' niggas can't be that official.

Death Row was thinking to himself that maybe they underestimated them niggas. Even though the YBM niggas hit the Young Goonz up, ain't nobody die. On the other hand, Craps got hit, plus three of Death Row young boys got smoked so all eyes were on him for the next move.

Shorty-D spoke up first, "If ya'll expected anything less than what happened, then it's obvious that ya'll ain't take nothing into consideration that I been telling ya'll about them niggas...I gotta call my boys and tell them to be on point, because they're in the dark."

"Fuck putting them on point tell them niggas to go blow that fucking Horseshoe off the Rock, let them know that the Young Goonz is on the top of the YBM shit list and to terminate on sight, " said Duke.

Death Row hung up the phone and said, "Yo, The Rock is on fire right now. They got the major crime's unit and asking questions. They snatching everybody up, gonna have to let shit die down before we bomb it's too hectic out there right now."

Sunny took a swig of his liquor then said, "Rest in peace to all our fallen soldiers. Y'all won't die in vain... Lord forgive us, cause we about to take the vengeance out of your hands for a minute."

"Let all the families know that we gonna cover the funeral expenses," said Duke.

"It should be them motherfucker's funerals." Death Row spazzed.

His loud outburst didn't sit right with Sunny, "Hold on my nigga, don't get hostile with us, my niggas plaid their part, popped off, and yapped something. Your niggas were the ones out there throwing leg shots, so you need to channel all that energy to your shooters if you want them Young Goon niggas in caskets."

Duke jumped up and calmed his comrades down, "Pella's ain't no need or time for that shit there. We gotta figure out our next move...I was thinking, ya'll know them Gateway niggas got that Horseshoe on their block. They gotta be getting that shit from one of the major niggas. We could lay on the Gateway niggas until one of them niggas show up to drop that bag off. At least that will keep the heat away from Hammels, which won't be a good look for us to react down there, that would be too obvious for the law to figure out.

Shorty-D was fed up, "I don't know how many niggas gotta die in ya'll camp before ya'll start hearing me. Ya'll think ya'll dealing with lil' niggas...I grew up with P-Killa and Foe, way before I was YBM, I was running around Hammels wilding out with them cats. Jail was the only thing that could separate us. So the same thing ya'll saw in me to appoint me as an O.G. Is the same shit that pumps through them niggas veins...all I'm saying is this, ya'll rush the gun and lives is lost. If ya'll think we could lay on the Gateway niggas in hopes to catch one of them dropping the bag off, then ya'll niggas crazy...them niggas ain't gonna be nowhere near that bag."

The YBM crew was all muscle, they had been winning all these years due to their guerrilla tactics and the fact that they were over a thousand niggas strong in FarRockaway alone. They never were tested in this type of capacity.

Not to say that the YBM crew wasn't thinkers, because they could definitely think past go. The problem was them having to outthink a crew of thinkers, and that's exactly what the Young

Goonz were...Thinkers.

Death Row took Shorty-D's advice, "Well fuck it. Let's step in the minds of the enemy. If Sunny youngsters popped off at the showcase then I'm sure I gotta think it was the same niggas that aired Mott Ave out, so why the fuck would they gun niggas down in Edgemere and Redfern. If they were on some kill all YBM niggas shit, then why not just ride down on Shorty-D people in Hammels, like why take the risk they took?"

"Man, fuck all this trying to figure these niggas out shit. When the heat dies down and the smoke clears, we burning that pussy ass Horseshoe down," said Sunny.

"Did you hear anything that came outta Shorty-D's mouth? We gotta think on this one. Do you know that those niggas drove a fucking D.T. car through Edgemere, right up to one of my buildings, jumped out, and started blazing?" Death Row said with a look of seriousness on his face.

Nobody in the room knew the details of the Edgemere shooting, and what Death Row just told them caused a moment of silence with each of the O.G.'s trying to grasp a visual of what he just said, because that shit sounding kind of disturbing.

The YBM crew was ten steps behind, still trying to figure out their next move. So they stuck with what came natural to them, which was good ol' violence. "We going back to the hood in three days, we gonna show these niggas who run this town of ours...we put FarRock on the map...us," said Duke.

D, call your squad and tell them to keep tabs on them marks. I wanna know their every move for the next three days...we gonna teach these niggas about pissing in the wind." Death Row explained.

Homicide Detective Anthony Bell was getting nowhere fast in

his investigation. Three days of questioning possible witnesses and still no leads left Bell frustrated and annoyed. His most trusted confidential informants had their ears to the streets, but nobody was talking.

The media was chalking it up as gang violence, which was another way of saying fuck the hood. If five bodies had dropped in one day in Sunny Side Queens, it would have been all types of rewards for information, they would be checking for any links of terrorism.

Detective Bell was in charge of the shooting that took place on Mott Ave also, Due to the innocent bystander that was killed. When Bell heard that, it was Jiggy Jack and the Young Goonz, who put the showcase together he was overly ecstatic.

Bell hated the Young Goonz with a passion and he vowed to take them down once and for all, by any means necessary. Bell was deep into the Mott Ave shooting when all hell broke loose the next day, with the five homicides.

The five murders were a priority on some ghetto high profile shit, so the Young Goonz investigation had to be put on the back burner.

The five dead guys were all members of the notorious Young Black Mafia and Detective Bell knew each of the young men personally. At one time or another, each one of decease had been suspects in other homicides.

Bell decided to go down to Peninsula Hospital on Beach 54th Street and question some of the survivors. One of the guys were still in a coma, while the others were fresh out of surgery and still groggy.

Bell got the room numbers of each of the victims and would return to the hospital after they were out of the recovery unit.

Bell drove through Redfern Projects and noticed the crowd standing around a makeshift memorial in the front of the Chinese restaurant.

Young Goonz

A few guys already had R.I.P. shirts on, with a picture of their slain friend or family member on it. After sitting there observing the local tenants paying their respects to the memorial Detective Bell was just about to leave the location when he saw David Kelly a.k.a. Duke exit a black Yukon and embraced the somberly looking crowd. Bell sat up erect in his seat, grabbed his binoculars, and focused in on Duke. Being a 17-year-old veteran on the force Bell was reading Duke's body language and it was safe to assume that Duke was telling his mob to get ready for war. Well at least that's what his gut was telling him. Whatever it was that was about to go down. Bell planned to be the one to crack the case wide open.

CHAPTER TEN

Shorty-D was back in Hammels with mixed emotions. He explained to his soldiers exactly what transpired between the Young Goonz and their YBM affiliates. His soldiers were amped up and ready to ride. Logic and common sense have no home in the minds of these young crazy lil' bastards from the hood.

Shorty-D felt that he and his team didn't start this war, but they had the heavy burden of finishing it.

"Listen, when the Young Goonz retaliated, they didn't aim their guns at us. So before we jump out of the window let me find out where them niggas heads is at as far as us," explained Shorty-D.

One of Shorty-D top guns who went by the name Crook said, "YBM is YBM, violate one then you violated all...ain't that what you taught us."

"Yeah, but right is right and wrong is wrong. We gonna ride with the family of course, but we not gonna dumb out on some wild and reckless shit. So nothing's going down in Hammels unless I make the call. Are we clear on that?"

The bottom line was this, Shorty-D ran the YBMs in Hammels Projects and what he said was law. None of the other O.G.'s had the authority to tell his crew what or whatnot to do but him.

Shorty-D did remind his boys to stay on point and keep their eyes open at all times. After they were informed of what was what, Shorty-D led his crew down the stairs to the front of their building 85-02.

It was important to let his presence be known in Hammels. They were definitely ripped up and ready to let them hammers bang if they had to. Shorty-D had to show his leadership, so he was right there on the front line.

A dope fiend that wasn't too familiar with Hammels Projects walked up to the YBM crew and said it. Ya'll got that Horseshoe?"

"Hell no bitch. Beat it," screamed Pit, another one of Shorty-D shooters. All the traffic was bypassing their building and heading straight for the Horseshoe as usual. Now with the beef brewing, the money the Young Goonz was getting was intensified. Not only were they taking all the dope money, they were still getting 85 percent of the crack and weed money too.

The Young Goonz stop making deliveries, so the rush was coming from every direction. They had two runners in each of the three buildings. One building had the dope; one had the crack, while the other had the weed.

Shorty-D was stuck in between a rock and a dope spot, and he knew he had to do something quick. What...he didn't know, but something had to give." Look at all this fucking money," was the only thing running through his mind.

C-Dollars rented a club in Brooklyn for five hours to shoot a video. The club was packed with the Young Goonz only. No bitches, no other niggas, just the Young Goonz. Nah, this video was for something else. It was more like a statement for the whole FarRock to see. It was an all-black affair...well kind of. The director screamed, "Action," and it was on, "It's your boy C-Dollars, but ya'll know that...what I wanna do today, is introduce ya'll to the head hunters, because ya'll might not know them. Head Hunters, I'm gonna need ya'll help on this one...when I say we line em' up. I need ya'll to say. We lay on em. See where I'm going with this... aight. Let's get it... WE LINE em' UP (LAY ON DO RUN

UP ON em' (SPRAY ON EM) POP A BOTTLE (CELEBRATE) THEN WE SAY A PRAY FOR EM/ WE LINE em' UP (LAY ON EM) RUN UP ON em' (SPRAY ON EM) POP A BOTTLE (CELEBRATE) THEN WE SAY A PRAY FOR EM.

For the next few hours, the Young Goonz flashed money and talked hella shit to the cameras. C-Dollars swung his brand new black diamond YG chain in front of the camera to show the haters that his money was unlimited. This was a cocky move on the Young Goonz part, but like everything else they do it would serve its purpose in the very near future.

After the video shoot, the Young Goonz figured it was time to go back to FarRock. A week had passed since the five murders and now it was time to show their faces in the hood.

The celebrating and partying came to an abrupt end and now it was back to the concrete desert. When they pulled UP to the Horseshoe three cars and four SUVs deep the mood changed drastically. It was like an off and on switch with the Young Goonz. One minute they were young, full of energy, laughing and joking around, then the next minute they were calculated cold-blooded murders.

The shooters were posted up and ready, while everybody else stood around conversing with each other. One of the trucks was blasting the latest Dot mix tape called, "Connect with the Dot." C-Dollars was handing out CD's with Jiggy Jack to everybody that passed by. They were out there fronting like they were promoting their music, when in all actuality, they were waiting on somebody to act like they don't know how to act.

"What's good Ma, here take one of our new C.Ds. It's called Fear is not a factor," said Jiggy Jack.

Home girl said thank you then turned to C-Dollars and said

are you all right, I heard ya'll got shot on Mott Ave. Where Precise, tell him I said hit my phone and I'll make the pain go away."

C-Dollars laughed and said, "Okay, I'll definitely let him know that, just make sure you listen to that C.D, Precise is on track nine."

Thuggy Thug noticed Shorty-D and the YBM crew standing in the front of their building looking toward the Horseshoe. Thuggy Thug being the hot head that he was lifted both of his hands in the air to say, "Wussup."

Shorty-D, who still lived by the jail code that all call outs is mandatory, so he told his team to come on and they walked to the Horseshoe.

"First nigga false move, put a slug in his head," said as the YBM 'approached the Horseshoe. Shorty-D was telling his shooters the same shit.

"Wussup Thuggy Thug, somebody scored a touchdown or something?" Asked Shorty-D.

"You lost me," replied Thuggy Thug, knowing exactly what the hell Shorty-D was saying.

"You through your hands up like somebody scored a touch down." Nah...ain't nobody score no touch down, but if ya'll trying to catch something I gotta mean arm."

Foe came out of 84-18 and was surprised to see the YBM crew in the Horseshoe. Shorty-D, what brings you around these parts my nigga?"Asked Foe.

"That's what I'm trying to figure out, ask your boy Thuggy Thug he the one that invited us over.

One of Shorty-D soldiers that went by the name Ty said to Messhall.

"Keep your hands where I could see them before I get lumpy."

Who the fuck you think you talking to stupid face." Messhall replied with a dangerous grin on his face.

Right at that moment Chillz and D-Block came out of 84-12

with big guns in hand. G-Pac and Smokey came out of 84-16 with big guns in hand too. Rah came out of 84-18 with the automatic shotgun, better known as the street sweeper.

Messhall looked Ty right in the eyes, "And what you was saying again." The YBM crew was boxed in, but dying never scared nobody, so they stood their ground like the gangstas whom they felt they were.

Foe took control of the situation quick easy, easy fellas. Put the guns away. Shorty-D, take your people back to your building and I'm gonna come over there and holla at you my nigga."

Shorty-D had respect for Foe, plus he knew he walked into a trap, so he told his soldiers, "Move out," but not before Ice grillin Jiggy Jack.

When the YBMs walked back to their building, P-Killa said to Foe, "Yeah, they feeling a certain kind of way."

"Yeah, I could feel it in the air...I'm bout to go over there and give them niggas a warning." Foe replied.

"Na, that was their warning, next time they come this way it's gonna get messy out here...fuck them niggas," said G-Pac.

Foe jumped in the whip and drove around the block to the front of the YBM building. When he pulled up he could tell that they were over there talking mad shit.

Foe beeped the horn, called Shorty-D's name without getting out of the car. When Shorty-D realized it was Foe, he walked to the car.

"Get in," said Foe. Shorty-D was skeptical about leaving his crew, for all he knew Foe could have been trying to get him away from the building so the Young Goonz could come air shit out. "Don't pull off," said Shorty-D.

"What you don't trust me my nigga."

"It ain't about trust; I gotta make sure my people are safe...too much shit been popping off lately."

"Check it...I know you know what went down, so I could understand why ya'll on the defensive side of things, but I could assure you that you and your niggas over here are good. Now if ya'll loyalty to ya'll movement is causing ya'll to turn the blind eye on the fact that them niggas violated, then this conversation is unnecessary."

"I did hear about what happened on Mott Ave. but what I don't understand is this. What did that have to do with my people from Edgemere and Redfern?"

Foe was too swift on his toes to admit that the Young Goonz committed five murders.

"Listen, I ain't got no knowledge of that, but me and you go back to far and I would hate to hear that something happened to you out here."

Shorty-D chuckled then said, "You think I'm gonna let one of them lil' niggas run up on me and leave me slumped on these streets...you should know me better than that Foe."

"Yeah I do, and I would hate to hear that Shorty-D and his youngens laid one of my Goonz down."

"Well you better talk to them lil' niggas."

"Now you talking reckless, so let me say this...niggas is itching to scratch something, so if anybody get a body bluff in, they gonna end UD in Daffney's funeral home. And that's a fact."

Shorty-D never heard Foe be so direct on some murder shit and it kind of caught him off guard. "Me and my niggas ain't got nothing to do with what went down, but if ya'll think Thuggy or anybody gonna give us a call out and we ain't gonna respond, then ya'll wrong. The tension is too thick to be backing down, so the complex is what the complex is."

"I can't control my niggas actions because we all got our own minds. So if things do happen to take a turn for the worst, just know that's not what I personally wanted...in fact, the only reason why we are having this conversation, is for us to give Tall an opportunity to let us know where ya'll stand," said Foe calm as can be.

"As long as nobody throw no shots over here, then nobody

won't throw none over there."

"Say no more...so you cosigning for your niggas right?"

"I'm cosigning for my YBMs in Hammels...yeah."

After they gave each other dap and departed, Foe headed back to the Horseshoe and let the Young Goonz know that Shorty-D and his crew didn't want any drama, but they weren't gonna let niggas walk over them. "Fuck them niggas, but if you say they get a pass, then that's what it is...If one of them niggas get out of line and harm one of ours, then you know it's gonna be on you to handle it. Right?" said P-Killa.

"Say no more, my G," replied Foe.

Benzo from the Black Cowboys were on Jamaica Avenue doing a little shopping with his baby mother. They were hitting up all the hot spots, but when his B.M. went inside a shoe store inside the Coliseum mall, Benzo dipped off into the Hall of fame booth to cop some new mix tapes. When he walked in the booth, the dudes that were working there jumped to their feet to show him some love, not that they knew him personally, it was because Benzo was wearing a Young Goonz sweat hood.

There were Young Goonz posters on the wall, along with other up-and-coming Queens rappers. Benzo had all the Young Goonz C.D.'s, so he brought some other dudes shit that he didn't know. Benzo was kicking it with one of the dudes that worked in the booth when Death Row and two of his YBM bell ringers from the 40's Project Gilette and Fats walked in Benzo knew that Gilette and Fats were live wires and his hammer was in the car.

Death Row said, "Oh shit. I ain't know you was a Young Goon too." Benzo wasn't about to clam up at all, "And I didn't know you was a comedian." Benzo replied.

"But if you think about it, he looks good in that hoodie. I mean it fit you, because I don't see no difference from the Young Goonz and the Black Cowboys. So wear it proud," said Gilette.

Benzo laughed and said, "I'll rather wear this then them black suits ya'll been wearing lately."

The shit was just about to pop off when Benzo baby moms walked in the store. When she saw Death Row, she knew things could get ugly, she grabbed Benzo by the arm and said, "Come on Boo, let's get out of here, I ain't feeling too good."

"Aight go start the car. I'll be there in a second."

"No come on." She wasn't about to leave her man there outnumbered, Death Row told Benzo, "Be careful wearing that hoodie in the Edge, somebody might mistake you for the enemy and walk up on you and give you a hug."

"I'll keep that in mind," said Benzo as he walked out of the booth with his baby mother.

Lex and T.I. were two bitches from Hammels Projects that was far from bitches, in fact, the only thing feminine about them was the multiple women they had been fighting for their affection. They both rocked three sixty waves with low Caesar haircuts and their shits was spinning. They rocked the flyest men's clothing, and jewelry from Benny and Co.

Lex and T.I. weren't down with the Young Goonz directly, but if they were violated in the least bit. A motherfucker could kiss their monkey ass good bye. They were considered extended family and their ghetto pass extended throughout the whole FarRockaway.

Lex had the females flocking, but just like any other nigga. She had a wifey who lived in Edgemere Projects. Lex walked around most of the time with her grill broke down, not like Snoop from "The Wire," but like Lex from FarRock.

Everywhere she went, she had that chip on her shoulder for no damn reason at all.

On this particular Day Lex was in Ocean Village taking all the paper when this lame nigga name S.L. pressed her.

"Damn Lex, you ain't got no respect for my hood. You just out here snatching all the bread like niggas ain't gotta eat...what it ain't no money in Hammels."

"Fuck is you talking bout' nigga. Who the fuck is you to be questioning Lex?"

S.L. was a punk his whole childhood and Lex knew it. He did a bid for some lame shit, put on some weight, and now he was home trying to throw it around.

"I don't know how it was going down when I was gone, but I'm home now so you need to take your business elsewhere."

Lex laughed in S.L.'s face and said, "Suck my dick."

Right at that moment a fiend walked up to Lex and said, "Yo Lex, let me get five."

"Go in the building."

S.L. lost the little clientele that he had before the bid and his ribs were touching.

"Since you wanna be a nigga so bad, the next time I catch you grinding in the Viii I'm gonna treat you like a nigga."

Lex didn't even entertain S.L.'s last statement. She went into that building and bust that head.

After she made the sale, she hit T.I. on the phone, "What's good my nigga," asked T.I.

"Code 89," Lex replied plain and simple.

"Where you at?" "Ocean Village."

"Aight, I'm on my way."

After T.I. hung up, she was wondering what the hell Lex done got into now. T.I. grabbed the P-89 Ruger then headed out of the door. T.I. wasn't on that gangsta shit that Lex was on. She considered herself a ladies' man, but Lex was her right hand man, and if it was drama with Lex then it was drama with her.

T.I. pulled up in Ocean Village parking lot ten minutes later. She had that feeling that shit was about to get crazy. T.I. felt that nobody needed a hammer in Ocean Village; this was the less violent area in the whole FarRockaway. When T.I. got inside the apartment, her bitch was cooking steaks, smoking haze and sipping on a glass of Nuvo, while Lex's bitch was cleaning the living room.

Lex pulled T.I. in the back room, "Yo I'mma push this bitch nigga face off tonight."

"Who." T.I. asked almost not even wanting to know.

"That bird ass nigga S.L. that just came home from up north, talking bout' Lex can't eat. That nigga must have bumped his mother fucking head on the pull up bar." T.I. saw Lex in this zone before and wished it was something she could say to change Lex mind, but T.I. wasn't in the habit of wasting her breath, so she wiped her prints off the P-89, handed it to Lex and asked, "You gotta mask?"

"Fuck a mask, I want this nigga to see my face before he dies." This bitch is crazy. T.I. thought.

Later that night, around two o'clock in the morning Lex and T.I. slid out of the crib, leaving their bitches in the bed sleep. T.I. was shaken. She really didn't want anything to do with this shit but she would never leave Lex hanging. Never.

Lex told T.I. to go and get the car ready. T.I. was so happy she didn't have to go with Lex, she damn near ran to the car.

T.I. sat in the car chain smoking Newport's just waiting to hear that pop.

S.L. was in the lobby of his building counting his little chump change that it took him all damn day to make when Lex walked in the building with a black leather baseball jacket and a black fitted cap to match. S.L. didn't realize that Lex wasn't a dude until she spoke, because the brim of her cap came down low to her eyes.

"What up gangsta...what's that hot shit you was saying earlier."

S.L. laughed, "Yo you really think you a dude, coming up in

here questioning me like you some type of G."

Lex not being the one for talking in situations like this, backed the hammer out and said, "Remember where you heard it first. Bitches." Boom.

The panic and shock that raced across S.L.'s face when the hollow tip chewed through his chest was Priceless as he dropped to his knees. Lex was just about to put one in his head when she heard him mumble something that wasn't audible.

"What nigga...I can't hear you." Lex got closer to hear what S.L. was trying to say.

"Im...sor...sorry." S.L. said finding it impossible to breathe.

"You sorry. You sorry, fuck your apology bitch, you bitch ass pussy ass mutha fuka. Lex was so enraged that she started kicking the fuck outta S.L. bird ass.

Somebody screamed down the stairs, "Hey what's going on down there. I'm calling the cops."

Lex kicked S.L. one last time in the chest then ran out of the building and jumped in the car with T.I. "Co my nigga go." When they pulled up in the Horseshoe T.I. asked, "Did you get the nigga."

"Yeah. You ain't hear the shot?"

"Nah son, I couldn't hear shit with my heart beating so loud."

They both laughed as Lex sparked the blunt. Lex took two pulls without exhaling and said, "

The shot was kind of muffled because I put the blicky right to the nigga chest when I popped him."

"You think he dead," asked T.I. sounding a little nervous.

"I don't know, but I bet he sorry for fucking with the kid."

CHAPTER ELEVEN

S.L. was in Peninsula Hospital's recovery room after the doctors removed fragments from his chest cavity and pancreas. He was handcuffed to the bed due to the twenty-three bags of crack that was found on his person.

Detective Bell heard about the shooting and wanted to see if was in any way connected to the five murders.

When Detective Bell walked into the room holding the twenty-three crack rock rocks, S.L's heart dropped inside his bedpan.

Bell went straight for the jugular, "Criminal possession of a control substance in the third degree. And a curfew violation, sounds like a straight disregard of your conditions upon release. Shit, you only be out of the can for what. Eight days. I hope you got laid enough buddy to hold you for the next five years because you're screwed. Big time."

Water welled up in S.L.'s eyes when the reality of going right back to jail sunk in.

"Unless you wanna help yourself out. I could make all this petty shit go down the god damn toilet."

S.L. didn't miss a beat, "Okay, please I'll tell you whatever you wanna know. I ain't trying to go back to jail...please." S.L. sobbed.

Detective Bell hated snitches; they took the adrenaline out of his job. Bell got his rocks off by solving cases the good ol' fashion way with good police work. But you know what they say, "A good detective is only as good as his informants.

"Okay but let's get one thing straight, don't bullshit me, I get enough of that at home with the wife. If I feel that your bullshitting me, I'm out that door, just like I do the old lady. And right there in that small claustrophobic hospital room, a rat was born.

Detective Bell pulled out his scratch pad and asked, "Are you currently a member of the Young Black Mafia."

"No sir."

"Do you know who runs the YBM organization in Ocean Village?"

"I don't know his real name, but everybody call's him Death Row."

"I got one last questioned to see where we go from here...Can you infiltrate, well let me say it like this cause infiltrate is such an ugly word. Can you get down with the YBM crew, then get me some information on these murders?"

S.L. wasted no time answering in the affirmative. "Hell yeah, they been trying to get me down with them every sense I came home."

"Good. Now for the matter at hand, who shot you, Mr. McRay?"

"Come on Bell, If I tell you that, then the word gonna go around the hood that I'm a rat, tthen the YBM crew ain't gonna wanna fuck with me." S.L. whined.

"Let me do the thinking. You just do the talking."

Two days later Duke was in Hammels Projects at one of Shorty-D's apartments looking out of the window at the Horseshoe. He felt that it was time for him and his team to peel one of these niggas cabbage back. His shooters sat stationary in a getaway car a block away from the projects by the boardwalk. They waited on Duke's instructions.

Shorty-D didn't agree to let Duke do a steak out at his crib, but what could he say when Duke showed up at his door seven o' clock in the morning.

Shorty-D was indirectly trying to discourage Duke, "I'm telling you my nigga, them niggas don't be showing their face in that Horseshoe that much...you might see one or two lil' niggas, but the niggas you want don't be out here every day."

"I'm not gonna be able to rest until I slump one of these bitch made, cornball ass niggas," said Duke in a low voice that was almost a whisper.

For the last hour, Duke watched what looked like a million dollars' worth of sales go in and out of the Horseshoe.

"You know what apartment all of them fiends going to cop at?" Duke asked.

"Nah, them niggas be switching up." Shorty-D lied, knowing that the fiends are copping right there in the lobbies.

It was just turning nine o' clock in the morning and Duke was getting hungry.

"Let's go across the street to the restaurant and get something to eat."

Shorty-D wasn't trying to be seen in Hammels with Duke after he already had an agreement with the Young Goonz.

"Nah my dude, stay focus. I could send my bitch to get us some food."

On some G shit, I'm starting to see what you saying. Those niggas are somewhere in the cut, while the Horseshoe is bubbling...I'm bout' to head back to the Fern and rethink this shit."

Duke called his shooters and told them to swing around to the restaurant on Beach 87th Street, across the street from Hammels. Duke had on a level three bulletproof vest on with a Glock 23 on his hip. He gave Shorty-D dap and a hug then left the apartment.

Shorty-D couldn't understand if Duke had a death wish, or if he just made a habit out of moving reckless. Whatever it was, Shorty-D was just glad that the nigga left his crib.

But little did he know. It would have been better if Duke stayed a little while longer.

P-Killa and Looch were sitting in the restaurant on Beach

87th Street having breakfast and discussing Young Goonz business.

"C-Dollars and Young Bash had a sit down with Whitey last night... Everything is good and powerful. Holla at Stink and B.G, once everybody is taking care of in the hood we gonna take a trip O.T," said P-Killa.

"Did Jiggy Jack say anything about the coming home party for Sha the God, Grecco, Crazy Mone, and Mone...I think we should throw it at Sue's Rendezvous. The bitches in that motherfucker are flawless. If I just came home from jail, Sue's would like heaven, with a bunch of butt naked angels shaking their asses," said Looch as he reminisced about the last time he was at the famous strip club in Mount Vernon.

"I don't know how Jiggy Jack plan on doing it for them. He ain't letting the cat out of the bag yet, cause of that shit that popped off at the showcase. Whatever he does, I know it's gonna be crazy. And I'mma be right there. We just gotta be on extra point," replied P-Killa.

P-Killa thought he saw a ghost, "You gotta be fucking kidding me, look what the wind just blew it."

Looch turned his head to see what P-Killa was talking about and it seemed like him and Duke locked eyes at the same time, and both of their faces said it all, when their grills broke down instantly. Duke made a quick u-turn and walked out of the restaurant. When he got outside his shooters were parked right next to his 2009 Jaguar, "P-Killa and Looch are in there eating, when they come out make me proud. That's the nigga Looch Benz right there." Duke point to the silver CLS500 then got in his whip and peeled off fast.

P-Killa watched the Jag speed past the restaurant's window, but he was totally oblivious to the car full of killers who waited for him and Looch to exit the restaurant.

Looch paid the bill and said, "Let's get the fuck outta here before that nigga double back."

"You got the blicky in the whip right?' P-Killa asked.

"You already know."

When they made it out of the restaurant, they walked about half the distance to the car when the young killas with depraved indifferences for human lives ran up on them.

P-Killa instincts kicked in when he saw the hoodies and the hammers; he pushed Looch and screamed, "Bounce."

P-Killa shuffled left, shuffled right, and then dipped behind park cars in the parking lot. He heard so many shots that his legs got wobbly, but experience is the best teacher, so he shook the jitters off and kept running.

Looch, on the other hand, never stood a chance. When P-Killa pushed him and told him to Bounce is brain froze up and didn't send the message to his feet to run. Looch froze, but shorty didn't. The lil' nigga raised his gun to Looch head and squeezed the hair pen trigger. Boom.

When the shots finally stopped P-Killa heard tires screeching off. P-Killa stood up. He didn't see Looch, so he figured he got away too, until he heard the shrieking scream of a female. He ran to the middle of the street where Looch laid in a puddle of blood that leaked from his face. The sight was harsh on P-Killa's eyes, so he turned his head and started screaming, "Call the ambulance. Call the fucking ambulance."

Five minutes later the whole hood came running to the parking lot. The ambulance arrived a few minutes after and everyone watched in shock as the EMT workers went to work on Looch trying to keep him alive.

The Young Goonz was pulling up in cars one at a time, and now they stood out there deep.

P-Killa explained to them who was responsible for the hit and Foe started spazzing out. "What the fuck is ya'll doing, eating in the hood, in the middle of a fucking war...fuck is ya'll niggas stupid or ya'll just slipping."

"Watch your fucking mouth nigga, don't come at me like I'm a fucking lame. Address me like a G nigga."

"Then move like a G, G's don't get caught with their fucking heads down."

D-Block came running, jumped in between Foe and P-Killa,

"Yo chill. It ain't looking good; a slug went straight through his eye...If my nigga die."

Detective Bell pulled up and that was the cue for the Young Goonz to break the fuck out. Looch was already en route to the hospital, so there was a need to stick around. The Young Goonz went straight to the Horseshoe.

Everybody listened as P-Killa broke down exactly how it went down. That's when a little smut bitch from Hammels named Diamond walked up and said, "D-Block let me holla at you."

"Not right now, burn it up." D-Block said real disrespectful.

"But it's important, I seen what happened."

D-Block already knew what happened, but decided to hear her out. Diamond was in a car parked in the front of Shorty-D's building with a nigga from Bay Towers. She just had finished deep throating the nigga to death when she saw Duke come out of Shorty-D's building. She knew Duke real well, in fact, she couldn't stand his ass after he nutted in her mouth and never called her ass again.

Diamond explained to D-Block how she saw Duke come out of the building, and she saw him talking to the dudes in the car right before they shot Looch.

D Block had heard enough, "Aight good looking, my bad for spazzing on you too...Look, don't tell nobody what you just told me, or what you saw okay."

Diamond said all right and was about to leave. D-Block went in his pocket counted out four hundred dollars and said, "Nobody right?"

"Nobody...trust me, I ain't stupid, and thanks for the money, but you ain't have too. The Young Goonz show me too much love for me not to say what I saw to ya'll."

D-Block told the rest of the Young Goonz what Diamond said she saw right after she walked away. P-Killa looked at Foe and said, "Yeah, talk that G shit now. The same nigga, Yo man, said he don't want no drama, now he got niggas out here laying on us. Live with on your conscience.

Young Bash and Dot pulled up in the Horseshoe with concern looks on their faces, almost anticipating somebody to shake their head and say that he didn't make it.

"How is he?" Dot asked.

"Nobody knows yet." G-Pac replied.

Detective Bell came speeding through the Horseshoe, with a blue and white squad car trailing his unmark car. He jumped out of the car and walked toward the Young Goonz. Nobody was in the mood to be fucked with.

Bell walked passed the crowd when he saw Lex, he pulled his department issued Glock and screamed, "Freeze; don't you move...put your hands in the air and leave them there."

The Young Goonz was looking at Bell like he lost his damn mind. They thought that Bell was mistaking Lex for a dude or something. Until he put the cuffs on her and read her rights, using her government name. Lex calmly asked, "What am I being arrested for?"

Bell tightened the cuffs, and then said, "Attempted murder in the first degree."

Lex turned to T.I. and said, "Call my wife, tell her I said call my lawyer."

After the cops left the Horseshoe Young Bash asked T.I. "What the fuck was all of that about?"

T.I. shook her head then said, "Long story."

When it's your time to go, it's your time to go. But it definitely wasn't Looch time to head to the upper room. The Bullet knocked out his right eye and exited his temple. Looch head swelled up the size of a basketball. The doctors were afraid that if the swelling didn't go down in seventy-two hours, there could be some brain damage.

The doctor came out and explained to Looche's family and C-Dollars his conditions. He was definitely going to live, which was great news, but it was too early to determine the lifelong effects of his injuries.

C-Dollars was furious, and vowed to put something in the dirt himself. Once upon a time, before the money, Ice, and European cars C-Dollars was running around FarRock letting his hammer fly. He went from a gun slinging two-bit hustler; to a six-figure nigga that could push the button and have the Young Goonz murder a nigga like it's nothing. You could take the Goon out of the hood, but he could always come back. C-Dollars weren't dealing with emotions, because it was all fair in the concrete desert. He respected how the YBM niggas answered back the way they did, as long as they respected how he was about to give it up.

C-Dollars left the hospital and drove straight to Gateway to holla at B.G. and Jah.

When he pulled up B.G. jumped in the whip with him, "Don't talk in the car my nigga." C-Dollars said as he pulled off. He drove to the Olive Garden located in Times Square. There was no need in getting a table, so they ordered drinks and sat at the bar.

B.G. knew all about the Young Goonz and YBM war, but his only concern was getting his hands on the dope. His block ran out two days ago and the fiends already started car pooling it to Hammels Projects.

C-Dollars took a sip of his shot of Nutron then got down to it.

"This is what it is, me my niggas is putting a hefty price on a nigga head, so ya'll gonna have to miss at least two re-ups. Everything we got gonna have to go to the streets, so we could cover the bill."

This was the last thing that B.G. wanted to hear, but being the opportunist that he was, missing the two re-up's went in one ear and out of the other. What stuck in his head was the hefty price that they were putting on a nigga's helmet. B.G. didn't want to sound thirsty, so he came out as smooth as possible when he said. "Not for nothing, but whoever ya'll gonna spend the money on ain't my business. But if I can't get the work because the money is needed to handle that problem, then whoever that problem is, got a problem with me because he's stopping my flow. And I'll love to handle that problem for that hefty price, plus keep my block clicking."

C-Dollars stirred the Ice in his drink, while staring at it like he was in deep thought, or heavy contemplation then said, "I don't know if you wanna get yourself involved with a caliber of shit that paying all that money for."

"How much bread ya'll talking bout'?"

"We cashing out...a hundred grand." C-Dollars said like if any hood nigga with them kind of numbers thrown at him would refuse.

"Damn boy. Fuck ya'll niggas trying to get a cop off fed." B.G. joked C-Dollars didn't laugh though, he took another sip of his drink and said, "Nah, ain't no cop...We putting that on the nigga Duke-head."
The shit sounded too easy to B.G. there had to be a catch, "Not for nothing, but that's a nice piece of changes for some light work...what's the catch my nigga?"

"There's no catch, but what we want done ain't no regular hood shit."

"It can't be nothing I ain't do before, Plus I promised P-Killa loyalty over royalty. So..."

"Cool, but trust me you never even thought about doing no shit like this...this is what we want done."

After C-Dollars explained exactly how he wanted Duke to die, B.G. had to admit it to himself that he never did no shit like that before, nor did he ever thought about doing it...but he was going to do it, or at least try for all that paper.

"We giving fifty up front to put a rush on it. My niggas outta town would be here in the morning if I proposition them, so let me know now if you could handle it."

"Shit...it might be done before them niggas could even get here." On the drive back to FarRock, sense there was no talking in the car B.G. had time to think. HE wondered if all that shit about not giving up the dope was a hoax just to get him to take the hit. He remembered what Stink told about these niggas being real smart when it came to this street shit. Yeah, those niggas could wipe their ass with a hundred grand, but fuck it. I live for this shit.

B.G. casually stole a glance at C-Dollars and for the first time in a long time he saw a nigga just as dangerous as him and Jah, if not more dangerous...but in a whole different way.

CHAPTER TWELVE

This was Lex second violent offense so the judge in Queens Criminal Court set bail at 150,000 cash no bond. Which meant the only way out would be to pay that 150,000, dollar for dollar, then it would be all types of hearings to show proof of where the money came from, to make sure that's it's legit and not drug money.

Lex's lawyer David Castro was a well-respected criminal attorney in Queens County. So he could gain access of certain documents before him or his clients were entitled to have them.

Castro entered the bullpen area and called Lex by her government name.

"Back here Castro," shouted Lex from the last bullpen in the back.

After they greeted Castro quickly explained to Lex what was going on so that he could get out of that funky ass holding area. "Listen, this totally weak. The guy who was shot that he went down the stairs in his apartment building to check the mail box three o' clock in the morning and was robbed by two guys wearing face mask, he claimed that the guy shot him when he discovered that he only had three dollars on him.

Lex laughed, "So why the hell they lock me up for."

"I was just about to get to that, it seems that they have a witness that claims she saw you running away from the scene right after she heard the shot...Do you know a lady name Mary Atkins."

"Nah, but I could find out."

Well, you need to find out before next week when this

case goes before the Grand Jury. I did background check and her rap sheets tells me that she's a drug addict, she's been in and out of jail for the past ten years with charges ranging from trespassing all the way to prostitution. I had to pull a few strings to get this information, so that mean this is an off the record conversation that never happened. And I'm sure you remember that all off the record conversations have its own set price."

Lex smiled and said, "What conversation."

When Lex got back to the women's house on Rikers Island, she went straight to the phone and Dre. All the phones on Rikers are monitored so Lex used one of the pen numbers she brought from a fiend for three Newport's that she smuggled into the jail, to make the call.

Lex explained everything to Dre, She was adamant about the fiend not making it to court for the Grand Jury. Lex knew If the fiend make it to testify, she would be indicted, which meant she would have to cop out to some jail time or take the case to trial if she couldn't make the 150,000 dollar cash bail.

When Lex told Dre the fiend's name, he lied and said he didn't know who she was. Dre knew exactly who Scary Mary was. The word around Ocean Village was that she was rat, but nobody ever had any proof, until now.

Before Lex hung up, she told Dre, "Yo, find out who that bitch is, then come pick me up from Court next week."

Dre knew exactly what Lex was implying, but he had a better idea.

That following Saturday, two days before Lex case was to go in front of the Grand jury. That night Dre was walking around Ocean Village looking for Scary Mary. Dre was a low-key smooth nigga. His main hustle was exotic weed, which held him maintain his low profile.

Dre was still on parole at the time. He did a three-year bid when his dope spot was raided in Hammels Projects. The police found two guns and some dope and the rest is history.

He walked around Ocean Village until he ran into Scary Mary, "Mary, wussup ma, I need you to test some boy for me, but if you ain't gonna keep it real then I'll find somebody else."

"Now baby, you know I'll keep it real and let you know what it's hitting for.

Dre didn't want to be seen going inside the building with Mary, so he told her to meet him upstairs on third floor where he had a get low crib at. When they got inside the apartment, Mary asked Dre, "When you get back in the game, I thought you were leaving the hard shit alone."

"Man, it's hard out here for a pimp." Replied Dre.

"I know that's right baby, Okay I'm ready." Scary Mary tied up her arm to find one of her damaged veins. Little did she know that Dre cut the dope sulfuric and battery acid.

When Mary shot the poison in her vain, she instantly knew that something was wrong. First, her whole body froze in stiffness. She fell out of the chair and began to violently shake with convulsions.

Dre pulled up a chair, sat down calmly, poured himself a glass of Patron, sparked his blunt, and watched as Scary Mary pissed her pants and foam from the mouth.

Ten minutes later, she was dead as a doorknob. Four o' clock Sunday morning, pre picked Mary's body up, carried her down the back stairs-case where he laid her down on the second floor landing.

Scary Mary's body was found eight o' clock that morning. The tenants were awakening by the loud sirens. Nosey neighbors were already whispering that Mary overdosed on the steps.

Dre was standing right there among the crowd, smoking a Newport like nothing happened a few hours ago. The only thing that was on Dre's mind was he might have to lay the nigga S.L. down next, because there was no way in the world he was going to let the nigga front on Lex. He already had the one up on S.L; he was fucking his baby mother when he was up north. Dre made her except his collect call and talk to him while he beat off all over her face...and she loved it.

Detective Bell came out of the building looking distressed. Mary Atkins was more than just a confidential informant to Bell. Their relationship went back ten years. Bell watched as the drugs added wear and tear year after year. He knew that the money he gave her went to drugs, but he also knew that she became so dependent on the drugs that she would go to any extreme to get it, so he rather gave to her himself.

Dre looked at Bell and thought, "Rat poison motherfucka."

Later that night, back in Hammels projects the Young Goonz was in the Horseshoe plotting on Shorty-D and his crew.

"Let's just walk over there and spin a few of them niggas tops off. Bird ass broke ass niggas." Smokey stated like if it was just as simple as saying it.

"I ain't trying to spend the rest of my life in the can for one of them dirty niggas. Its better ways of doing shit my dude." D-Block explained.

"I'm saying, we gave them sluts the pass and this is how they thank us...Looch could have died. Let's just press the niggas to the concrete—I'm feeling what Smokey feeling," said Thuggy Thug, always being the one to come with the battery already in his back.

"Yeah, but P-Killa said that they wanted us to fall back, cause they didn't want us to make it hot before they bust the next move." D-Block said trying to stick to the script.

"Fuck that, I'm riding...whoever with me say Boom," said Smokey as he looked through the window of the lobby inside of 84-12.

"Boom," said Thuggy Thug.

"Boom," said Chillz.

D-Block was reluctant to say Boom, but at the end of a deep breath, he said, "Boom."

"Aight, then it's settled. Go grip up. Me and Chillz gonna creep through the back way staircase of their building, catch them bitches slipping in the lobby. If those niggas get lucky and make it out that building D-Block, you and Thuggy Thug come around the front and trip them niggas up...feel me." Smokey thought he put together a foolproof plan in three minutes of talking and no minutes of thinking.

When the war is on in the hood and the enemy lives literally 60 feet away in the next building death is promised. Death shows the reality of the opposition's determination. Because everybody knows, it's real when somebody dies.

Smokey put his hood over his head, tied a scarf around the bottom of his face, and then walked out of the building. Chillz was two steps behind him when they entered the back door of the YBM building.

Chillz was thirsty to touch something up. He was about to show the YBM crew that G stands for Goonz. The Young Goonz lived by many principles, and one them was, "Friends of my enemies is also my enemies."

Smokey and Chillz crept through 85-02; they walked up the back steps, and then came down the front steps with their guns out, ready to squeeze.

Three YBM soldiers; none of them not even sixteen years old yet was in the lobby. They were rolling dice for fun, because they damn sure didn't have any money to bet.

Smokey and Chillz bust through the staircase door, catching the lil' niggas off guard.

"Don't fucking run. If you run I'ma shoot," screamed Chillz.

The young punks dropped everything in their hands and threw them straight in the air.

Chillz grabbed one of the lil' niggas by the collar and said, "Where the fuck is Shorty-D at," the youngster was shaking like a leaf.

"I don't know man; he ain't out here...get off me."

Chillz smacked him in the eye with the 9mm, which left a deep gash that blood poured out of instantly.

"I'm gonna ask your lil' bitch ass one more time, then I'mma kill you if you lie to me again," said Chillz with a deranged look on his face that he put on just to scare the lil' nigga up.

Lil' man was scared to death already; he ain't never experienced no grown man shit like this before.

"Please don't shoot me, I don't know where he's at, but I could call him."

Little did Smokey and Chillz know; a blue and white patrol car was pulling up to the side of 85-02. The cops got out of the car and were heading towards the entrance of the building. They had a call for a domestic dispute, and they were on their way to the apartment.

G-Pac and D-Block had no way to warn them because the building knocked the service out on their Nextel phones, so they thought of the only logical thing to do in a situation like this.

G-Pac put his hood over his head, pulled out of the 40 cal, pointed to the sky, and emptied the clip.

The cops stopped dead in their tracks and drew their guns out of their holsters. They could see flashes coming from the nuzzle of a gun coming from the Horseshoe. Off of impulse, they jumped in the squad car and sped to the Horseshoe.

Little man in the building was just about to dial Shorty-D's number when he and everybody else in the building heard the forty going off.

The lil' niggas nerves were so bad that he dropped the phone, and damn near fainted. He thought Chillz shot his ass.

Smokey and Chillz didn't know what the fuck was going on. Smokey was just about to peek his head out of the building, but those thoughts were cut short fast when they heard the sirens blaring real close to the building.

It was time to think fast for the Young Goonz. The last thing they wanted was for the YBM niggas to come running down the stairs and find them in their lobby violating two lil' niggas. If shit pop off, and they got to shoot their way out of the lobby, they would be running right into the cops with smoking guns.

There was nothing they could do but wait it out and keep their guns on the little niggas. More cop cars could be heard speeding past the building, so Chillz and Smokey situation wasn't getting any better.   "Aight...this what we gonna do, everybody in the elevator. Now, let's move." Smokey demanded.

The little niggas did exactly what they were told to do. Smokey and Chillz took them to the roof and made them sit on the floor while they waited for shit to die down. After about a good twenty minutes, Smokey peeked his head over the roof's fence and saw all the cop cars leaving the projects.

They marched the lil' niggas back down the stairs. They were just about to send Shorty-D a message with a couple of leg shots, but that turned out to be unnecessary. Shorty-D and three of his shooters walked in the building.

Everything happened in fast forward. Chillz might be as blind as a bat, but the bright lobby lights gave him a good enough look at Shorty-D's face. He didn't blink, nor did he hesitate. Chillz just let it go, "Boom Boom...Boom Boom Boom." All of his shots missed, and the YBM crew could back pedal up out of the building.

Once outside of the building one of Shorty-D's shooters started blasting eratically at the lobby door pop pop pop pop...pop pop pop pop pop. That's when all hell broke loose, G-Pac and D-Block must have heard the shots, and they came running around 85-02 blazing. The YBM crew returned fire and it was on.

Smokey and Chillz ran back up the steps and came back out of the back way entrance, the same way they crept through the building.

Chillz blind ass threw two shots at D-Block by mistake. "Nah nigga, that's us," screamed Smokey.

One of the benefits of living in any of the projects in FarRockaway was that you could hear the cop's sirens echoing under the A Train station way before they reached the projects.

And that was the Young Goonz cue; they ran back to the

Horseshoe and split up into three buildings.

The police that just left the projects minutes ago was back taping off the YAM building. There was over fifty yellow cups next to shell casings...but not one person was shot.

S.L found a way to have a sit down with Death Row, two days later he successfully wiggled his way into the YBM crew. S.L. had more hidden agendas then a little bit.

Bell been blowing g his phone up every day, so he figured he'd give him a call.

I'm in, give me some time to hear something. I ain't trying to be asking niggas D.A. questions...motherfuckers get suspicious and kill my ass."

"Either way your ass is on the line, get me what I want or you'll be back in the Messhall eating rice Diablo and soup of the week. Oh yeah, just so you know, your lil' girlfriend is home. Mary couldn't make it to the Grand Jury."

S.L. hung up the phone and was already plotting on using his new YBM status to get Lex gay ass murdered. That same night S.L. was standing in front of his building in Ocean Village sipping on an ensure, lying his ass off to this nigga name Face, who has been repping YBM for years.

"Two niggas ran up in the building talking bout' respect the jooks...you heard. One nigga got the skatty while the other nigga tried digging my pockets. You heard. Soon as the nigga got close to me, I sized em' up, and then hook on the busta...you heard. The nigga must have had a glass jaw, because the nigga went straight out. After that nigga hit the ground, I rush the one that had the skatty. I almost disarmed the bozo, but the nigga got a lucky shot off and caught me in the chest...you heard, but you know I'm built like that. I chased the niggas out of the building, but the niggas were fast as flick. You heard. Word to everything I love, I lit a cigarette and called me a cab." Face was caught up in S.L.'s bullshit story. It wasn't just what he was saying, it was the way he dramatized the story with extra emphasis that made the shit sound official. Just like the typical jail nigga!

"Damn My nigga, that was some straight gangsta shit you did...but check it, you good now. Nobody violates YBM so you ain't gotta worry about shit now. It's one for all, and all for one. You heard," said Face, meaning every word he said.

S.L. took a sip of his ensure and said, "That's WUSSUD, first nigga front getting murdered...YBM to the death...you heard."

Face never knew S.L. for being no gunslinger, but he figured that being in jail must have brought the beast out of S.L.

"Hurry up and heal up too, cause we at war. And when Death Row says it's time to ride out, don't ask no questions and don't be late," said Face.

"I'm always ready. Who we ay war wit, cause I seen when ya'll went to them funerals. Who the fuck had the heart to transgress against us?" S.L. asked.

Face knew exactly who killed his affiliates, but running his mouth was never in his DNA. "Just know this...they died for repping YBM, the same thing that your repping now. So it's ride or be rode on...bite or be bitten...feel me?"

S.L. wasn't riding or biting on shit, he was just trying to get enough information to get Detective Bell off his back and out of his life. All he had to do was fake it until he made it. Well at least that's what he thought.

CHAPTER THIRTEEN

Two weeks past since the Young Goonz shot up Shorty-D's building in Hammels Projects. The tension was thick enough to cut with a knife.

Shorty-D and Sunny circled Hammels in a rented Ford Explorer with tinted windows.

The shooters were in Shorty-D's crib waiting on the call. Sunny had two carloads of his knuckle heads parked behind the Horseshoe on Beach Channel Drive.

Sunny was astonished when he saw all the fiends going in and out of the Horseshoe. He saw fiends from Redfern, Gateway, Central Ave, Mott Ave, 25th Street, The 40s, Edgemere, Ocean Village, The 60s, the 100s, and other motherfuckers that didn't even look like they were from FarRock. "God damn. This can't be...I wonder what these niggas are pulling in daily. We should have just come to the table with these dudes instead of starting a war."

Shorty-D looked at Sunny like he had three heads. "I'mma act like I didn't just hear that...cause I been telling ya'll that shit from the jump. Ya'll wanted to press the issue the wrong way. Death Row and Duke lost soldiers. I almost walked into my coffin, what you think you and your solders is next on their to do list, so now you saying this war shit is senseless." Shorty-D barked.

"Take it easy gangsta, I was just talking shit, I didn't think you were gonna take shit all personal and jump down my fucking throat."

"All I'm saying is this. It's too late to even be talking bout' what we should have, could have done. Them niggas ain't playing with it, they trying to leave us stinking."

Sunny couldn't focus on nothing Shorty-D was saying. He

was too busy estimating how much money was flowing through the Horseshoe.

While the O.G.'s were watching the money, the Young Goonz was spending it. Within the last two, to three weeks, three Young Goonz were released from prison. Sha the God got his conviction reversed after appealing his 25 to life sentence because he did not get a fair trial, due to the district attorney systematically keeping blacks from sitting on his jury.

Sha the God was a beast in more aspects than one. He was a stick up kid, a boxer, a shooter, and a Young Goon.

Crazy Mone came home about a week after Sha the God. Crazy Mone wasn't originally a Young Goon, but his loyalty to Foe is what eventually brought him to the family. When Foe was doing one of his bids, he kept hearing how Crazy Mone was keeping it gangsta on the streets, so he reached out to him and those niggas been rocking every sense.

Grecco was another Young Goon to come home not expecting the war that was going on. Grecco was turning it up in the pen. He had beef with everybody. It's easy to be a G in the streets with a big ass 45. ACP in your hand, but when your back is to the wall and all you got is a razor, a knuckle game, and your heart, the facade is over. Grecco was as tough as nails, and to top it off, he was screaming Young Goonz every time he shook it with a nigga or a C.O. Grecco lived for conflict. The war was right up his lane because while he was bidding one of the YBM niggas from Mott Ave was fucking is sister and put hands on her. Whenever he ran into a YBM nigga in the pen, he broke his face.

The Young Goonz rented the club on wheels to go pick up the last Young Goon to come home. M-One did an eleven-year bid off a nine to life sentence for a murder that one of the other Young Goonz committed. M-One held it down, did the time and now the journey was over.

When M-One walked out of the front door of Arthur Kill

Correctional facility, he saw Foe standing next to the Navi.

"Oh shit...they done fucked up now, they let the beast out of the mother fucking cage." Foe screamed.

"AAAAAAH," screamed M-One. "I'm still standing. They couldn't break me my nigga... they couldn't break me."

The childhood friends embraced each other with gangsta love right there in the front of the jail. "Let's get the fuck outta here before they say they made a mistake." Foe joked.

"This your boat my nigga?" M-One asked as they walked to the Navigator.

"Nah, but wait til' you see what's inside." When Foe opened the door, everybody screamed, "SUPRISE," and all you heard were corks popping. The welcome home celebration was on. Many of the dudes come home from jail, but when you're a Young Goon, coming home is like winning the lottery. Minus the war it was a blessing to be a member of the Young Goonz, and that's exactly how M-One, Sha the God, Grecco, and Crazy Mone were feeling in the stretch, plushed out Navigator.

The first stop of the shopping spree was 5th Avenue. From there they went uptown to 125th Street. The last spot they hit was Jamaica Avenue. It was five o' clock so M-One decided to go make his first report to his parole officer on Merrick Blvd. He had 24 hours to report but why come back to the Ave. tomorrow, knowing that he was about to party all night long.

The Young Goonz pulled up on Merrick Blvd too flashy for any P.O. not to get on some bullshit, if they saw somebody on their caseload getting out of the Navigator. M-One jumped out like the world was his.

After eleven years in the joint, he felt like it was high time to shine. When M-One entered the building, Crazy Mone and Foe started kicking it in the whip.

"Damn son, we ain't been in the town for a minute. I had been hearing bits and pieces about this war with the YBM. All this shit is new to me. I read about the five murders that happened, but I just brush it off as some FarRock shit. I didn't know the team was involved, but check it. If shit get funky, I'mma show you why they call me crazy Mone."

"You ain't gotta show me what I already know. It's deeper than that. You been gone for hot minute but many things changed. I kept my ear to the streets when I was up north, and your name was definitely ringing.

But to keep it official my dude, it's a new mind frame for this movement...and death or jail ain't in manuscript, so if you with me, then I need you here with me, mentally as well as my second set of eyes and ears."

"I'm fucking with this Young Goonz shit on the strength of you; my Loyalty is to loyalty, not money. I'm not impressed by bright lights and big cars, all I ask is that niggas keep it funky with me at all times," said Crazy Mone.

"I only ask, and expect one thing from you my dude."

"And what's that?"

"Just be a G around me."

Crazy Mone laughed, then said, "I was born with my clothes on."

Foe didn't know what the hell Crazy Mone meant by that, but he knew he would find out soon.

"Yo Gecco, wussup my nigga...wussup." Foe screamed over the music.

"You know me...I'm on it. Me and Sha the God just made a little bet." Grecco screamed.

"Oh yeah, I want in. What ya'll betting on," asked Foe.

Sha the God screamed, "I bet this nigga that I smoke one of them YBM lames before he do."

Foe looked at Grecco, then back at Sha the God and thought, "These niggas is straight fucking insane. Who the fuck sits around betting on niggas lives...fresh out of jail...only the Young Goonz.

"Guess what the loser gotta do Foe?" Grecco asked.

"What. What do the loser gotta do?" Foe replied.

"The loser gotta smoke two of them niggas."

The Young Goonz erupted with laughter, like it was only a joke. But the real, and there would be no ass betting.

Sha the God just gave 25 to life on an appeal and the only thing he's been talking about since he got out was killing motherfuckers.

M-One walked out of the parole building, jumped in the Navi, and screamed, "Where the Hoes at."

After they left, Jamaica Ave Foe saw M-One staring out of the window as they drove through Queens. Foe wondered what was going through M-One's mind after doing eleven years for a murder he didn't commit. He knew that it wasn't the time or place to pick his brain so he just asked M-One, "Everything cool with your P.O."

M-One said, "So far," and everything else faded as day turned to night.

The Young Goonz ended up at a strip club in Chinatown, which was one of Jiggy Jacks on the low spots. He went in the back of the club with this Chinese dude name G-Kay. They talked in private for a few, and then they partied.

Later that night, Jiggy jack instructed the driver of the Navigator to drive to the Hilton Hotel where he had a suite on reserve. The after Party started and M-One was still screaming, "Where the hoes at."

Then, there was a knock at the door. Fifteen exotic Asian bitches walked in. And they all had on black sexy outfits.

M-One screamed, "Oh my fucking God," as he was double-teamed and groped all the way to one of the rooms.

The after party turned into a drunken orgy with Chinese chicks.

Loc stripped butt ass naked and was chasing bitches around the suite screaming, "Sucky Sucky."

M-One, Sha the God, Grecco, and Crazy Mone had their own rooms. Each of them had two Asian sensations a piece. The Young Goonz was living like rappers and trappers. The night was theirs and they enjoyed it.

Foe was about to walk in the bathroom. He noticed that one of the Young Goonz dropped their I-Phone. He would have walked right past it if it weren't lighting up from an incoming call. Foe recognized it to be C Dollars phone. When he saw

B.G.'s name on the screen, he answered it. "What's good B.G, this Foe, C-Dollars kind of caught up right now; you want me to tell him something."

'Yeah, just tell him I said...gravity gravity gravity!"

Duke got out his car in Redfern Projects parking lot. It was a little past three o' clock in the morning and all he wanted to do was get inside his crib and kick them heavy ass Timberlands off his feet.

A cold chill ran down his spine on the way to his building. Duke put his hand on the nickel-plated 357 Magnum and span around fast. There wasn't a soul in sight, he just had that feeling that killers get... like karma is around every corner. Duke pulled his gun out and walked cautiously inside the lobby of his building. Everything was quiet. Paranoia is the best defense a nigga with murder beef could have in the hood. Duke got in the elevator, pushed his floor, and took the ride up. The door slid open and he walked off the elevator. When Duke entered his apartment, he went straight to his king-size bed and crashed. What seems to Duke like a five-year coma, was only an eight-minute cat nap. He was awakened by his cell phone on blast. Duke started to the shit against the wall but when he saw that it was his baby mother calling that late he sat up and answered it, "Yo what happened." Duke asked with a little panic in his voice.

"The baby had an asthma attack in her sleep. I'm in the ambulance meet me at St. Johns Hospital."

Duke jumped up and ran out of the door. He was running full speed down the stairs, still putting on his jacket when he reached the lobby. Duke's first instinct was to reach for his hammer when he saw two niggas standing in his lobby, but once he saw that it was the Gateway niggas B.G. and Jah, he thought he was good. Not that it mattered anyway because he left the gun in the crib. All was on his mind was getting to that hospital.

Duke said Pardon me," as he tried to go around Jah, who was blocking the entrance.

But instead of moving to the side, Jah pushed Duke back.

Duke was confused. The shit wasn't registering. "Ayo what the f," was the last thing Duke said before everything went black on him.

B.G. knocked him cold with the butt of 45 Colt. "Get his leas." B.G. said in a hurry up.

They dragged Duke unconscious body on to the elevator, rode up to the roof, dragged him off the elevator, and then tied his behind his back. Jah cocked back his gloved hand and smacked the fire out of Duke. "Wake the fuck up."

Duke made a grunt then opened his eyes. The pain that shot to his head was excruciating. "Wut...da...fuck." Duke could utter.

"Hundred grand on your head...nothing personal," said B.G. in all honesty. "Wait. I got more than that just let me live." Duke pleaded.

He had to try something; nobody knows what they would say if they knew that this might be the last thing they would ever say.

As Duke started to gain full consciousness things started to look even weirder, he was wondering why the Gateway niggas had on YBM sweaters on. And why the hell was he still alive on the roof of his building, and what the hell Jah was doing with one of the mini camcorders.

"So what ya'll saying—it's non-negotiable." Duke asked in one last attempt to save his life.

"Yeah, pretty much it's a wrap." Jah stated as he pulled the roll of duct tape out of his back pocket.

"Fuck it. But before ya'll do it, my son just had an asthma attack, can one of ya'll call and see if my seed is aight...I won't be able to rest right...feel me."

Jah walked up to Duke as he sat upright and wrapped the duct tape around his mouth, all the way around his head. Duke knew it made absolutely no sense to try to struggle. After Jah secured the tape around Duke's mouth, he searched Duke's pocket, pull out of the cell phone, and asked Duke, "The last call you got was Kia, is that your baby moms?"

Duke nodded his head yeah, and watched as Jah dialed the phoned his baby mother.

"Hello. No this ain't Duke. I'm parking the car for him. He's running in the hospital right now. Please tell me everything all right with the little one."

There was a long pause that caused Duke eyes to bulge out of the sockets he tried to get up but B.G. held him down. All Duke wanted more than his own life was that cell phone.

"Okay, well I'm sorry to hear that I'm on my way in." Jah hung up the phone and with the saddest face B.G. ever saw on him, Jah said, "I'm sorry to tell you this..., but your son didn't make it. He died ten minutes ago. There was nothing you would have been able to do."

Duke slumped his shoulders, and cried like a baby. He went into another world mentally, and lost all sense of time and reality. He saw Jah put on the mask. He saw B.G. pointing the camcorder at him, and he saw that it was a full moon.

Jah stood next to duke and started talking into the camera, "YBM... motherfucker. This is what happened when you steal from the YBM family. O.G. or foot soldier the penalty is death. I looked up to this nigga right here. We would have died for this snake..., and the thanks we get. Well, it's time to pay the piper. For all those that's affiliated or want to be a part of this movement, take a good look at what not to be...YBM to the death and this ex-YBM O.G. Is about to die a horrible death.

The YBM sweater that Jah had on really made this whole facade believable.

B.G. slipped on his mask, then propped the camcorder on a smoke pipe.

They both walked over to Duke, who was still crying, and picked him up over their heads like a rag doll. "Y.B.M, Y.B.M, Y.B.M," is what Jah and B.G. chanted then threw Duke over the gate and off the roof.

As B.G. ran to get the camcorder, he heard Duke's body smack the ground. The crunch, thud, smack sound almost made B.G. throw up, but he knew better then to leave his DNA on that roof, so he chucked it up as him and Jah ran down the steps and out of the building.

Duke laid mangled on the ground. His eyeballs popped out of his and damn near every bone in his body was broken...only in FarRock!

When JAH and B.G. pulled up on Gateway, they sat in the car and smoked a blunt in silence. After a good ten minutes of sitting there, B.G. said. "Damn. That's fucked up."

"Well that's how they wanted it done right," said Jah.

"Man I ain't talking bout' that nigga...I'm talking bout' his son dying right before he died."

Jah crazy ass bursted out laughing. "You think that shit is funny my nigga?" B.G. asked, getting vexed at Jah. B.G. loved the kids and felt no kid deserved to be harmed by another person or natural causes.

"That nigga son ain't die...his baby mother said that shorty was aight and that they were already on their way back home...I just told that nigga that." Jah laughed even harder just thinking about the look on Duke's face when he thought his son died.

B.G. looked at Jah as he laughed and thought, "What would make a man's heart so damn cold." (FARROCK) ****

72 hours later, Detective Bell and Lieutenant Alex Stucky from the Major Crimes Unit was holding a conference meeting at the 101st precinct. They just got finished watching the YouTube video of Duke's murder.

"Over two million hits in two freaking days... this mess is getting more views then the Iraq beheadings." Lieutenant Stucky stated to thirty or more officers that sat in the meeting. Everyone was feeling the pressure from the brass.

Detective Bell stood up and walked to the board that held thumb tacked pictures of all the known YBM members.

Duke, Death Row, Shorty-D, and Death Row's pictures

were at the top of the food chain. Duke's picture had a big red X on it.

"These guys here run a very tight lip organization, and after watching this video, I guess it would be safe to assume that nobody in this crew would be talking to us anytime soon."

Bell pointed at S.L.'s picture with a laser pen, "I have this one guy on the inside of this organization—I'm not too confident how reliable this guy will turn out to be, but I'm sure I'll gat enough to at least get an idea of what's going on within the group. So familiarize yourself with his face, because he's not to be detained under any circumstances without contacting me first.

I've been investigating these guys for quite some time now, and I'm assuming that there's a power struggle going on. You are all aware of the five homicides that occurred a few weeks ago, which was considered the deadliest day in the History of FarRockaway Queens.

Well, three members from Death Row's crew were murdered, and the other two murder victims were from Duke's crew. The 911 calls are only two minutes apart, so these incidents occurred around the same time. Sources say that Death Row is one mean son of a bitch and rules with an iron fist.

I'm not sure, but this guy here." Bell pointed to Bless picture with the big red X on it. "Was killed the day after he was released from prison. He was one of Duke's guys, but like I said this was a few months back so I can't say."

As Detective Bell spoke for the next hour, each name he mentioned, he pointed to the picture of the individual.

Detective Bell and Lieutenant Stucky wrapped up the conference and was getting ready to do a Q & A with the press.

Stucky whispered in Bell's ear, "You got to have the balls of a damn elephant to post something this horrific on the goddamn internet."

Bell whispered back, "Three words. Young Black Mafia."

As soon as they entered the room, the news cameras lit up and the questions from the media started.

"Detective Bell, do you have any leads or suspects in the assassination of David Kelly A.K.A. O.G. Duke?" The blonde hair reporter from channel 9 news asked.

Well at the moment, I'm not at liberty to say. The details in this case have to be dealt with in a delicate manner." Bell answered.

"Is there any indications that this murder is connected to the five murders that you are investigating," another reporter asked.

"At this time...let me just say this, it's very early in this investigation."

"Is the department doing anything to prevent any retaliations, Mr. Kelly was a prominent member of a dangerous organization," this question was asked by a representative of the Mayor's office.

"We will do everything in our power to secure the safety of the local residents throughout the entire Rockaway's."

The blonde hair reporter from the channel nine news jumped in,

"Lieutenant Stucky. With the Major Crime Unit now involved in this case, how is it that no arrest has been made, or any strong leads with the five murders...and how much longer would it take before the FBI step in?"

"Well with any organization as big as the Young Black Mafia, the proper steps will be taking. I'm confident that these guys won't last too much longer on the streets to commit these acts of violence...whoever's responsible will be brought to justice in reasonable time...Thank you, no more questions." Lieutenant Stucky said as pleasant as he could be to the media, who always pissed him off with their line of questioning.

"One last quest Lieutenant, please," the blonde asked.

"Go ahead." Now a disgruntle Stucky replied.

"Is there any fear that YouTubeing a murder will start a new trend...of murdering for the public's entertainment?"

"Absolutely not, these guys are street thugs...not terrorist."

Young Goonz

CHAPTER FOURTEEN

The YBM boys from Redfern Projects were in frenzy mode for the past three days. The liquor mixed with the pain caused all out riots. The YBM boys from the Mott Avenue area caused chaos; they flipped over cars and lit stores on fire. Some of the crew members walked the streets watching the YouTube video on their cell phones, and the more they watched it the angrier they got.

All they knew was that Death Row, Sunny, and Shorty-D were the only ones capable of making all of that caliber against an O.G. They were loyal to Duke first, then to the YBM movement.

D.B., who has been repping YBM before most of the Redfern crew, came home two days ago, and to see the video of his best friend since the first grade was too much for his stomach to handle. So he vowed to never watch it.

D.B. felt the only right thing to do was to step in Duke's shoes and revenge his brother's death. He was ready to lead by example, and be the first one to ride for his fallen comrade. D.B. had many on his plate; he had to go to war with the whole YBM and the Young Goonz. He felt that he was built for the task. No more being a soldier. It was time for him to lead +a team to the top...or the slaughterhouse.

Just when the Redfern crew was getting more out of control in the middle of the projects, seven van loads of YBM soldiers pulled up with the three remaining O.G.'s leading the pack.

As the vans emptied out, they were surrounded by the angry mob. The police stood around in riot formations, at this point there wasn't anything they could do but watch.

Death Row, Sunny, and Shorty-D climbed on the roof of one of the vans. The O.G.'s and the crew they brought with them were outnumbered by far, but they were ready for whatever.

Death Row waved his hand for the crowd to quiet down so he could speak. The angry mob wasn't trying to hear shit at first, but after about three minutes, Death Row got his chance to be heard.

"If anybody in this mother fucking crowd is stupid enough to think we would do some shit like that to our beloved brother, come up here right now, and shoot me in my motherfucking head. I'm willing to die out here tonight to prove my loyalty to my brother. This ain't no hoax nigga. I'll rather be in a better place with my brother then to be out here turning guns on my own family...so if you feel we killed duke over some fucking money or any other reason, then bring your mothafucking ass up here and send me with him."

"Don't temp me," said a voice from the crowd.

"Who said that? Fuck all that talking, show me you believe we did that shit, cause if I believed any of you niggas killed Duke, I would put one in your head right in front of these faggot ass cops, then do my time like the true O.G. that I be."

"I said it motherfucker," said D.B. as he walked up to the vans with a few of Duke's top Goonies.

Death Row knew all about D.B. and his reparation for repping YBM in the jails, plus he knew that all Duke talked about for the last few months was his nigga D.B. coming home. Death Row jumped down off the van and walked straight up to D.B, pulled his gun out, handed it to D.B. and said. "We didn't do it my nigga, word to Duke. Now if you don't believe me, then suck my dick nigga, and I'll see you in hell...squeeze nigga, I know the jail house rules...never invite a nigga to your dick if you ain't ready to die right...well I'm ready."

D.B. noticed the tears welling up in Death Row's eyes and right then and there, he knew that somebody else killed Duke.

"Who did my nigga like that," D.B. asked as tears welled up in his eyes too.

Sunny came through the crowd and embraced D.B. with an emotional hug.

"They ain't have to do my nigga like that" said Sunny as he began to cry on D.B.'s shoulder. The whole crowd moved in and embraced Sunny and D.B.

"Them Young Goonz did it. Duke lined one of their head niggas up. But we gonna get them bitches." Sunny sobbed in D.B's ear.

The YBM crew drank and poured out liquor all night. A few of them let off a few shots in the memory of Duke.

S.L. had his ears wide open, so when niggas got drunk and started telling the drunken truth, he heard it all. How Duke's death was retaliation for Looch being shot and how the Young Goonz was the ones who killed the five YBM members because of what popped off at the showcase.

S.L. got drunk and almost forgot that he was a rat that night. He was so caught up in the kill the Young Goonz movement that it took him a good five minutes to feel his cell phone vibrating in his pocket. S.L. dug the phone out of his pocket and read the text message that was displayed across the screen (Good job. I'll see you tomorrow. Look across the street, by the church.)

S.L. stuck the phone back in his pocket quickly, then glanced across the street where Detective Bell was parked, watching the YBM crew wild out.

The YBM crew broke day until it was time to go to Duke's wake and funeral service. The whole mob walked to Daffeny's funeral home.

So many people showed up that the cops were back out there in full riot formation. Duke was definitely loved by many. Blocks were closed off, due to the mass amount of people.

There were hundreds of R.I.P. Duke shirts being worn with different pictures of him on them. One dude had a big YBM flag walking through the crowd like if he was leading a marching band. This day was to be considered a celebration, not a loss. Everybody had their memories of a time Duke made them laugh or helped them out of jam. It was definitely a day to remember.

S.L. was attached to Face hip, knowing that he would be

able to ear-hustle enough information by playing him close. Face was the strongest member of the YBM crew in Ocean Village. By the end of the day, S.L. knew it all, more than he wanted to know. He wasn't built for this type of shit and couldn't wait to tell Bell what he knew so he could fall back from all that crazy gangsta shit, and he definitely wasn't fucking with the YBM crew any more.

After the funeral, the YBM crew marched through every project and side block throughout the whole FarRockaway. It seemed as if every stop they made. They would pick up fifty more people. The crowd was being followed by two helicopters. One was the NYPD, and the other was from the local News. The parade of family, YBM members, and YBM affiliates were just making their way to the back of Hammels Projects. They entered on Beach 81st street. As the crowd got closer and closer to the Horseshoe tempers and emotions started to flare up.

People started jumping on top of the parked cars in the Horseshoe, and that's when the riot squad moved in. The shit hit the fan when a rookie cop hit one of the YBM soldiers in the head with a nightstick.

The crowd was too much for the cops to handle. They were beating the shit out of them cops out there for about ten minutes, when the riot squad started shooting rubber bullets and tear gas into the crowd.

Death Row was in a tussle with two cops. They already had one of his wrist cuffed and they were getting the best of him. That's when S.L. came running out of nowhere and knocked one of the officers smooth out. S.L. was straight brolic, and when the other cop saw how hard his partner got hit, he didn't want no parts of S.L. He let Death Row go and ran like a bitch.

"Yeah, that's what the fuck I'm talking bout'. Step up to the plate at all times, this is what this YBM shit about." Death Row screamed to S.L. while they stood in the middle of the mayhem.

"You already know. YBM heavy hitter." S.L. replied, really feeling himself.

A whole hour of rioting finally ended. The Horseshoe was cleared out and about thirty people were arrested for inciting a riot.

All the O.G.'s and bell ringers went to one of Death Row apartments in Edgemere Projects to drink and plot on the Young Goonz. Death Row stood up, "Everybody lift your glasses, cups, bottles...To Duke...rest in peace bro...you'll be missed daily...salute."

The YBM crew watched the YouTube video repeatedly, trying to see if they could tell which two Young Goonz threw Duke off the roof. Once they realized that it would be impossible to tell, Sunny got up turned the computer off then said, "Fuck it. All of them niggas gonna get it. Straight like dat!"

The YBM crew wasn't the only ones focusing on their next move. Foe, P-Killa C-Dollars, Thuggy Thug, D-Block, and Jiggy Jack were at Looch crib in Hempstead Long Island laughing at the YouTube video of Duke's fall from grace.

Looch had the Slick Rick patch over his eye, but he only needed one eye to see Duke crying like a baby, looking scared to death.

"Shoot me in my motherfucking head; don't do a nigga like dat." D-Block joked. "I wonder if the nigga fainted before he hit the ground. I mean, what do you do, embrace yourself for the impact." Thuggy Thug asked while laughing at the same time.

"Man, fuck all that. We can't win today's game off yesterday's points. Them niggas probably circling Hammels as we speak, trying to catch one of us slipping. I'm thinking bout' striking again, cause it won't make it no worse. The war is already on. Mines well hunt the hunters." Foe rationalized.

"Nigga you know how hot it is in the Rock right now, all we gotta do is stay off the radar and let them niggas run around all reckless, trying to get some get back...the hood so hot them niggas gonna jam their self up head hunting us," said P-Killa.

"The doctor said after they take the stitches out and the swelling go down. They're gonna fit me for a glass eye," said Looch, already tired of Duke. The bottom line was he didn't have an eye and no amount of revenge in the world could give him his eye back.

C-Dollars felt his pain, "Fuck a glass eye...we gonna get you an iced out eyeball my nigga."

Everybody in the room laughed except Jiggy Jack. Jiggy Jack never found shit like that funny, if he wanted to laugh, he would take one of his bitches to a comedy show.

Plus his lawyer called him this morning and informed him that Detective Bell wanted to question him about the shooting that took place at the showcase. "Ya'll need to holla at them niggas from the 60s that started all this bull shit." Jiggy Jack said in an aggravated tone of voice.

"Don't worry; see this shit ain't about when it's about what and how we do what we do, because this shit ain't gonna last a life time. One day we gonna be looking back it all this shit, either from a cell, a suburb, or down from the sky. Follow what I'm saying," said P-Killa in a way that only he could say it.

"Let's just stay focus. And never sleep on the enemy." D-Block added, The Young Goonz didn't ask for this war, but they had been ready for it for some time now. There was no way a nigga could be living well in FarRock, without the unfortunate taking your success as an insult to their lame ass lives.

Riding on the YBM crew wasn't the hard part. Staying out of jail and the dirt was the real challenge. So far so good for the Young Goonz, but every warrior is wounded. So any day could be one of their last.

Bright and early the next morning, S.L. was in Detective Bell's office trying to decide how much of the truth he was going to reveal and how much he was going to keep to himself. He figured he would just feed him enough to get him out of his life.

"From what I heard, Duke sent some of his boys to rob

Looch and when Looch didn't give up his jewelry, one of them shot him in the head. The Young Goonz found out, killed Duke, and tried to make it look like the YBM boys did it for stealing money from their organization." S.L. explained to Bell.

"Sounds like a load of horse shit to me. Matter of fact, turn around you are under arrest for possession of crack cocaine in the third degree."

"Wait wait wait, I did exactly what you said. I could have got myself killed and now you don't wanna honor the agreement because you don't like how it sounds, just so you know I don't like how it sounds cause it sound like I could get killed. I'll rather do the time then to be out here getting thrown from a roof for some shit I ain't got nothing to do with."   "Calm down, let's say that horseshit is true...I wouldn't be able to get it to hold up in court because at this point it's just hearsay. I need concrete evidence to present to the district attorney."

"Well ain't nobody talking about that yet, but I did hear that they were targeted for being YBM members."

"So you mean to tell me that the YBMs are not at each other's throats and the ones that they are at odds with is the Young Goonz from Hammels projects." Bell asked bewilderly.

"Actual fact," said S.L. with a little more confidence as he was getting more comfortable being a rat.

'Well this opens a whole new can of worms...now I'm gonna need some evidence to support what you're saying, maybe we could get one of the guys on a wire."

"Shit, I don't know about no wire, you told me to get you some info, now you talking some other shit...I mean, do you have any consideration about my safety."

"Do I have any consideration...If I didn't you would already be in jail, so get me what I want or your going back. And that's the bottom line."

"I'mma keep it a hundred. I'll get you some info, but I ain't wearing no wire. you just gonna have to cuff me. If that ain't good enough—I'll even let you know when the YBMs is on their way to Hammels to get busy, but that wire shit ain't gonna happen."

Detective Bell never planned to make S.L wear a wire, which was just a scare tactic; he used to keep him in the rap trap. In fact, Bell was happier than a faggot with a bag of dicks to find out that the Young Goonz had something to do with Duke's murder.

"Okay, this is what we going to do. When the YBM crew plan on retaliating, I need the heads up at least thirty minutes in advance, if I could catch these guys on their way to Hammels maybe T could squeeze them for more information on this beef." Bell ordered letting S.L. that this what he was to do without question if he wanted to stay out of jail.

Forty-five minutes later S.L. was leaving the precinct. Jiggy Jack and his lawyer were on their way in. S.L.'s heart skipped a beat when he and Jiggy Jack locked eyes. He didn't know if his cover was blown, but at that point, he didn't give a fuck about too much of anything.

Jiggy Jack mind was occupied with this nonsense he had to deal with early in the morning. Nobody like walking into a precinct, not knowing if that would be their last time seeing the streets again.

Jiggy Jack's lawyer already briefed him on what questions to answer or not answer. Detective Bell and Lieutenant Stucky entered the interrogation room with a whole new swagger after learning what they now knew about the Young Goonz and the YBM war.

"Good morning gentlemen...we want to make this as quickly as possible so you guys could get out of here." Bell stated which caught Jiggy Jack off guard by his politeness. Jiggy Jack knew Bell for being more aggressive. "Maybe he was fronting because my lawyer was here." Is what he thought as he took a seat.

Even Jiggy Jack's lawyer felt that there was something weird about the interview; they were in and out of there in less than twenty minutes. They asked basic questions that Jiggy Jack responded in the negative. Claiming that he had no idea of what transpired.

"I don't know what the hell just happened in there, but I don't like it one bit...whatever it is you better cover your tracks real good just in case we got to pick twelve jurors and two alternates."

Jiggy Jack didn't want to hear shit about know trial, but realistically thinking he knew his lawyer was right, so for now on, he would be working on his defense and alibi's just in case.

What Jiggy Jack wasn't thinking about was S.L. S.L. called Death Row Immediately after crossing paths with him on his way out of the precinct.

Death Row just so happened to be in Ocean Village with Face plotting on circling Hammels Projects when they got the call from S.L.

Death row told S.L. to stay where he was and not to let Jiggy Jack out of his sight until he got there. Death Row and Face pulled up in a SUV 10 minutes later and told S.L. to get in.

They sat for about five minutes when they saw Jiggy Jack and his lawyer exit the precinct and get inside of a white 2010 Ford Taurus.

"Damn we can't get him now, that white dude he's with is that well known lawyer from Queens." S.L. said trying his best to get out of the predicament that he put himself in.

"Fuck that lawyer, we riding down on this nigga at the first red light. S.L. put that hoodie on and grabbed that skat from under your seat. It's already one in the head, safety already off."

S.L. almost threw up in the back seat when Death Row gave him the orders. He knew there was no backing down now. S.L. shot guns off the roof on New Years, but never did he shoot at anybody in his life. The nigga was so scared he farted in the back seat, and the smell was inhuman like.

"Goddamn nigga, you shitted on yourself." Death Row asked Eace.

"Nigga that wasn't me." Face honestly replied.

"One of you niggas did it. Crack a window in this bitch." S.L.

lied.

"G up my nigga, the light turning red. Jiggy Jack is in the passenger seat. Don't miss." Death Row demanded.

"The SUV stopped directly behind the Ford Taurus. S.L. jumped out with wobbly legs, instead of running up on the passenger window like he was told to do, S.L. stopped at the back of the Taurus and went ape shit...pop...pop pop...pop pop pop pop pop.

"What the fuck is he doing." Face screamed.

The window of the Taurus exploded as it sped off through the red light causing the oncoming cars to swerve and get out of the way.

Jiggy jack wasn't hit, but his lawyer took a shot to the back of his right shoulder. The lawyer pulled over and switched seats with Jiggy Jack.

They sped to St. John's hospital, which was the second time Jiggy Jack, had to bring somebody there with gunshot wounds in a month. Which was the easiest way to make a nigga hot in the hood?

First the showcase and now my lawyer...unfucking believable.

CHAPTER FIFTEEN

Back in Ocean Village, Death Row and Face was going in on S.L. bird ass.

"That was the dumbest shit I ever saw in my life... like, what was you thinking." Death Row asked. Before S.L. got a chance to answer Face said.

"All you had to do was walk right up to the passenger window and put one in the nigga head."

S.L. was an amazing body bluffer, "Nigga, I empty clips...that's what I do. S.L. spazzed, fronting like a motherfucker.

S.L. could have won an Oscar for performance of the year, because his lifestyle was one big act. He was soft as baby shit, but he fooled most. "That's not how you do it my nigga, the more shots you let go, the harder the getaway. Death Row explained.

"My bad, I got caught up in the moment...all I was thinking bout was Swiss cheesing that nigga for Duke." S.L. lied

Face was starting to question S.L.'s gangsta. Laying Jiggy Jack down was too important, and Face felt that he should have just handled the shit himself. Face looked at S.L. through squinted eyes then thought (This nigga ain't bout that life)...but he already vouched for the lame and didn't want Death Row to think he was slipping in his picking.

"Don't worry about it, it's a lesson learned in every fuck up. You gonna get a chance to redeem yourself in a minute, and lay one of them busta's down. Face said, already contemplating not letting S.L. off the hook that easy.

S.L. didn't like the nonnegotiable demand that Face just gave him, but he knew better then to voice his opinion after he just purposely fucked up the drop they had on Jiggy Jack.

The YBM crew was still on their rampage. Shorty-D and ten of his crew members walked through Hammels projects early the next morning. As they reached the Horseshoe, five cars of YBM soldiers pulled up.

They exited the cars and linked up with Shorty-D and his crew. The dope fiends were lined up as usual in the front of 84-16 and 84-18.

The YBM crew walked inside the lobby with their guns out, screaming, "Shop closed," to the dope fiend runners who was moving two bundles at a time. They let the fiends know that if they didn't leave the Horseshoe right now that they were gonna get shot up with some shit that'll make them more than lean.

The runners ran their asses out of the buildings and told the fiends that they had better get the hell out of dodge. It only took a minute and a half and the whole Horseshoe was cleared out.

Rah, Smokey, Messhall, and Buddah were in apartment 6E in 84-16 waiting for the runners to come up and reload on the bundles.

"Damn, what's taking Skeet so long with that long ass line out there; he only got two B's." Rah asked.

"I can't call it, but he should have been back up by now." Buddah replied.

Messhall got up to look out of the back room window. The Horseshoe looked like a ghost town, and Messhall instantly knew that something wasn't right.

"Yo get on point, I think we about to get raided. Yo, Buddah put the work in a bag then take it next door. Messhall said in a frantic, hurry the fuck up voice.

"What happened," Smokey asked as he came out of the kitchen."

"The whole fucking Horseshoe is cleared out. I looked out there 20 minutes ago and it was packed...plus Skeet ain't come reload." Messhall explained to Smokey.

"Well here take this too." Smokey took the 44 long off his hip and handed it to Buddah.

"Damn, what the hell you doing with that big shit on you like that?" Buddah replied as he grabbed the gun and put it the bag with the dope.

Buddah ran out of the apartment with a little over three hundred bundles of the Horseshoe dope and two loaded handguns inside a C-Town shopping bag.

The apartment that Buddah ran into windows had a different view of the projects. After Buddah stashed the bag in one of the closets, he slid the living room curtain to the side and peeked out of the window, which showed the front entrance of 84-16. Oh shit." Was what escaped Buddah's mouth when he saw all the YBM niggas in the front of the building.

Buddah ran out of the apartment to warn his niggas, but he did it without caution, which turned out to be a bad move. Two of Shorty-D's soldiers Ty and Pit were standing in the hallway.

Pit saw Buddah freeze up, and without thought, he fired three shots at close range with a Clock 40 Boom Boom Boom. The sound was deafening as the shots echoed through the hallway. Two shots taw through Buddah's chest, while the third shot went through his cheek.

Buddah died instantly. Ty and Pit ran down the steps so fast and reckless that Ty couldn't slow down in time, and ran head first into crack head Yolanda, who came geeking out of the second floor landing. They both crashed hard to the floor.

"Damn Ty, watch where you're going. You better not had broken my stem."

Yolanda's ears must have been clogged up with crack smoke because she didn't hear any of the shots that Ty just squeezed off.

Ty jumped up and ran out of the building.

Smokey, Rah, and Messhall heard the three shots and got shook. At first, the shots sounded like the cops banging the door down since that thought was already planted in their heads by Messhall. They sat there waiting for the door to fly open, but it never did.

"That shit kinda sounded like gun shots." Smokey said. He got up and looked through the peephole. Smokey unlocked the door and stuck his head out. The first thing he saw was splattered blood all over walls, and then he looked down and saw something he didn't want to see.

Buddah lay dead in a puddle of his blood. "Aww Hell No, Hell No." Smokey screamed. The Young Goonz ran down the hallway and stood over Buddah's lifeless body.

Messhall ran in the other apartment looking for the two hammers that Buddah just stashed. After he couldn't locate the guns, he went back in the hallway and started pacing around Buddah. "Oh them niggas violated. Them niggas violated."

"No emotions, no emotions...like P-Killa say... The rules of engagement, no emotions, "Rah said out loud to himself. Trying not to let his emotions get the best of him.

Messhall eyes started to water up, but somehow he managed to push the tears back into his face without letting one fall.

"Them niggas crept up in the building and laid Buddah down," was what Smokey was on the phone telling D-Block.

Minutes later 84-16 was a crime scene. Detective Bell was right there thinking to hinself   "Holy shit...S.L. was right. There's a war going on out here. "

Witnesses were already saying that it was a group of guys who wasn't from Hammels in the Horseshoe looking like they were up to no good.

Bell was willing to bet a dollar to a dime that the Redfern crew came down here and killed the young boy. He was on the right track, but definitely on the wrong train...well at least for now.

A week after Buddah's murder, the Young Goonz still hadn't responded. The beef was being talked about in every barbershop and beauty salon. The Young Goonz tactics were very different from the YBM's guerrilla tactics. Due to the YBM ways of war the whole beef was out in the open and when situations like this is out in the open the police always win.

The Young Goonz was very police conscience. They weren't trying to spend the rest of their lives in jail...life was too good to them for that, so they stayed out of The Rock for the past week or more.

The cops seemed to know everything that popped off and why at this point, but they couldn't prove shit, so there was a need to be in the hood being harassed by the dick heads.

The YBM crew in all Ignorance was spreading the word, that they ran the Young Goonz out of the Rock. Which was only making shit hotter. Gossipers were waiting to hear the next anything, so they could put their spin on the story, which normally causes the flames to spread.

The Young Goonz was well aware of how the D.A. in Queens County play. They were quick to put a body on a nigga and make him sit up on Rikers island for three years without bail. Then dismiss the charges right before the trial date gets set, knowing they never had shit on the nigga.

The Young Goonz was trying to avoid shit like that, while the YBM was drawing more and more attention to themselves. The Young Goonz were spread out, some out of town and the rest were in different boroughs throughout New York City.

C-Dollars continued to supply the Black Cowboys and the Gateway crew with the dope, but everybody agreed that changing the stamp on the bag would be in their best interest.

Tasty Tuesday. Tasty Tuesday was nick named that by P-Killa, which was the day that all FarRockaway parolees were to report on Merrick Blvd. Many of niggas were lined up leaving that building in the past. You know shit is real when niggas has to bring their fucking shooters to hold them down at the parole building, just to make it back home alive.

This Tuesday wasn't any different from the rest. Heavy tension was in the air. Sha the God, Grecco, M-One, and Crazy Mone had to report.

Foe sat in the passenger seat across the street from the parole building. Foe had his other half with him. Her nickname was Ooh Wop. She was from Maryland, and the history they had together put her on a level higher than the rest of his other females.

"You good Boo." Foe asked as he watched every car and pedestrian who moved on Merrick Blvd.

"Yeah Babes, I'm straight as long as I'm with you."

Thuggy Thug and D-Block were parked one block over, armed with two AP9's. Dre had to report too, so Lex was parked outside too. Waiting on him to come out of the building. Inside the building, there was about ten YBM niggas sitting in the waiting area. D.B. from Redfern Projects was on his bullshit as soon as the Young Goonz walked in.

It was like a championship face fighting contest going on. Sha the God didn't like D.B. and this was the first time they were in each other's presence in about five years, when they had words in the yard at Elmira Correctional facility.

Grecco crazy ass was sitting there laughing as he watched the You Tube Video of Duke's murder on his iPhone.

Crazy Mone asked S.L. "What you practiced that Ice grill in the mirror. Cause you been pussy, Face just letting anybody join the team huh."

S.L. laughed, then said, "Why ya'll niggas hiding for...thought ya'll was goons. But then again, what's a goon to a goblin?"

"Don't get banged with that busta, "M-One told Crazy

Mone. "I don't know one official nigga from Ocean Village ever."
Dre came out of the office with his P.O. and told him that he would see him in two weeks. He walked out of the parole building and heard a female calling his name. He didn't recognize Ooh Wop at first as she stood outside the car smoking a Newport.

"Oh you don't know me now."

Dre was skeptical at first but shorty looked too familiar not to go see who she was. When Dre got close enough he smiled, "Ooh Wop what the hell you doing in New York, wait let me guess, Foe in the trunk like the D.C. sniper."

Rolled the window down and said, "Get in." Dre jumped in the back seat, while Ooh Wop stayed outside. She didn't want to hear Foe's mouth about, "Them Stink ass cigarettes," as he called them.

"Click Clack Boom ...ya'll back on ya'll Bonnie and Clyde shit." You already know...them YBM niggas in there." Foe asked.

"Yeah, but I know you ain't bout to get crazy on this block. Half the P.O.'s in there is police of some sort.

"Nah...I'm just making sure my people get up out of here in one piece. Where your side kick Lex at?"

"Over there in the Magnum...probably hoping I hurry the fuck up."

"What she had got locked for that day in the Horseshoe, "

"She clapped that lame nigga S.L. from Ocean Village."

Foe laughed, "Crazy ass Lex. she owe me a couple dollars and scared to ask her for it, so I hate to see how she would treat the enemy, but fuck that lame nigga S.L. he repping IBM now, suddenly. That's cool by me though; see that's why this shit is so easy when it come to mashing on these birds. They have no experience in this type of terrain."

Ooh Wop stared at Foe through the window. She was ready to get in the car and sit down with her impatient ass.

Foe motioned for her to get in with the smoothest whip of his head.

"Yo, tell Lex I said wussup...I gotta keep my eyes on the block my

G."

"Aight, be careful, out here." Roe got out of the car, and then jumped in the Magnum with Lex.

"Who's that whip," Lex asked.

"The nigga Foe and Ooh Wop, Foe said get his bread to him or you going on his list."

"I had been on that list before...I ain't worried, Lex still alive. I'll knock that tall ass nigga out." Lex had mad love for Foe, They always did business, but they never paid each other what they owed each other. That was their little thing. Plus Lex had some bad bitches. And bad bitches always got some more bad bitches for friends, so...

"Nah...he just said wussup."

"What they doing up here?"

"Waiting on his people to come out, you know them niggas at war, so they on they shit right now...oh yeah, your boy S.L. up in there looking like a straight killa."

"Word...that nigga ain't got no Benz, why the fuck they call him S.L, broke ass nigga. That S.L. should stand for Sucka Lame...or Sorry Lex, bitch ass nigga, Matter fact, we waiting too. Shit get crazy we gonna get crazy right along with it."

Back inside the parole building, everybody was just finishing up with the P.O.'s. It was definitely one movement coming and going. They came together, and they left together.

Fifteen minutes later, everybody was back outside and cars were pulling up from all different angles.

YBM niggas came walking from one end of the block, and the Young Goonz came walking from the other.

Foe stayed in the car with Ooh Wop, he wasn't getting out unless he saw one of the O.G.'s, besides, he knew his niggas could handle it.

The P.O.'s must have gotten wind of the situation, because within minutes after everybody stepped out on Merrick Blvd, NYPD swarmed the block and made the crowd disperse.

Lex wiggled through the crowd and bumped S.L, as she walked passed him, she said, "Watch where you walking Sucka Lame."

S.L. was somewhere in between shook, and shocked as he watched Lex jump in the Magnum, then pull off.

Back at the precinct, crack head Yolanda was spilling the beans to Detective Bell. "No, I didn't see him kill Buddah, but right after it happened, Ty came running down the stairs and knocked me the hell over. Everybody know them boys got problems with each other, so what the hell is he doing speeding down the stairs right when Buddah got killed."

Bell dug into his pocket, gave Yolanda twenty punk ass dollars, and told her to keep her eyes and ears open. He knew he could ever use her as a material or character witness, Yolanda was just a good source of information. Her motivation was stronger than the devil...Crack!

Bell left the precinct, jumped in his unmarked car and headed toward Hammels Projects. He pulled over and parked in the same parking lot that Looch was shot in.

Bell lit up a Kool's light, rolled the window down, then loosened his tie.   The YBM crew saw Bell passed up across the street, "Homicide," Shorty-D warned. Pit got a little nervous, knowing he just laid Buddah down.

Pit slid into the building, but Bell wasn't thinking about him. He laid his eyes on Ty and wondered if he could crack the young punk, get him to talk so he could solve some of the murders that been happening in the Rokaway's.

The Young Goonz shut down shop in the Horseshoe, and the YBM crew still couldn't get any money in the hood. The YBM niggas from Hammels was weed money, liquor money dudes. They were content with being broke.

So the hate that they had for the Young Goonz was a total contradiction The Young Goonz felt that those niggas didn't want no money, because all the other YBM crews were eating. These niggas were doing petty stick up's trying to live off that bullshit.

Detective Bell sat up in his seat when he saw Ty walk up the Blvd to Sam and Eddie's corner store. Bell jumped the curb, and raced to the corner.

Shorty-D and his crew saw Bell jump the curb all crazy, so they ran out toward the street to get a better look at who they were fucking with. Two blue and whites came speeding up just as Bell jumped out of his car, drew his weapon.

Ty exited the store and walked into the, "FREEZE," that Bell screamed. Ty thought about running, but hearing all the sirens closing in on him. He couldn't do nothing but put his hands in the air, and comply with the Detective.

Shorty-D shouted, "Yo Bell, why you arresting my lil' brother."

"Oh don't worry; I'll be back for all you animals." Bell screamed with authority.

"Come on, cut the act this is not T.V. Tymeek. This is real life... murder in the first degree. We talking 25 to life easy if you go to trial. I even got two witnesses who saw you running from the scene of the crime seconds after they heard the shots."

"So. That don't mean I was the shooter."

And that's where he fucked up. Nobody teaches these young guys anymore. That silence is golden. Every word you say in the precinct puts you at the mercy of the listener.

"Well the witnesses, who are creditable good people never mentioned anybody name but yours.

"I don't care what they say, they're lying, and I'll take a lie detector test to prove it."

"Polygraphs are not admissible in the Court of law Tymeek...this is not the Maury show. Now if you telling me you were there, but you didn't pull the trigger, then that's a whole different story. Truthfully that complicates my job, because now I would have to investigate that matter, but at least 20 years from now I won't be kicking myself in the ass for sending the wrong kid to jail for a crime that he didn't commit."

Bell was leading Ty down that slippery slope. He could see

it in the young boy's eyes that he was about to crack like the liberty bell.

"I want you to sit here and think real hard about this...If the situation was reversed, would whoever killed Buddah do 25 to life for you Tymeek."

Bell walked out of the interrogation room. Ty got up out of the chair and started to pace the floor. He already made up his mind that there was no way in two worlds would he ever rat on Pit.

Ty was shaking like a stripper all the way to the precinct. He kept asking the same question repeatedly, "Bell what's this about,"

Bell kept giving him the same answer, "You'll find out once we get down to the station."

"Yeah, but you homicide. I ain't kill nobody, so what could you want with me." Ty complained.

They arrived at the precinct and Ty was still rambling about what he didn't do. Bell left him in the interrogation room by himself for forty-five minutes, to make him sweat.

Bell walked into the dense room with a folder in hand. The contents inside the folder had absolutely nothing to do with the investigation.

Bell placed a few pieces of miscellaneous papers that were on his desk in the folder seconds ago. "I got to be honest Tymeek. It's not looking too good for you.

I have three witnesses saying they saw you shoot and kill Brian Malone, you might know him as Buddah."

"I ain't kill Buddah, them motherfuckas is lying on me."

"Well it's going to be your word against theirs when it comes time for trial Tymeek."

"Trial—what you mean, trial for what."

"For Murder Tymeek, but you know you could take a plea... If you co-operate, I'll let the D.A. know that you did show remorse for the victim, and maybe he'll take a few years off your sentence.

Now the only way I could that is if you give me a written statement, showing some sort of compassion."

"Man I ain't confessing to no shit I didn't do, fuck them witnesses they lying."

Detective Bell was back at his desk when got the all from the front desk.

"All right, I'll be right there." Bell said then hung up the phone. Seconds later Bell was getting spazzed on by Tymeek's family. He assured them that Tymeek would be released real soon, that his name had come up in one of his investigations, and that he was only following procedure.

Bell headed back to the interrogation room with one last trick up his sleeve, it worked twice out of the eight times he tried it, so what the hell.

Bell walked in the room and told Ty to face the two-way mirror.

"For what, what's going on?"

"I'm about to conduct what's called a show up identification procedure, just face the mirror."

"Twenty seconds went by," Bell told Ty. "Now turn to the side."

On the other side of the mirror, stood a female cop who Bell had there to play the role. The lady cop pushed the intercom button and said, "That's him, "

Ty went crazy, "Bitch you lying. You ain't see me do shit." Ty spit on the window, turned to Bell then said, "I swear on my dead daddy that bitch lying."

Bell pressed the talk button and the fake witness, "Was he the shooter, or was it the other guy he was with."

"I'm not sure...I believe it was him, they both look alike."

Without thought Ty screamed at the mirror, "How the fuck we look alike and he's dark skin and I'm light skin you stupid bitch."

"That's twice he slipped up, "Bell thought.

"Thank you, you can leave now. I will forward all your information to the prosecutor's office. You should get a call next week when it's time for you to testify before the Grand Jury."

Ty started crying in frustration. Not that he was bitching up, he just couldn't believe that the bitch just lied and put a body on him.

Bell turned to Ty, "Look, I want to believe you but that's the fourth person that confirmed you as being either the shooter or the accomplice... now maybe if you could be honest about a few other things I could talk to My Boss and let you go. I'll just tell him I had to let you go until I obtain more evidence."

"I ain't no rat, so you could forget about that."

"I'm not asking you to drop the dime on your people...in fact, I don't have any qualms with the YBM crew...its them fucking Young Goonz that think they are untouchable."

"Man, fuck the Young Goonz, I tell you whatever you wanna know about them snakes if you get me out of here today."

"Did they kill the five YBM boys from Redfern and Edgemere Projects that day it."

"Yeah, that's why the war is on...and they killed Duke, trying to make it look like we did it."

"Why would they kill five people? There has to be a reason."

"It all started at the showcase..."

For the next fifteen minutes, Ty broke it all down, of course making the YBM crew look like the victims even though Bell put it all together in between the lines. The YBM crew fucked with the wrong dudes this time around. They were just lucky that Bell had absolutely no empathy for the Young Goonz.

At this point, Bell could give to shits about Buddah's murder, or the person that killed him. What he learned from Ty was priceless, "Listen, I'm not telling my boss about any of this, just take my card, and the next time you see them bastards do anything, you give me a call."

"So I could go." Ty asked in a shaky voice.

"Give me your word that you'll help me bring the Young Goonz down and I'll walk you out that door right now."

Young Goonz

"You got my word, on my momma. Like I said, Fuck the Young Goonz."

Seconds later Ty walked out of the precinct with his head held up high. He didn't consider what he agreed to as snitching." Fuck the Young Goonz...I'mma do it for O.G. Duke," is what he thought, as he got in the car with his mother and his nappy headed lil' girlfriend.

The car pulled off...and Duke turned in his grave.

CHAPTER SIXTEEN

"Them niggas shot my fucking lawyer. That shit is all over the news with my name attached to the shit, as the...how they said it...the intended target." Jiggy Jack was pissed beyond pissed.

"I don't see how you let them niggas creep up on you, as much as you be on point." D-Block stated.

"You know I stay in my rear view. My lawyer drove me to the precinct, but trust me nobody followed us."

D-Block took a swig of his Yak right before saying, "Shit, somebody saw you go in, or come outta that precinct."

That's when hit Jiggy Jack ' Oh shit. That bird ass nigga from Ocean Village was leaving the precinct when I was going in with my lawyer...what's the brolic nigga name L.S, S.B." Jiggy Jack asked. II Who S.L." Foe asked.

"Yeah, that's the nigga name. He YBM too."

Foe laughed, "Yeah that nigga YBM...that's the nigga Lex clapped the other day, on some real disrespectful shit."

"Yo don't sleep on Lex that bitch G'd up," said Young Bash in all seriousness.

"I got a line on any nigga from Ocean Village, I'm a send that nigga something in a minute." Foe said.

"Did anybody hear from Sha the God lately?" Jiggy Jack asked.

"Yeah, he laying on them niggas in the 60s at some bitch crib, he told me he was gonna catch the nigga Sunny slipping." Nitty replied.

"Yo, Gunz and Loc were wilding out on my Brooklyn niggas

last night at the dice game. Loc was drunk as fuck; he rolls an ace, pulls his dick out and starts peeing on the dice."

Thuggy Thug laughed so hard he spat all the liquor out his mouth. Everything was funny to this nigga, no matter how serious, or how stupid it was, he always found humor in it.

"Fuck all that shit. them niggas shot my lawyer.' Jiggy Jack reminded his niggas.

"Objection," screamed Thuggy Thug as he laughed so hard tears rolled down his cheeks.

"I don't think that was funny at all," said Jiggy Jack, which caused Thuggy Thug to laugh even harder.

"I know one thing, we gonna have to open back up in the Horseshoe. Everything is coming along good in the Block Bully movement and management...so bread is gonna be needed when it time for all of us to put The Rock behind us. This Peninsula of a rock ain't gonna be the death of us, and twenty-five to life ain't in my legacy vision, so that money gotta keep flowing. Nitty said, always having a vision of a better way of living.

Shit seemed to be taking forever to get out of the hood, but Nitty always knew that it was just one come up away from happening.

The mere mentioning of the Horseshoe caused Thuggy Thug to stop laughing and pay better attention to the conversation.

D-Block, being swift on his toes suggested, "We could just move the lines back to the Bang out building, and if them niggas try walking to the back, niggas could cut em' in half when they passed the Horseshoe. We gonna see them coming from a mile away."

"We can't go to war and get money at the same time, but we gonna have to, cause FarRock is beneath niggas of a certain caliber...and we them Niggas. Let these grimy niggas stay out here for the rest of their lives, their story won't end no different from the rest of the motherfuckas that never made it out." Nitty spoke with determination in his voice.

"We could end this shit quick if we just focus on the O.G.'s, let's put all our resources together and off these niggas, or at least send them in hiding," said Foe as he blew rings of purple haze smoke across the bar, which was irritating Looch eye.

"Ya'll niggas killing me with that smoke." Looch said as he pulled out his phone and called one of his shorties, who was an R.N. a Jamaica Hospital. He asked her did she wanna play Nurse and sick patient. And just like that he was giving his niggas daps then left the bar.

The Young Goonz was holding the little get together in an up-scale, Illegal gambling spot in Manhattan. They didn't have to worry about bumping into the YBM crew, because, "Them niggas is local," like Jiggy Jack always would say.

Foe raised his glass up and the rest of the team did the same, after a brief paused Foe said two words, "To Buddah, "

"To Buddah," said the rest of the Young Goonz in union. They all threw back their drinks, then kicked it for the rest of the night about all types of shit.

"Good news," said Death Row to all the top bell ringers in the YBM camp. "I ran into Duke's man Chico at the funeral, he told me to give him a call. So happy to inform all of ya'll that my testers just confirmed that we have the best dope in the whole NYC."

The YBM crew went crazy in cheer to the best news they heard in months. They all knew that better dope meant levarage in everything. Including the war with the Young Goonz.

Death Row looked at Shorty-D, Sunny, Face, Fats, Gilette, and D.B then said, "It's now or never...ya'll gotta go hard on ya'll teams, this shit here is gonna sell itself. We gotta build the bank back up. Each of you has to take this opportunity and be the bosses ya'll claim to be."

"How we gonna focus on the money when we got these niggas trying to line us up every chance they get." Sunny asked, not wanting to take any chance with them Young Goonz.

"Like I said leverage my G...the money gonna give us leverage on them bustas." Death Row answered.

"I thought our numbers gave us leverage, but they showed us that our numbers hold no weight. Plus to keep it official with you, I'm not satisfied with the young boy Buddah being smoked...I don't feel compensated. That lil' nigga don't match my nigga Duke's status, in fact, it's an insult to the O.G. to focus on anything but killing them niggas. So ya'll can chase paper, me my niggas gonna chase them niggas to their graves. After one of their major niggas eat the dirt, then and only then will me and my team focus on the money." D.B. said, which had pissed

Face off, who didn't like it when Death Row word wasn't taken as law said, "Your team, I don't remember nobody appointing you O.G. nigga." Face spazzed.

"It ain't about no big I's and little U's, so pardon me for not sounding all hyped the fuck up about no dope when niggas threw my dude off the fucking roof, and put that shit online where his family would see it."

Face had been following orders so long that he never had a voice in the YBM matters. D.B. had a voice, whether niggas liked it or not. Duke was his boy since the sandbox, and war was the only thing that was on his mind. All of Duke's soldiers had already flocked to D.B, so what the rest of the O.G.'s felt was more important at the time, mattered not to D.B.

"Nobody said the war was over, what my G was saying is; now we have a better advantage. We over a thousand niggas strong in FarRock alone, everybody ain't gotta be on the grind. We gonna take paper out them niggas pocket, and we gonna be riding down on them niggas at the same time...daily. The beef is for life with them niggas, and that's a fact." Face said with somewhat a hint of irritation. "If you want the position of constant rain on the lames, then so be it," said Shorty-D. "Oh, so you giving out positions now." D.B. asked Shorty-D.

Shorty-D turned to Death Row, "Yo what's wrong with this dude. He need to learn to respect rank, and watch who the fuck he talking to."

Shorty-D had enough pressure on his back with the Young Goonz being so close to his home base to be hearing D.B. defiant, stubborn ass. Death Row winked at Shorty-D without D.B. seeing, then said, "The only thing wrong with him is, He's reminding me too much of my nigga

Duke right now...D.B. nobody's telling you what or what not to do, what Shorty-D was saying is can't none of us stop you, or try to stop you from bombing on the enemy...it just don't take everybody to do it at the same time, we got too many different factions for that."

Death Row didn't want to start no inner strife in the camp at a time when shit was about to get better, one day D.B. gonna wish he followed rank instead of disrespecting O.C. Shorty-D like he did. And Death Row was gonna make sure of it.

"The death of the Young Goonz will be when this war will end. Matter of fact, that's what we stamping on the bag...WAR," Death Row said as he rubbed his hands together, knowing The Young Black Mafia was about to reign supreme once again.

One of Death Row testers came running out of the back room high as a kite in the middle of a windstorm, "Call the ambulance. Carol just overdosed back there. Man I don't think she's brea..." the dope fiend nodded off in mid-sentence, right there in the middle of the living r o o m.

"Fuck the ambulance. Let the bitch die, then put the word out on the street that we got that killa shit." Death Row said to his people.

And that's exactly what happened, Carol died and, "WAR," flooded the streets of FarRockaway like Katrina flooded New Orleans.

As the tables turned, the unfortunate becomes fortunate. No more getting the short end of the stick, the YBM crew was getting all the money in The Rock, and they felt like the hood

was there's again.

Money had a way of calming niggas down. Death Row wasn't even thinking about the Young Goonz as he sat on the hood of the Benty GT, that it only took him two months to get.

Even D.B. and the Redfern crew had to get a slice of the pie. After running around FarRock for two straight months without spotting any of the major niggas from the Young Goonz camp, B.G. decided to pull back and get some of that paper too.

Face and S.L. were doing extraordinary numbers in Ocean Village. Sunny team was natural born hustlers, so one could only imagine what they were pulling in.

What shocked the YBM O.G.'s most of all was how much money Shorty-D was finally bringing in the Horseshoe dope was so yesterday, that the fiends would park their cars in the Horseshoe, get out and walk to the YBM building.

Dope fiends are loyal to one thing only and that's the bag. If a nigga was selling dope to support his child and his child's mother was a dope head and another niggas dope was better than her baby father's was, she would spend that money with the other nigga instead of letting the money go to the support of her child.

Death Row sat on the corner of Beach 54th Street catching stunts in his new whip. He had a fresh tattoo on his neck that said R.I.P. O.G. DUKE.

Death Row felt like he was the illest nigga in FarRock as he thought, "The Rock is mine."

CHAPTER SEVENTEEN

The YBM crew might of shut FarRock down as far as the dope game, but like C-Dollars said on his latest mix tape, "We on vacation, "

Actually, the Young Goonz was out of town trapping in some of the roughest cities, and some of the richest Counties. Whitey's dope was the best they ever had, and in some spots, they were making two hundred and fifty dollars off each bundle.

The Young Goonz was stacking their paper up, plus sending money home to all the Young Goonz that couldn't leave New York because of Parole.

They were still ten steps ahead of the YBM crew, but from the outside looking in, an onlooker would swear on his mother's life that the YBM boys took over the world and ran the Young Goonz out of FarRock.

It was obvious that the YBM crew wasn't sending any missies at the Young Goonz that was still in FarRock. On numerous occasions, they bumped heads with each other and ain't nothing pop off.

The Young Goonz had a vision, and they were sticking to the script... well. Most of them was sticking to the script.

Sha the God, Grecco, Crazy Mone, and M-one was on parole, so they were pretty much stuck in the hood. Thuggy Thug was right out there with them, for the love of drama.

"Man I don't give a fuck what nobody said—I'm cooking one of these niggas tonight." Grecco said.

"You talking my language now. You know our bet is still on."

Sha the God replied.

"Let's flat line one of them niggas from the 60s tonight, ya'll know they be in the front of that bodega on the back street. Crazy Mone suggested.

M-One wasn't thinking about doing nothing that could send him back up north.

"We could just drive by and air shit out with the Mac's, they won't be expecting no shit like that," said Thuggy Thug.

It wasn't about money with all the Young Goonz, these niggas here were infatuated with violence. They felt that one body didn't make you a killer. It just meant that you have killed before.

Uncivilized logic is expected and accepted in an uncivilized environment, and hands down that's exactly what FarRock is.

G-Pac pulled up in the Horseshoe with one of his shorties behind the wheel. "Click Clack Boom," said G-Pac as he stuck his head out of the passenger side window.

Thuggy Thug walked over to the car and gave G-Pac the Young Goonz get money dap.

"I just passed the five four, your man skid bid out there flossin with his back to the world like he ain't got a problem in the world." G-Pac had a way of nick naming niggas he didn't like the opposite of what their real name was, that's why he called Death Row skid bid.

"That's cool, we gonna show them niggas some love tonight." Thuggy Thug explained in a way that G-Pac shorty couldn't understand. She really didn't give a fuck about nothing but getting some dick before G-Pac disappeared again for months.

If she only knew that their conversation was about killing niggas, she probably would have passed out. She was a good girl that fell for a Young Goon, typical ghetto love story."

"Who sponsoring that movie?" G-Pac asked.

"We are, it's an independent film."

G-Pac looked pass Thuggy Thug and saw Crazy Mone, Grecco and M-One Aight, just make sure everybody's on point for the negative feedback, cause it's gonna come."

After a few more words were exchanged G-Pac told his shorty to pull off.

A few dope fiends were walking past the Horseshoe. Crazy Mone overheard one of them saying, "Girrrl, that WAR had me nodding so hard last night that I damn near kissed my pussy."

The other fiends laughed at the joke, as they made their way to the YBM building.

"Yo. What's shaking with them niggas over there? What they think we forgot about Buddah or something, they getting their little money like the beef is dead. Fuck them niggas from the 60s, we could focus on them on a later note," said Crazy Mone.

"I really don't give a fuck, I'm just tired of talking bout' it...I'm ready to feed the beast, whether it's the 60s niggas, or these niggas... let's just lay something down tonight." Grecco spazzed.

M-One just did an 11-year bid and wanted to live a little, but unfortunately, he came home in the middle of a war with his niggas. 11 years straight ain't no joke, in no way, shape, form or fashion...and life on parole was even more hectic, which is enough to change a niggas whole mind set. The fear of going back to jail after doing all that time is greater than the fear of death. M-One wasn't taking any chances, he wouldn't smoke weed at all, and the only time he would break curfew was when he had some new pussy lined up.

He couldn't understand how Sha the God could be so gun crazy after giving back a 25 to life sentence. There are so many dudes up north that lost all of their appeals, that would give their right arm and left leg to give their life sentence back, and Sha the God was ready to kill more niggas, with no concern of the consequences.

"Why I never hear ya'll niggas talking bout' pussy, all ya'll wanna do is cook a nigga...I wanna cook a bitch a nice meal, then blow her motherfucking back out. I got 11 years worth of catching up to do." M-One said to his niggas.

"I don't know about you. But I fuck three times before I even leave the crib in the morning, and sometimes it be three different bitches." Sha the God joked.

Grecco got hyped up, "Yo I can't even fuck one bitch no more, that shit don't do nothing for me. I get a ménage at least four times a week."

"Nigga stop lying...but yo', y'all know who got some good ass pussy, that nigga Gilette baby moms, that live in 84-16...that lil' bitch a freak." Crazy Mone bragged.

"I hope you don't be in that bitch crib, I heard that nigga Gilette be trying to creep through. On some five in the morning shit...and the boy definitely let his hammer off," said Thuggy Thug.

"I wish I would catch one of them YBM niggas creeping through this Horseshoe, plus I keep the big bad wolf on me. I'll shoot that nigga, Am I your, and the motherfucking seed." Crazy Mone replied with a bizarre look in his eyes.

One minute the Young Goonz would be talking about killing shit, and then they'll be talking about pussy, then money, and then back to killing. The Young Goonz had what you could call a, "Intermittent Explosive Disorder," intermittent- means (off and on) according to an English dictionary. Explosive- means to break, destroy, damage & cause harm to. Within a sporadic time frame of let's say zero to sixty.

It's intermittent (off and on) because the Young Goonz don't spazz out all the time; But when triggered, "Explosive," is their only and normal response. Society deems it as a 'disorder'. "Because to deny yourself the opportunity to rationalize and to instantly explode puts such society at a grave risk of danger. Yeah, the Young Goonz had some deep-rooted mental issues.

"Yo what the fuck is going on over there, "

There was a commotion in the front of the YBM building, close to where the street was.

"Ya'll niggas get on point, I'mma swing around to the parking lot and see what the fuck them stupid niggas doing," said Thuggy Thug as he ran to the tinted hooptie that was parked in the Horseshoe.

It only took Thuggy Thug about a minute to swing around the projects, and parked in that same parking lot that Looch got shot in. Three of the youngest YBM soldiers from Shorty-D crew were beefing with the Jamaican dollar van man driver. The young boys basically jumped out of the van without paying, and Rude Boy jumped out behind them spazzin, "Lickle blud clod, idiot bwoy...giv me, me mun nee," said the dread in a heavy Jamaican accent.

These lil' bastards had money, they just wasn't paying the dread. Shorty-D and the rest of the level headed YBM boys were in the crib counting money or else they would have paid the dread and smacked the lil' niggas upside their heads for making the building hot.

Lil' Monster was nine years old, and off the fucking hook. He picked up an empty beer bottle and smashed it across the dread face, causing blood to gush out profusely.

"What the hell you-bad lil' asses did to that man," screamed a girl name Brina that live in the YBM building.

The dread jump his ass in his van and jetted straight to the emergency room.

Brina grabbed Lil' Monster by his collar and dragged him up the steps to Shorty-D's crib.

"Get off me, you dick eating, pussy licking bitch." Lil' Monster screamed as he unsuccessfully tried to wiggle free.

When Brina finally got him to Shorty-D's crib, Shorty-D was so focus on counting money that he snatched the door open, listened to Brina spazz out, grabbed Lil' Monster in the crib and thank Brina for bringing him up stairs

"What's wrong wit' you boy," asked Shorty-D right after closing the door.

"I'mma YBM gangta...Lil' Monster nigga." Shorty D laughed and gave the lil' nigga dap.

Thuggy Thug was laughing his ass off when he saw the young boy split the dread wig open. When Thuggy got back to the Horseshoe, he was still laughing as he told M-One, Grecco, Crazy Mone, and Sha the God what just transpired.

Sha the God had that look on his face that he gets whenever he's in deep thought.

"Oh them niggas done fucked up now," said Sha the God.

Dangerous minds would be the best way to describe the Young Goonz. The shit that these niggas would think of in a tenth of a second was amazing.

All Grecco wanted to know was, "Is it going down tonight or what?"

"Oh it's going down my nigga, check it..." For the next 20 minutes Sha the God explained to them what they were gonna do. The Young Goonz jumped in the hooptie and headed to Mott Avenue.

Shorty-D had counted more money than he ever counted in his life, and for the first time ever he was feeling the drug game. He put the re-up money to the side, and then split the ends with his team. After each one of them had their earnings, Shorty-D made each one of them take a grand of their money and put in the pot for the runners and look outs, who were YBM soldiers also.

"This is the life that everybody asked for," Shorty-D screamed, quoting Kanye West. "Yo, somebody go up the block and get the biggest bottle of Yak in that bitch, matter fact...get two, This shit cause for a celebration.

Shorty-D and his crew left the apartment and posted up in the front of 85-02. As the night went on the YBM crew got more and more intoxicated, and rowdy.

The shooters were gripped up, but they were drunk too, so they never noticed Thuggy Thug pull up in the parking lot in the tinted up hoop ride and park. Something they would have easily noticed on a regular night.

Thuggy Thug pulled the prepaid boost mobile out of his pocket and chirped Sha the God.

"Can you see what I see?" Thuggy Thug sang over the phone.

"Aight clocked the dick heads, they're in a squad car. Let me know how much time I got, they should be circling the projects every 20 minutes. Sha the God inquired.

"The big fish is out too, so you already know."

Thuggy Thug clocked the police three times at about 18 minutes a lap, give or take a minute or two.

Thuggy Thug hit Sha the God's phone with the information and told him when I hit you back just move in on em."

After the patrol car made two more rounds, Thuggy Thug gave Sha the God the green light. Sha the God parked behind the YBM building, he had on a big Jamaican hat, the ones that come with the fake dread locks attached to it. He had his whole face wrapped in gauge bandages. The only thing that was left exposed was his eyes and his mouth.

Sha the God put on the Illest Jamaican walk and walked right up to the YBM building, only leaving about 20 feet between him and the YBM crew, then screamed out, "Where duh pussy whole that chop up my face."

Lil' Monster wasn't out there, but Shorty-D remembered what transpired earlier, when Brina came to his crib spazzin.

"Step off rude boy...this ain't what you want." Shorty-D said in a calm but threatening tone.

"Whatcha talk bout, step off...hun?"

The YBM crew pulled out their guns, but they were baited into focusing in the wrong direction. Grecco and Crazy Mone came around the opposite corner and woke the mother fucking neighbors up. There were sixteen Pops and nine Booms that rang through Hammels Projects.

Crazy Mone and Grecco wore all black with Jamaican flags wrapped around their faces. The YBM shooters were so caught off guard that they never had a chance to return fire. They had to get low first, then try to bust back.

The Young Goonz didn't know if they got Shorty-D or not, but as they ran away from the YBM building they heard niggas screaming in pain.

When the smoke cleared a 13-year-old YBM soldier laid dead and three others were hit, including Shorty-D, who got hit in the elbow with one of Greco's 45 copper tops. The pain Shorty-D was in was unbearable and the only thing that was on his mind was whipping Lil' Monster's ass.

CHAPTER EIGHTEEN

etective Bell was woke out of his bed 3:45 in the morning to go to Hammels Projects where another kid was murdered. The young boy was a member of the YBM crew and Bell was already convinced that the Young Goonz was responsible for the shooting, and nobody was going be willing to talk.

The crime scene unit had the YBM building taped off and they started collecting possible evidence, and taking pictures. Bell lit one of his Kool's and drew a picture wn his mind of what went down in the front of 85-02.

He read the reports from the medical examiner that noted the possible cause of death was due to the bullet that entered the young boy's left arm traveling straight through the armpit, entering the upper rib cage, with no signs of an exit wound.

The crowd of onlookers talked amongst themselves. Some of the tenants complained to the police, that they weren't doing their jobs good enough to prevent their kids from being killed. The police complained that nobody was willing to step up, testify, and help get the murderers off the streets.

Bell was tired of it all. He had about ten open homicides and couldn't get one arrest.

M-One heard all the shots from his bedroom window. A few minutes later, he heard all the sirens blaring through the hood. He let an hour go past before he called Thuggy Thug's phone,

"Ya'll good?" M-One asked.

Yeah we out here in Brooklyn, chilling with Dot rapping ass," said Thuggy Thug.

After the conversation ended, M-One pulled out his prayer rug and asked Allah to forgive his friends, for what they know not.

The next morning Sha the God and Grecco were beefing over the bet they made, "Son I want my money...you not ass betting me, straight up," said Grecco in frustration.

"How the fuck you know your bullet killed the lil' nigga that shit don't count. Unless I see the autopsy report." Sha the God stated, and felt that he had a valid point.

"Aight fuck it, we going to the 60s tonight, not to shit on Crazy Mone aim, but I saw my bullets hitting them niggas...so I'mma just slump something in the 60s."

"Grecco you a bug out, straight up my nigga...like something ain't working right in your dome."

"You the bug out. Ain't shit wrong with me. You read a few books in jail now you think you God, your ass was nuts before you went to jail." Crazy Mone and Young Bash were tired of hearing them beef about that crazy shit while they tried to listen to the music. "Why don't one of ya'll call the hood and see what they saying about last night. Cause we don't know if that stunt we pulled worked or not," said Crazy Mone.

Not that he had any worries about the YBM crew finding out that it was them, he just wanted to know if the police caught wind of it. Just in case, he had to run again. Crazy Mone never had a problem with running from the authorities.

P-Killa and Foe were having a heated argument about what occurred at the YBM building two nights ago.

"I thought we made it clear that shit was to die down until further noticed." P-Killa said, clearly pissed the fuck off.

Foe chuckled, "Further notice. You be talking a whole different language my nigga. You might could talk to the lil' little niggas like that and they'll listen. But stop means go to certain niggas that don't live by rules or commands."

"What part of die down that you don't understand—it's almost like you be justifying niggas wrong, which only motivate niggas to keep doing wrong. But you don't hear me though."

Foe screwed his face up right before saying, "Well if firing on enemies is wrong, then I'm about to change my name."

P-Killa got more and more frustrated by the minute, he never liked to be challenged, but Foe was nobody's yes man. "Your art of war is suspect." P-Killa said trying to get under Foe's skin.

"Fuck the art of war, its 2010, I follow the art of Foe, F...0...E, Fire...on...Enemies. Foe stated, breaking down the acronym of his name, which he loved to do.

"You brought Grecco and Crazy Mone in this family and they need to know that when it's agreed upon, nobody violates the call." P-Killa barked.

"Don't put this on me cause niggas is out there steady mobbing, and if I'm not mistaken, which I know I'm not. Sha the God orchestrated the band, and Grecco and Crazy Mone just sung along. From what you told me Sha the God was a thinker, and truth be told I like how he put it together, them lames don't even know that it was us, so what's your beef really about... that you didn't make the call." Foe put many of emphasis on the word, "You," raising his voice at the same time.

"Son stop yelling at me," said P-Killa.

"What you gonna do if I don't?"

"Beat you up, like I used to do when we were little."

"We ain't little no more. buss a move nigga." Foe joked as he threw his hands up and squared up.

Foe and P-Killa threw a few playful jabs at each other, the same way they did when they were twelve years old.

"Nah, but real talk. Them niggas gotta be easy out there." P-Killa said trying to catch his breath.

"Look...these niggas is fresh out of the pen, you know how it is. Years and years of stress and aggravation, let downs and disappointments, bitches with you one minute, then gone the next. C.O.'s oppressing a nigga just cause they could, so when a nigga get home it's like PAY BACK MOTHERFUCKAS. Foe explained, speaking off personal experience that P-Killa was also able to relate to.

"Yeah you right, cause I came home ready to kill shit too. You know what I hated most of all when I was doing that time. When I call home and ask a motherfucka to do the simplest shit. and what they say. "I got you." Foe replied.

"And do the shit ever get done?"

"Hell No," Foe answered again, knowing P-Killa spoke the truth, then added, "And the shit a nigga be needing done, he would be able to do in five minutes if he was free."

"Word. I don't see how a nigga could do life under those circumstances, if the cops got me dead to right, and I know I'm facing life...nothing personal, but I'm trying to shoot my way out of the jam. Fuck that, I'll rather die and take one of them with me then to spend the rest of my life in jail depending on niggas and no good bitches." P-Killa stated in the most sincere tone that Foe ever heard come from his nigga.

"How you feel about sending somebody to holla at the nigga S.L. for that shit he pulled with Jiggy Jack and his lawyer," asked Foe, as if he heard nothing P-Killa said about letting the heat die down.

"Everything in due time my nigga...everything in due time." P-Killa replied.

They left the plush honeycomb hideout that was located on the upper east side of Manhattan that P-Killa rented a year ago.

They went straight to a nice up-scale strip cub in Harlem where they made it rain like it was nothing, because it wasn't.

Foe took a badass Spanish chick in the V.I.P. room for an exclusive lap dance. Mami straddled Foe and went to work on the boy. "Goddamn girl," was all Foe could say as she grinded to the music. It didn't take Foe long to swell up with her sitting strategically on his dick.

"Ay Papi...you gonna make me cum on myself," the stripper said in the sexiest, suductive Spanish accent. She grinded even harder with a little too much concentration. "This bitch really trying to get her shit off and make me pay for it, then have me walk away with the blue balls...Hell No." Foe thought.

She had her arms hugged around Foe's neck as she rubbed her soaking wet thong all over his stiffness. A small moan escaped from her mouth, "Umm," That's when Foe started to push her off him.

"Wait Papi wait. Let me just," she said in Foe's ear, panting heavily, "Nah Ma...it ain't fun if I can't get none."

That shit turned her on even more, never had she been told, "No," before. She was used to having her way, at work, and in her personal life. She went back to the locker room, washed up and changed her costume.

For the first time since she was dancing at the club, she caught feelings for a stranger. She always heard other girls talking about it, but she thought they were stupid gold digging bitches, that the job was just business. Absolutely no feelings.

P-Killa was kicking it with a red bone stripper that went by the stage name Cherry. Cherry was from the Bronx, her body was so amazing that it looked face.

Foe walked up to them and smacked Cherry on her ass causing it to jiggle.

"If you gonna hit it, hit it hard nigga." Cherry said looking over her shoulder at Foe.

Foe smiled at her comment then asked P-Killa, "What's good?"

"I found what I'm looking for. I'm ready to bounce." P-Killa said with arm around Cherry's waist.

The D.J. screamed over the music, "Coming to the stage. and hopefully on the stage...the one and only. Priceless. The crowd went nuts when the Spanish stripper that Foe had in the V.I.P. room walked on stage.

"I don't get down like that, but this bitch right here gets my pussy wet every time I see her perform...I just wanna lick her one time, just to see if she taste as good as she looks." Cherry admitted.

Foe walked through the crowd, right in the front of the middle of the stage and watched as Priceless started to perform. Niggas were throwing money before she even touched the pole.

When Priceless saw Foe standing in the front of the stage she abandoned her normal act, walked up to him, and started to sway her hips side to side. Her movements were so seductive that Foe was in somewhat of a trance, that he hope she didn't notice.

Priceless popped one perfectly shaped tittie out of her bikini top. The crowd was in a frenzy but she never took her eyes off of Foe's eyes.

She laid on the floor right in front of Foe and contorted her body in all different kinds of position. Sexual positions that is, never breaking eye contact with Foe.

Her flexibility was every man's fantasy, college tuitions were blown on Priceless. But Priceless was her name for a reason; she was not for sale, no matter how much niggas offered.

She crawled on all fours right up to Foe and asked, "You miss me Papi?"

Foe smirked and shook his head, "NO," but the look in his eyes told the truth and she said, "Yes you do."

Priceless put both of her legs behind her head and shook her whole body, as she laid flat on her back for two minutes straight. Foe was so close to her that he could see her juices dripper out of the side of her thong, down her ass cheeks.

"Scared you might like it Papi," she taunted, as niggas poured more and more money on top of her. Foe was about to spin off and leave when Priceless let one leg down from the back of her head. She placed one hand inside of her thong and began to masturbate, biting her bottom lip as she stared in Foe's eyes.

Priceless use the leg she let down to push money off the stage with her foot where Foe stood.

"Anything for you Papi. Anything," was what she was saying as she began to cum. Niggas were hating the fact that the bitch had the nerve to kick their paper to the nigga. Foe heard one dude say, "That nigga better be a part of her show. Word."

The music went off, Priceless stood up, and put her titties back in her top, her helper ran on the stage with a cardboard box collecting the piles of cash that littered the stage.

"You know I'm mad at you right?" Priceless said to Foe after walking off the stage, with the sexiest pout Foe had ever seen.

"You don't even know me...so how you mad at me?" Foe asked. "For that bullshit you pulled in the V.I.P. room."

"Don't know what you talking bout Mama, "Foe screamed to her helper, "Don't forget this money over here."

"No Papi...that's for you."

"Do I look like I need your money? Besides, you earned it with that performance."

"So that mean you enjoyed Papi...because it was for you."

"It was aight...but don't beat me in my head with all that it was for me stuff."

Priceless wasn't used to this type of resistance, "Come here Pi, let me tell you something in your ear." Foe walked closer to the Latin Goddess and gave her his ear. "Next time I tell you something is for you, you better take it...you said I've earned the money Pi, well when I was performing I really used your face to get off, I was picturing it in my culo."

Foe grabbed her lightly by her chin, turned her head to the side, and whispered back in her ear, "One day I'm gonna get off all over your face Mami." Foe blew a sensual breath in Priceless ear causing her to shudder. Foe picked up one of the bills off the floor, wrote his number on it, dropped it back on the floor with the rest of the money and mixed it with the rest of the money, "Like I said...you earned it." Foe walked away without looking back, knowing she was going to pick the money up now that his number was in there somewhere...and that she did.

Priceless got back to her dressing room and couldn't believe how she behaved for the stranger. She logged his number in her phone and she smacked herself in her forhead realizing she never got his name.

P-Killa, Foe, and Cherry were in the parking lot about to leave the strip club. Cherry couldn't stop talking about Priceless performance,

"I swear on my child, she never did no shit like that as long as I been working here. That stuck up ass girl must be really feeling you."

Face was getting tired of hearing S.L. talking all that gangsta shit for the past hour, "My nigga, I saw your last one and I'm not impressed."

S.L. being the ultimate body bluffer was all hyped up. "What, we could go to Hammels right now. Bet I lay the first one of them chumps we see the fuck down."

Face laughed, "Son you be talking like you got mad bodies, you ain't never kill nothing, or let nothing die nigga...you shot a civilian by mistake, and now you think you an official gun clapper...nah my dude it don't work like that." Face said causing the rest of the young YBM soldiers to laugh. He was purposely clowning S.L. because Death Row wasn't around and he wasn't feeling S.L. war story telling ass any more.

"Fuck all that, we could grip up right now, and I'll show you how I give it up...wussup you driving?" S.L. asked in the heat of the moment.

"Don't front for me, because I'll call you on it." Face replied.

"Call it nigga...call it." S.L. was the illest; all bark with a poodle a bite.

"Aight grip up, we riding." Face said as he made up his mind to see where S.L. heart was.

"You ain't saying nothing but a word killa...what you think I'mma back down or something." S.L. asked.

"Why you still talking killa, grip up...I'mma swing the whip around."

S.L. heart sunk when he realized that the joking was over and Face was dead ass serious.

"I can't get to my skat right now, you know I'm on parole, I don't be leaving them shits in my crib. My little slide bitch get off of work in two hours, when she get home I'll grab the joints up, then we could bounce."

Face wasn't about to let S.L. off the hook that easy, "Nah I got something for you, come on."

"Damn...that didn't work." S.L. thought. Twenty minutes later, Face's lil' soldier came to the parking lot in Ocean Village where they sat and past a book bag through the window with two ratchets in it.

Five minutes after that they were parked on the Beach 84th Street behind the Horseshoe, in the same spot that B.G. and Jah lay when they flamed Chillz.

"Why you so quiet my nigga...you aight." Face teased.

"Who me, I'm good, as long as this skat is operable."

"You do know how to work one of these right. up is for safety, down is to shoot. It's already one in the head so you good, you ain't gotta cock it." When Face passed S.L. the Lima, he noticed that S.L. hand was shaking. Face peeped it and was just about to pull off; knowing he forced the issue, when he already knew S.L. wasn't built for no shit like this.

But opportunity knocked, D-Block came out of 84-12. It was February cold; nobody was outside unless they were trying to get from point A to point B.

"Oh shit, there go the nigga D-Block...give me the hammer." Face demanded with his adrenaline on a million.

"Nah, I got this." S.L. said, motivated by something other than the shit that motivates real niggas in these types of situations.

He got out of the car, legs feeling like rubber bands. The closer he got to D-Block the more nervous he got. All he was thinking was, "One shot to the head," Like Death Row told him. "Up for safety. Down to shoot, one to the head."

D-Block saw the unfamiliar figure walking toward him; the dude was bundled up with a hood on. D-Block had a level three vest on, with a hammerless 38 special in his pocket, with his hand gripped tight around it.

The closer the dude got the more uneasy D-Block started to feel. S.L. was having hot flashes and he felt like he was about to pass out. He walked right up to D-Block still thinking, "Up for safety, down to shoot."

S.L. pulled the Lima out, which was already on down for shoot, but his mind went blank, he pushed up, closed his eyes and squeezed the trigger...but he heard no shot.

D-Block being on point saw the gun come out and dipped his head to the left just in time to hear the nigga gun click. He rushed S.L. and they began to tussle. What S.L. didn't see was D-Block had reached in his pocket and pulled the 38 out...BOOM.

The 38 slug flew past S.L.'s head and S.L. panicked.

Face was disgusted with what he just witnessed, he even considered leaving S.L., but when he heard the first shot, he stepped on the gas so hard that the tires screamed in the Horseshoe.

D-Block looked over S.L.'s shoulder and saw the car speeding toward them as they struggled with each other. D Block felt like he saw this movie before when Chillz was shot. He head bunted S.L. and dazed the nigga up off him.

The car was approaching fast so D-Block threw a wild shot at S.L. without aiming. The shot hit S.L. in the leg. S.L. dropped the Lima, fell on the ground, and screamed for his life.

S.L. hood came off his head during the struggle so D-Block knew exactly who he was. The car jumped the curb and was heading his way. D-Block emptied the clip at the vehicle. One shot shattered the windshield; the rest of the shots hit everything but the car.

Face saw D-Block running in the building as he jumped out of the whip.

He picked the Lima up with one hand and dragged S.L. bird ass with his other hand to the car, and got the fuck out of Hammels Projects.

"Take me to the hospital...I'm dying." S.L. cried.

"Where you hit at?"

"I don't know. My whole body on fire."

"What the fuck happen back there." Face spazzed.

"The gun jammed."

Face looked at the Lima in his lap, "This shit ain't jammed, it's on safety mothafucker."

Before S.L. could respond, five cop cars cut them off on Beach 71st street, right by the building 71-15.

"Pull over...turn the car off...and put your hands out of the window."

Face first thought was to bang at the pigs out of the window, but changed his mind quick when he saw S.L. crying like a bitch.

Face act like he was stashing the gun in the back seat, but what he really did was slide both of the guns under S.L.'s seat from the back.

"All this shit is this stupid niggas fault, so fuck it...and fuck him." Face thought as he turned the car off and stuck his hands out of the window.

One hour later, D-Block jumped out of the passenger seat of Slimo's 545 BMW in front of Jiggy Jack's crib in St. Albans Queens.

Two big crazy looking pit bulls were inside the crib terrorizing everybody that came through the door. Jiggy Jack had the wild animals trained so good that when he screamed, "Relax," they stopped barking and went straight to the back room.

Jiggy Jack and Foe were already in the crib when they got the call from Slimo saying he had to get D-Block out of the hood because some shit popped off.

"What happened now," Jiggy Jack asked, almost not even wanting to hear the shit. He was just plain fed up with all the drama.

"That same nigga S.L. that tried to air you out, just tried to kill me in the Horseshoe...I flipped the script on the nigga though and put a hot one in him...clapped the shit out that lame nigga." D-Block said as cool as violence could be explained.

"Did he die?" Jiggy Jack wanted to know.

"I can't call it; I don't even know where I hit the nigga at. But I don't think it was too serious cause the nigga was doing too much screaming, you know when a nigga is hit somewhere vital he be real calm and quiet, trying not to move and shit. Nigga just be laying there looking like he got a whole lot of shit on his mind."

"I'm tired of hearing this nigga name, I'mma handle this shit A.S.A.P. that lame just made it to the top of my to-do list." Foe said.

"Just put a quarter on his kufi...I'll cover it." Jiggy Jack said, like putting 25 grand on a nigga head was something light.

"Yeah, .cause we don't need the heat," D-Block stated.

Jiggy Jack looked at him with a sarcastic look, as if to say. Nigga you just made it hot.

"What. I was minding my business; he did it to his self."

"Slimo what's good my nigga, I ain't see you in a minute," asked Foe.

"You know me, working hard, with a light little hustle on the side... and taking care of my kids." Slimo was a few years older then the rest of the Young Goonz, he had his fair share of the streets, but his love and loyalty was never questionable. Call on Slimo and he'll be there.

Everybody in the crib phones started to ring almost at the same time, niggas wanted to know if D-Block was aight. Foe glanced at D-Block with a concerned look, knowing that the situation could have gone the other way. Foe couldn't Imagine D-Block being offed, so he shook the thought out of his mind. But the reality was what the reality was, and that's, one false move could be a niggas last in FarRock America.

D-Block caught Foe staring at him, "Fuck you looking nigga." Foe cracked a smile and said, "Click Clack."

"Boom," D-Block replied.

CHAPTER NINETEEN

"Fuck that, I ain't going in that Stink ass cell. The last time I was in this precinct, ya'll left me in that mother fucka with that broke toilet for five fucking hours. Toilet over flowing with crack head shit and vomit." Face complained to the police officer in the 100 precinct.

"Listen you little shit dick...this ain't Burger King and you can't have it your way...matter fact, come on." The cop dragged Face to the last bullpen all the way in the back.

"Now you don't have to worry about a toilet, cause it ain't one in there asshole. The cop pushed Face in the pen and locked it.

S.L. punk ass over reacted to the flesh wound in his leg. The doctors cleaned it up, patched him up and sent his ass to the precinct.

'What am I being arrested for. I'm the one that got shot." S.L. asked from the back seat of the squad car, never knowing when to shut up.

"They'll let you know at the station, I'm just in charge of transportation." The officer explained.

When they finally arrived at the precinct the cop put S.L. in the cell with the broken toilet in it, and told him. "Give me a sec, I'll find out what they charging you with."

The cop was back within minutes, "Criminal possession of two loaded fire arms in the second degree," was all he said, and then listened to S.L. spazz out.

"What...they ain't find no fucking gun on me, Hell no...I ain't trying to hear that shit.

Face heard S.L. spazzing out and was just about to scream down to him and tell him to shut the fuck up and don't say nothing, but then he heard S.L. scream out, "Call Detective Bell...let him know I'm back here, and I need to talk to him...it's Important."

The officer let S.L. know he had just saw Bell in the hallway at the soda machine and he would let him know that he wanted to speak to him. Face couldn't understand why S.L. was asking for the Homicide Detective, but he definitely was about to find out.

Yo Dre, what's good gangsta." Foe asked over the phone.

"Us, never them...easy like a Sunday morning." Dre replied. Where you at my G...cause I can't really phone bang." I'm in Ocean Village, why-you wanna meet up."

"Yeah, meet me at Fridays, the one in SheepsHead Bay."

"Aight, give me bout' a half. I be there."

"Forty five minutes later Dre walked in Fridays to find Foe flirting with a brown skin waitress with hazel eyes.

After ordering appetizers, Foe got straight to business, "Check it...somebody's so pissed off with that bird nigga S.L. from Ocean Village that they put 20 grand on the nigga head you want it? "

Dre fangs came right out.

"Do I want it, do the fif go Boom?" Dre joked. "I don't fuck with that nigga; you know I'm smashing his baby moms right?"

"Nah, I ain't know that, but check it...it would be better if this shit don't point back to The Young Goonz, cause we kind of hot right now. I mean...the whole Rock talking, it's gonna be tough. But nothings impossible...feel me, "

Foe pulled out a leather Gucci pouch and slid it across the table. Dre opened it, examined the contents, "This look like the whole dub."

"Why wouldn't it be my nigga? You family," Foe explained with a little smile on his face.

After they finished their meal, they ordered drinks. Dre told Foe how S.L. bitched up when Lex popped him. They shared a laughed, then Foe." S.L. phone rang.

"Talk about it."

"Is that how you answer your phone?"

"Who dis?"

"It's Jasmine, "

"I'm sorry, but you got the wrong,,

"Papi... It's me Priceless," she said in that voice that tickled Foe's ear.   Foe knew exactly who she was as soon as he heard her voice. He just decided to to mess with her for a minute.

"I'm sorry, but I'm not Papi...and I don't know a Jasmine or Priceless." She laughed and said, "I know you fronting now Pi...nobody, and I mean nobody forgets Priceless."

"Cipher...don't get gassed." Foe mimicked one of Funk Master Flex famous sayings. Priceless thought it was funny and said, "Stop playing Pi...wussup.' te Nah, I'm just fucking with you...Look I'm in the middle of a business dinner, can I call you back in a little bit."

"Okay...but I don't like waiting...later."

Foe hung up the phone, "My bad my nigga, let's get the fuck outta here." They walked to the parking lot, embraced each other, said a few more words, and then went their separate ways.

Detective Bell walked in the bullpen area after reading all the reports on S.L. and Face arrest. "So you need my help again. You promised me that the next time the YBM crew was on their way to retaliate I would be the first to know, can you Imagine how disrespected I feel, when I find out that one of my C.I.'s get shot in Hammels projects and get caught fleeing from the scene with two loaded hand guns on him." Bell stated in a real cop-like sarcastic tone.

"I got caught in a catch 22, if I didn't go to Hammels I might have got killed...They were trying to see how much they could trust me. It's like a test they do...that's how I got shot...they wanted me to

shoot somebody, but I just couldn't pull the trigger, I ain't no killa."
S.L. lied so good that Bell felt a bit of sympathy for him, but of course, he didn't let S.L. know it.

"Well, I guess our deal is off the table now anyway since you got caught with two guns." Bell explained

"I didn't get caught with no gun." S.L. cried.

"This DD5 report says otherwise...it says here that they found two automatic hand guns loaded to capacity, under the passenger seat."

"That nigga put them shits under there."

"Well that'll be your word against his in court."

Bell turned to leave and the straight bitch came out of S.L. "Wait... I'LL testify against Lex for shooting me." S.L. spoke in a panic pace.

"It's too late, you already gave a conflicting statement saying you was robbed at gun point and shot by a guy you never saw before. If you recant, after catching a case for weapons her lawyer will eat you alive. Plus you never honored our agreement; I got absolutely nothing out of our last deal. Goodbye." Bell reached for the doorknob and S.L. screamed, "Wait. Please, I'll wear the wire. I'll get Death Row on the wire talking bout' the five homicides."

It took everything in Face's power not to start spazzin out. He heard everything S.L. said and he knew the nigga was about to take down the whole YBM crew if he didn't do something quick.

S.L. was removed from the bullpens and taken to Bell's office. About a hour later, Face was taken to central bookings, he was only charged with a traffic violation that justified the search of the vehicle.

After all the paper work was done, Face was let out of the back door. He ran up Queens Blvd, offering people a hundred dollars to use their cell phone for a minute.

Most people thought he was crazy so they kept it moving. He found a female that thought he was cute and she let him use her phone.

Face dialed Death Row's number and was praying that he didn't talk to S.L. yet.

"Who this?"

"It's me Face, I just got out of the bookings, the nigga S.L. eating cheese on the team hard body, don't chop it up with son, he trying to get you on a wire."

"Slow down my nigga. Where you at. Aight, stay right there, I'm on my way.

The next morning Death Row and Face went to Lex and T.I. bitches crib in Ocean Village. T.I. answered the door, not expecting to see them.

"What's the problem?" T.I. asked.

"Ain't no problem, we come in peace—is Lex here?" Death Row asked.

"Nah...she ain't here, why wussup." T.I. lied. Lex was standing behind the door with her P-89 gripped tight. She knew S.L. was down with these niggas, so she wasn't taking any chances.

Death Row knew he was getting nowhere with T.I, so he decided to keep it funky, "This is what it is...I respect gangsta shit, cause I'm a gangsta...I just found out that I might have a busta in my camp."

T.I. cut him off before he could get to his point. "I'm saying, what that got to do with Lex."

"It's like this, something happen to a nigga, and he told me this gangsta story how he got wounded in an uphill battle with two dudes, but now I'm hearing a rumor that Lex lift the nigga skirt...I don't got no hard feelings against Lex, like I said, I respect gangsta shit." Death Row explained.

Lex swung around the door so fast that Death Row and Face jumped back.

"Yeah, I rode on the nigga; he told me I couldn't eat...so I had to get it how I live."

Face turned to Death Row and said told you, that nigga ain't no good, "Then Face told Lex, "You could put that away, welcome here for all that."

"Just so you know, that nigga is no longer a member of the Young Black Mafia. Death Row explained to Lex right before him and Face got on the elevator.

Death Row and Face walked out of the building, to the crowd of YBM soldiers. "Listen up. S.L. Is a rat, and no longer is he a part of our family...There's a good chance that the nigga is wired for sound, so don't even talk to him, plus there's a good possibility that the cops got their eyes on him, for his own protection. So what I suggest is every time ya'll see the nigga, put hands and feets on him." Death Row stated to the YBM crew, who hung onto his every word.

Face was about to address the crew when one of the young boys said, "Here the nigga come right now." The crew looked in the direction that shorty pointed. S.L. had a cane in his hand as he walked up to the YBM crew.

"YBM G's...wussup?" S.L. said to all the cold stares.

Nobody greeted S.L; Face twisted is grill up and asked, "What happened in court?"

"They said some shit about illegal search and seizer, so they couldn't charge me with nothin...what happen with you my nigga."

"How you ain't get charge if they had a reason to pull the car over, they were responding to a shooting and they had the description of the car, and they found skats under your seat." Face continued to press S.L.

"How the fuck did they get under my seat in the first place." S.L.

"Don't talk to my big bro like that you fucking rat," said one of the young boys.

"Rat. who the fuck you calling a rat lil' nigga." Something wasn't right, what the hell these nigga know about me ratting," S.L. thought.

Death row and Face walked off and the YBM soldiers beat the fuck out of S.L. bird ass. It was blood and feathers all over the place. One lil' nigga was beating S.L. over the head with hs own cane, and then started to stomp his leg where he was shot at.

"I'm putting cases on all you bitches." Screamed S.L. right before he was kicked unconscious by an aCG boot to the temple.

Dre watched the whole situation unfold from his window. He didn't know why they were whipping S.L.'s ass, and he didn't care. The more people that crowded around, the better it was for Dre, and what he planned on doing.

CHAPTER TWENTY

Two days after S.L.'s royal ass whooping Dre saw S.L.'s baby mother at the supermarket located in Ocean Village's complex.

"Wussup stranger. You miss me?" Asked Dre.

"You know I do, this nigga got me stuck up in that fucking house like a hostage...I hate him."

Everybody knew S.L. was a rat, and that he was hiding out in his baby mother's apartment, scared to death to come outside.

"You gotta be careful around that nigga, you know them YBM boys talking about killing him right...the longer he hides in your crib, the more I worry about you and your daughter. What kind of man would put his family in danger." Dre laid it on thick, trying to scare her enough to kick S.L. out so he could gangsta lean him.

"I already told that motherfucka, he supposed to be leaving tonight.

I don't want them crazy ass niggas shooting my door up like they did that girl Tiffany, trying to kill her brotha."

Dre was hardly listening to her, "But anyway. You know I miss that mouth right?"

"I bet you do...but what that gotta do with what I'm going through Dre?"

"My bad, I just don't wanna talk about him. Take a quick ride with me. "I can't. This nigga gonna be tripping If I don't hurry back."

"So. Let him trip, it'll be too late by then." Dre pleaded.

"Let me get this straight, you gonna nut down my throat, my pussy gonna get all wet for nothing...then I gotta go put up with his bullshit.""

"You said he leaving tonight right. Well hit me after he leave and I'll come through I beat that thing up."

"Nigga stop lying, once you get your shit off your ass ain't gonna holla, how many times you think I'mma fall for that one Dre."

Dre pulled her close to him, gave her a tight hug, and whispered in her ear, "Please, "

"Come on nigga...where your car at."

Later that night, around 3:45 in the morning S.L. baby moms texted Dre this message (He's about to leave...you promised :) Bitches are so sneaky that she didn't realize what she just did by sending that text message.

Nobody was outside in Ocean Village. Dre was parked on the outskirt, waiting for S.L. to try and sneak out of the building. A cab pulled up 20 minutes later. S.L limped his punk ass out of the building, looking in every direction danger could come from.

Dre peeped him from a distance. He got out of the car and squatted behind the row of cars that was parked on Rockaway Beach Blvd.

The closer S.L. got to the street where the cab waited, Dre would move up one car closer toward the cab.

S.L. was so fucking scared that he forgot about the pain in his leg, and started running to the cab.

Just as he reached the cab and reached for the door handle, Dre seemed to come out of thin air. When S.L. felt the cold steel press against his temple, he closed his eyes and pissed down his legs at the same time...BOOOOM.

One shot from the Glock 23 blew S.L. brains out of the other side of his head.

All because he didn't want to do the time for 21 dimes. The cab driver thought somebody was trying to rob him when heard the shot, so he peeled off fast as fuck.

Dre bent down, put the Glock in S.L.'s rat mouth...BOOOOM.

Ten unsolved murders and two dead confidential informants in one year had Detective Bell in hot water. He was on the verge of being demoted.

Bell had just left out of an intense meeting with the higher ups and the Queens District Attorney. They chewed Bell a new asshole. The D.A. had suggested, rather ordered Bell to work with the Narc's who just launched a long-term investigation in the Rockaway's.

Bell wasn't too fond about it, but he wasn't in any position to argue. When he walked into the TAC meeting that was being held by the Narcotic division he felt out of place. The room was filled with undercover officer that was dressed up like drug addicts, while the field team was dressed in street clothes.

Bell read the name that was written across the chalkboard to himself. "Operation Good Neighbor, "The lead Detective was Mike Demillio, he ran this same operation in over a dozen crime infested areas, and helped solve a few murders.

The primary objective was for the undercover to identify as many drug dealers as possible, by buying from them without making the arrest like the standard Buy and Bust operation. This was a Buy and walk type of operation. Then when the supervisor felt confident on the conviction rate, they would bring the case down with what they call the, "Take Down where the undercover would make confirmatory Identifications of the subjects that they purchased narcotics from in the past.

Demillio was giving his briefing and Bell listened half-heartedly. Okay guy's, same routine, give your subject a J.D. name (John Doe), that matches his or her distinctive features...so if the guy is 300 pounds then he should be called J.D. Fat Man in your buy reports.

Young Goonz

There are two groups of individuals that we're targeting in this in investigation, The Young Black Mafia and The Young Goonz. Some of these guys are a little more organized then others...we want them all.

If they got drug addicts pushing the drugs, then we need to build relationships with those addicts until they lead us to the dealers.

I did some back ground checks on these guys and I must inform you all, that these is the most violent groups that I've encountered in my ten years as a Detective.

Each undercover will be assigned a ghost officer, who would be the first responder in an emergency...

Bell raised his hand like if he was back in grade school. Demillio smiled then said to the rest of the officers. "This is Homicide Detective Anthony Demillio; he has been investigating these guys for some time now. Do you have a question Detective."

"Yes, I was just wondering why it is called operation Good Neighbor.

"I was just about to get to that. We have three empty apartments in Hammels Projects. One located in 85-02, the YBM building, and two in the horseshoe, 84-12, and 84-18, which is the Young Goonz buildings.

As selected, my undercover will move into these buildings under the impression that they are new tenant. For the first month, they will behave as regular neighbors, they will check their mailboxes, and shop at the local Supermarket, plus utilize the laundry mat...All in the undercover capacity.

After the 30 day period the undercovers will began to purchase drugs. Demillio explained to Bell.

"Well I understand the tactic totally, what I'm having a hard time with is the term Good Neighbor. Because if we were Good Neighbors the last thing we would want is to see these guy's buying more guns with money funded by the N.Y.P.D, surely they will use those same guns to kill whoever get in their way

Cops and the real good neighbors included.

Then in a few months, they will be standing in front of a Judge with a non-violent drug offense and be back on the streets ready to kill again with the same gun they used the buy money to purchase."

"I can't do both of our jobs for one pay check." Demillio joked, "Plus, whenever we bring this case down, there will be over fifty arrest made, and somebody will be looking for a deal. And you will solve some of those unsolved mysteries." The room of officers laughed at the jab Demillio threw at Bell, he was the only one that didn't find the humor in dead kids.

"No, but in all serious, somebody will talk about the murders. They always do."

"So what do you do for a living?"

"I'mma porn star." Priceless burst out laughing at Foe's joke.

"Oh yeah. What's your screen name Papi?"

"Sea biscuit!"

"Sea biscuit huh. Do you got like a specialty or like a signature move or something?" Priceless asked in between laughs.

"Yeah, it's called the Doggy Bounce Broken hind legs." Priceless almost choked she laughed so hard.

"You are crazy Pi. I like a man that could make me laugh."

Foe smirked, "Truth be told Ma, I don't get to laugh that often. So when I fine time to relax, I guess my real personality tends to come out."

"Good, I'm glad you can relax around me, because I been thinking about you many...it's kind of weird."

"Well, I've been told that I have a special effect on people."

Priceless made a silly face then said, "Cipher don't get gassed."

That caught Foe off guard and he cracked up laughing, "Don't be jacking slang Ma...I seen the same shit happen to

Kane."

Foe phone been ringing every five minutes from the moment they entered Pasta Lovers on Queens Blvd. He pretty much sent everybody straight to voice mail until he noticed DuPont's 313 number kept popping up. DuPont was in Detroit and to blow Foe's phone up the way he was doing, Foe figured it had to be an emergency.

"Do you mind Ma? I gotta take this." He asked.

"A gansta with manners. How tough and sexy, you are too much Pi."

Foe spoke into the Phone, "Tonight. I don't know, I hate trying to book a flight in a short notice, let me hit you back."

Priceless had her bottom lip poked out in the sexiest pout. "What's wrong with you?" he asked.

"You leaving me."

"You wanna come."

"Where?"

"With me."

"On a plane?"

"Why you scared." Foe teased.

"I ain't scared of nothing but being broke Pi."

Foe smiled, paid for their dinner, then said. "Niccce." (Fabulous voice)

Five hours later, Foe and Priceless was landing in Michigan... Foe boy DuPont was waiting for them when they arrived. He was pushing a brand new Range Rover sport, charcoal black, with 22-inch rims.

DuPont jumped out smoking a back and mild, "Aaaah...what's good you fly ass nigga."

"From FarRock to the Midwest like it's nothing...cause it ain't." Foe responded.

"Oh my fucking God, who is this?" Asked DuPont with his eyes glued on Priceless picture perfect frame.

"This right here is my future. Jasmine, Jasmine this is

DuPont, DuPont Jasmine." Priceless was flattered that Foe used her real name and not her stage name to introduce her, but she recognized game with all that... my future shit.

"It's gonna be about three hours to the grand opening, I didn't tell nobody you was coming. Bo gonna be happy as fuck to see you."

"Aight drop me off at my crib, and I'll meet you down there," said Foe.

"Did this nigga just say his crib, "Priceless thought. Thirty minutes later DuPont pulled up to a house on the West side of Detroit on Marlow Street, right off of Fenkle Street, which technically is six mile.

Priceless noticed the Cadillac CTS in the driveway looking wet from the way it was shinning. She wanted to ask so many questions, but she figured if she kept her cool everything would come to the light soon enough.

Foe was flossing; never had he let any female in this crib before, not even Babe. Foe had another crib on the East side of Detroit for all of that.

It wasn't that he trusted her; he just knew exactly what he was doing... Foe always did. When they got inside the house, Priceless juices distilled from her sweet spot.

The crib was plushed out; Foe kicked his Timbs off and asked her, "You want a drink Ma?"

"What, trying to get me drunk and have your way with me Pi."

"Actually...I hate drunken sex; I was just trying to show some hospitality."

"There you go again with them manners." Priceless blushed.

"I'm just being myself, look, I'm about to get in the shower, the towels and wash rags is in that closet, we gotta get out of here in a few."

Foe was extra comfortable with stripping down to his boxers right in front of Priceless. Besides, he was in his house. "Can I get in with you Pi." Priceless asked as she started to remove her clothes too, not waiting for Foe's answer.

Priceless undressed slow and methodically, holding serious eye contact with Foe. He took it as a challenge, not once looking at her naked body as soon as they both were fully naked Foe grabbed her hand and lead her to the bathroom. There were wall-to-wall mirrors all over the bathroom and Foe was able to view Priceless whole body, front and back at the same time. He noticed that her nipples were stiffer then they were the night that they were at the strip club.

Priceless noticed Foe's stiffness and her breathing became heavy as they stepped in the shower. She handed Foe the rag and Dove body wash, "Wash my back for me Pi...please." She turned around and the butter pecan complexion, and the fatness of her ass almost caused Foe to make a bad decision, but he maintained his composure and started to lather her up.

After he washed her back, he soaped one ass cheek at a time. She giggled knowing how hard it had to be for him to be back there without bending her over.

"Your turn Papi," was what she said as she turned around. When she saw I soldier standing at attention her knees got weak, she had to brace herself on the wall, "You monster, "Was all she said as she got her head together and started to wash Foe's body.

She felt sorry for her twat because she was definitely going to let Foe break it off in her.

CHAPTER TWENTY-ONE

Foe 's boy Bo was opening his strip club that night. It was a major accomplishment for a dude that came from nothing, so Foe had to fly in for the occasion. The club was named, "Wiggles," and as soon as Foe and Priceless pulled up to the grand opening, she knew she was in her element.

Everybody was still out front when they got out of the car. Bo was standing there smiling with a huge pair of scissors in his hand, Bo saw Foe and his excitement couldn't be hidden, "OOOH Shit. The mothafucking dangerous Don is back in the three one three, Oh it's going down...power moves baby. I told you. I told you, Matter fact let's go cut this ribbon and jump this shit off." Bo was hyped up, he didn't let Foe get a word in he was one a million, but fuck it, tonight was his night.

Priceless was taking it all in. She realized that Foe wasn't just any ol' body and was glad she met his smooth ass. She couldn't wait to go inside and see how the dancers in the D differed from what she was used to.

The inside of the club was amazing, Bo did his thing, and he had a good reason to be proud of himself. All the N2L crew was there to show Bo love, and to spend big bucks. Nothing to lose was some Major dudes in Detroit city when it came to the underground music world and their money was up. They showed Foe love, knowing that he was Bo and DuPont people from New York, plus Priceless made motherfuckers want to say hello.

They headed straight to V.I.P, which was full of ballers, players, and even pimps.

Priceless was in her own world when Foe walked up behind her, "You ain't getting home sick already right?" Foe asked.

"No, I'm good...just watching these girls get short changed by all these ballers."

"Nah it ain't like that. Every nigga in this spot done saw it all and most of them done it all, so titties and ass ain't really gonna impress them." Foe explained as he looked down at the crowd.

"So not true Pi...the problem is this, they are selling sex Pi, instead of selling the Illusion. These girls are some of the sexiest girls I've seen in a long time, and they got moves. But the key to this business is not sex. It's seduction."

"So what you're saying is niggas want what they can't have more then what they can have?"

"Yup."

"Damn Ma that's kind of deep...but why is that?"

"Because that other head don't have no brain. It's dumb." Priceless joked, causing Foe to laugh. He was glad he brought her; she was giving him a different perspective on strippers. There's a lesson to be learned in all aspects of life, and Foe loved to learn.

DuPont came over and embraced Foe, "Is this living or what. You need to stop playing with it, and move down here for good...fuck the hood, me and Bo ain't never going back."

"Listen my nigga, I ain't got a home phone number, I live on the road, I go to FarRock just to visit and show love to the team."

DuPont looked past Foe and said, "Uh oh. Here comes trouble."

Babe came strutting their way. She was looking flawless as usual, with her Gucci frames and a floor length Mink.

"Hey fellas," was all she said with that look in her eyes that she learned from studying Tyra Banks.

Priceless peeped Babe's swagga from head to toe wittiest one blink of the eye and silently gave her props.

"What brings you out in this kind of environment?" Foe

asked indirectly, knowing one of Babe's people done tipped her off that Foe was in town.

Babe noticed Priceless was standing a little to close to Foe, so she decided to respond in a more blatant way, "Well I heard Bo was opening a new spot, so I came down here to show him some love on the strength of you, daddy."

Foe didn't miss a beat, "That's so sexy of you. I could always count on you Boo."

"Hey DuPont, I heard your new song on the radio the other night, that thing is hitting." Babe was born and raised on the East side of Detroit so her accent mixed with her hood slang always was a turn on for Foe.

"No doubt, you know how N2L east do it," said DuPont.

"Ay why ya'll being rude. Hello my name is Babe." She extended her hand to Priceless. Priceless Spanish accent caught Babe off guard

"Hi Mami, I'M Priceless, what you dance here?"

"No, do you?" Babe asked in defense mode.

"No Mami...I dance in New York, I'm visiting your city for the first time, and I'm loving it."

Babe was mad that Foe brought a Bitch from New York to the D, but she had too much class to let it show. Babe took a sip of her Nuvo, looking over her glass at Foe.

Bo came over with two bottles in his hand, a cigar in his mouth, with the biggest Kool-aid smile on his face, "What ya'll think. am I sitting on a gold mind or what?"

"No doubt my dude. Let me introduce you to one of my business advisers, she know all about this line of work...Priceless, this is my dude Bo. Bo this is Priceless. She had a few ideas that I think you might be interested in.

After the formal greeting Priceless spoke for 20 minutes straight about what niggas didn't mind spending their money on. Even Babe was taking down a few mental notes to use in her personal life. "You have to teach your girls how to create a compelling spectacle...think about it, men are turned on to what they see first. Then their next thought is, "I wanna beat that." So like I said the illusion comes first. It's the aura, that's the manifestation of the chocha Pi." Priceless preached.

"So what you saying is make em' feel like the more they spend the Closer they gonna get to the pussy." Bo asked causing Priceless to laugh.

"Something like that, but it's deeper than that. This ain't something I learned over night, you gotta really understand men to understand what I'm saying...men don't study other men, women do."

"So let me ask you this. Even though these dudes had been throwing money all night, you saying they ain't throwing enough." Bo asked, really starting to enjoy the science of the conversation.

"Papi, they gotta make them throw it all, then go home, get more and throw it all again."

"Maybe in New York sweetie, this is Detroit, the land of the Pimps. Babe said, trying to get the attention off Priceless. But Priceless just laughed at her comment, "Pimps is the biggest tricks...because they don't have to work hard for their money. It's a cycle sweetie.

Foe knew Babe like the back of his hand, he knew she wasn't feeling Priceless at all, but he didn't think she was going to say what she said next.

"Well why don't you show us how it's done in New York."

"Nah, we didn't come here for all that." Foe stated, a little too quick for Babe.

"What's the big deal? She'll just be teaching Bo girls how to bring in the real doe." Babe pressed.

Priceless wanted to shut Babe's ass up so bad, but she didn't want to step out of line with Foe.

"We got a whole basement full of brand new costumes. You could show me what you talking bout'. Make these niggas cash out and I'll put you in charge of training these girls. if that's okay with you Foe. Bo suggested.

"Papi let me help your friend be successful...jump this thing off the right way. After I'm done this will be the hottest spot in Detroit City."

Foe cracked a smile, smacked Priceless on the ass, "Get em' gurrl." Priceless left the V.I.P. area with Bo; they went down the steps and disappeared into the crowd.

"What's wrong with you? Why you showing off?" Foe asked Babe before she got the chance to try to slide off.

"What I do daddy?" Babe was trying to act all innocent, but she wasn't fooling nobody...especially not Foe.

"Who told you I was in town.

"Nobody I."

"Oh, we lying now. When we started that." Foe asked seriously.

"I'm sorry daddy...you know this my city, one of my bitches that's on you, work's at the airport...so when she saw you, she got all moist and hit my phone."

"Why are you antagonizing my guest, you making me look bad?"

"You look just fine to me." Babe said as she walked up close to Foe, he could smell her perfume but he wasn't about to fall for that.

"How if I bring you to New York and some chick you don't know start coming at you sideways. you think I would allow that. Never."

"Yeah you right daddy. I guess I got a little jealous."

"You got jealous of a stripper...think about what you saying Babe."

"She ain't no ordinary stripper and you know that...or she wouldn't be down here. so when did we start lying. like you said."

They conversation was interrupted when the D.J. put on Drake's song, "Houston Lanta Vegas," all the lights went out, except for one spot light that illuminated the stage.

There was no introduction, Priceless came out crawling on the stage, and she had on a black spandex cat suit with a four-foot long tail that stood up straight in the air with a curl at the tip.

It seemed as if the whole club stopped what they were doing and focused on the stage. Priceless worked that mother fucking stage like the professional that she was. The crowd motivated her, the more hype they got the more she envisioned Foe blowing g her back out.

The D.J. switched the song to an up tempo booty shaking song, Priceless ripped off the sweaty cat suit and tossed it in the crowd, which almost started a riot. Her ass swallowed her thong, she wasn't even dancing, yet she was just walking from one end of the stage to other. She knew that the six-inch heels had her ass wiggling all over the stage.

Priceless grabbed the mic from the D.J. then screamed, "Welcome to club wiggles."

She walked to the edge of the stage and made it shake, pop, clap, and wiggle. The stage had so much money on it that she had to watch her step before she slip and fall. She wouldn't get close enough for niggas to touch her, she would play the dude that was tossing the most money at her close, and let him get the best view of her goodies. One Dude pulled out a crazy stack of hundred dollar bills and Priceless flocked right to him, lie on her back, and put both of her legs behind her neck. Dude couldn't grope her but he felt like the man because she was with him.

Ego's came into play and the bidding frenzy began...it was crazy, the type of money that was being thrown on that stage. It wasn't even about Priceless any more; she knew her crowd and plaid the ballers against the players.

The D.J. switched the song to Trey Songs, "You gonna think I invented sex," Priceless already had this planned. She dragged a chair to the middle of the stage and niggas went fucking nuts, pulling out loads of cash trying to get chose for the exclusive lap dance.

The more money they threw, the more she pretended like she was going to choose one of them. Instead she pointed up at the V.I.P. at Foe. She turned that same pointer finger upside down and made the come here motion to Foe.

Babe was standing right next to Foe, but at this point all the hate she had for Priceless was replaced with respect. Priceless was a beast and Babe had no choice but to respect her hustle.

Right before Foe left the V.I.P. area Babe whispered something in Foe's ear and squeezed his dick. Priceless saw it and took it as a challenge; she decided to show Babe what she was made of.

As soon as Foe got on the stage she grabbed his hand and walked him to the chair. Every few steps she took she would look back to make sure he was looking at the way her ass was jiggling. And he was.

The lap dance that she gave Foe is still being talked about and watched on YouTube to this day. To try to explain the moves she put on Foe is impossible, but the way it ended was nothing other than epic.

Priceless had sat in Foe's lap, facing him. She put her flexible legs over his shoulders, one at a time. He looked down to see her twat bulging out under her thong.

"What did your little girl friend whisper in your ear Papi...huh?"

"Oh yeah...she told me to tell you that she don't mind sharing me with you."

Priceless leaned all the way back until her head hung over Foe knees. She tilted her head way back until her eyes connected with Babe's, grabbed her titties, and started flicking her tongue at Babe in a suggestive way, at the same time she started to bounce on Foe's dick that was hard as a diving board under his jeans.

Foe wasn't aware that Priceless hasn't been sexually active in the past 11 months, and that the dry humping had her seconds away from the big, "O."

The song was ending right as Priceless began to cry out, "You gon' think I invented sex. YO."

So the crowd heard her when she said, "Em. Bout to, I'm bout' to...I'm Cuuummmminnn."

The crowd was cheering like the Detroit Lions just won the Super Bowl. It was straight pandemonium as Priceless laid there shaking, with her body going into convulsions and spasms.

Foe had to hold her legs apart to keep her from breaking his damn neck. When Priceless was finally able to pull herself together, she stood up to walk to the edge of the stage and her knees buckled. She fell down to one knee and every nigga in the club felt like he personally put that work in, they cheered even harder, still throwing money on the stage. Foe got up and helped her to her feet. She bowed to the crowd and gave Bow two thumbs up.

There was over 137 thousand dollars in assorted bills at her feet and she was speechless. She never got that much money for a performance in all her years of dancing and she was shocked.

Bo ran on the stage and grabbed the mic, "Thank ya'll for coming out God bless and good night." Sounding like fake ass Russell Simmons.

Niggas were going so crazy for Priceless that she and Foe had to be ushered out of the back door.

Babe was mad as hell that she wasn't leaving with them, But she had to, "Join the club," on that one, literally.

Priceless leaned her seat all the way back in the Cadillac. She balled her body up under one of Foe's sweaters that she got from the back seat.

"Why you so quiet?" Foe asked.

"That shit was embarrassing." She replied.

"Embarrassing...they loved you."

"I ain't talking bout' them Pi...I'm talking about you." I don't get it. What do you mean Ma?"

"I just don't want you to think that I be doing shit like that in New York...cause I don't."

"Why you care what I think?"

"Because you...I don't know."

"Because I'm what...say it."

"I just think that you are different Pi. That's all."

"Oh you think. Well before this night is over your gonna know that I'm nothing like what you used to."

"Papi, I got a confession... I haven't had sex in a long time, and from what I seen in that shower, you look like your gonna kill me."

"How long has it's been Mami."

"11 months 2 weeks and 3 days."

"Don't worry Ma, my love don't hurt."

That night Foe did the opposite of what every man wanted to do to her, he made love to her...all night long. Priceless bit, scratched, screamed and curse in Spanish every time he made her cum.

Her chocha (as she called it) was so tight that it pulled the condom off twice. Foe thought, "This gotta be the best pussy I ever had in my life."

It was so good that Foe didn't even remember falling sleep. He woke up three hours later, it was 7:30 in the morning, and he started his normal routine that he been doing since his days of incarceration. 300 hundred sit-up's and five hundred push up's to start his day.

Priceless was in a coma, she looked like an angel as she slept. Foe couldn't help his self so he had to take one last peek under the sheets at her naked body. He wanted to wake her up and bend it up one more time but he had shit to do.

Foe Texted Priceless this message as he was leaving the house. (Gotta handle B.I. everything you need is in there, hit me when u wake up.)

Foe drove to the East side of Detroit to one of his trap houses that was run by his Detroit niggas. He made sure everything was good then drove to Babe's house.

Foe had the key so he walked in like a nigga had better not be up in here. Babe was in the bed sleep with her hair wrapped in a scarf.

Foe was something like a chef, well not a chef but he did know his way around the kitchen. He made homemade French toast, scramble eggs, and turkey sausages. The French toast had slices of strawberries and whip cream on the top of it.

The aroma woke Babe out of her sleep, "Good morning daddy."

"Top of the morning...go wash up, then come have breakfast with me.

"She get's the dick. And I get the grits." Babe stated as she walked into the bathroom.

"I didn't make no grits." Foe yelled from the kitchen.

All Babe could do was laugh as she brushed her teeth. Only Foe could get away with some shit like that, she thought.

They sat there and ate, while they small talked. Babe wanted to ask Foe how his night went but she wasn't trying to play herself. Foe phone sounded off letting him know he just received a text message. He read the message, and then slid his phone across the table to Babe.

Babe looked at him funny before picking the phone up, "It's for you." Babe read the message (Ask Babe did she enjoy the show...muah...LOL) Babe slid the phone back across the table then asked Foe, "So I guess she's the newest member on the team huh."

Foe smiled, "You already know."

CHAPTER TWENTY-TWO

B ack in FarRock Sha the God was up early in the morning, driving around the 60s looking for Sunny. Two of Sunny's soldiers had a long dope line that extended around the block. "Cop and Go," screamed the YBM soldier that Sha the God figured was the look out and the one with the blicky on him. Sha the God decided to park across the street and wait to see what the wind would blow in.

The two young boys were taking in a nice piece of change. Sha the God fangs came out, not that he needed the bread, he just missed the rush he used to get when he was sticking motherfuckers up. He got tired of sitting stationary after a hour. He concluded that Sunny wasn't gonna show, but he couldn't leave without doing something.

He got out of the car, put his hood on, and rolled up his left sleeve.

He walked up and got on the back of the dope line. There were only a few fiends ahead of him. Sha the God scratched his arm, and emulated the dope fiend nod.

After the two fiends in front of him scored their dope and walked off, Sha the God dug in his front pockets like he was searching for his money, but still with his head down. "Hurry the fuck up nigga. We shutting down," one of the boys spazzed.

Sha the God dug in his back pockets and said, "Oh here it go." He pulled out a brocky 357 snub nose and grabbed the closest one to him. "Run and I'mma kill you," was what he told the other lil' nigga.

"Take the money. We respect the jooks par," said the young boy he was holding.

"How many people in the crib?" Sha the God asked.

"Nobody in there, just take the money." The lil' nigga was shitting bricks.

"Walk...nice and slow, if somebody in there you catching the first one to the back of the head...so let me ask you again, "Are you sure nobody is inside?" "Yeah I'm sure, but ain't no money in there."

Sha the God knew that he was on pressed time when he got inside the crib, so he made the lil' niggas strip down to their boxers and seems, while he put all their clothes and money in a garbage bag.

"Ya'll know ya'll gonna die if ya'll don't tell me where I could find Sunny at right."

The YBM boys looked at each other, and for the first time they realized that this wasn't a joke.

"You just gonna have to kill me, cause I ain't telling you shit bitch," said the brave one.

Sha the God walked right to where he laid, pointed the cannon to his head, and squeezed...BOOM.

The other lil' nigga tried to jump up, but got smashed in the back of the head with the 357.

"Where's Sunny?" Sha the God said in the calmest voice. The smell of blood flooded the room and the lil' nigga was on the verge of passing out.

The lil' nigga was tough. He must have felt like he was gonna die anyway, so he looked up at Sha the God and said, "Suck my dick...YBM to the death."

BOOOM BOOM BOOM. One to the head and two to the chest put him to rest.

Sha the God walked to the window and peeked out. Everything looked cool, Right before he walked out of the YBM crib, he took one of the socks out of the bag, dipped it in the lil' niggas blood and wrote on the wall in big red letters, "WAR."

He did not intend to collect the bet money from Grecco, because he wasn't telling a soul what he did.

As soon as the story hit the news later that night, all the YOUNG Goonz had a pretty good idea who did that crazy shit in the 60s. Only one nigga in the team would stand in a crib with two dead bodies on the floor and take the time to write WAR on the wall and that was Sha the God.

Shorty-D, Death Row, D.B. and Sunny were back to the drawing board.

"How the fuck these niggas manage to keep picking us off. They done took so many of us that I lost count, and we only smoked one of them niggas...how." Death Row asked with a look of disgust on his face.

"Focusing on the money and taking our eyes off of the unfinished beef, that's how." D.B. explained.

"Shorty-D, you know these niggas better than all of us, and I never hear you offering no insight on these bustas." D.B said in frustration.

"How much insight you want. I told ya'll from the beginning not to fuck with these niggas, so let me point a few things out. We don't know which Young Goonz is doing what. When the shit popped off at the showcase and those niggas ran through the Edge and the Fern, I think that was the shooters that be in the Horseshoe. Thuggy Thug and them, But when Looch was shot. I think P-Killa and Foe threw Duke off the roof, or stood there and watched, cause we don't know how many of them was there. See it's like this, when you see some reckless shit go down, then you know it's the wild ones, but when you see some real smart shit happen where can't nobody say who did what, then that's the thinkers."

When that bird nigga bust that move on Jiggy and his lawyer, they probably didn't figure it out that he was involved. But as soon as he tried to cook the nigga D-Block his stupid ass got parked...I think D-Block did it himself, you can't sleep on D-Block he reminds me of FOE and P-Killa when they were his age." Shorty-D explained. If nobody listened to him before, they were listening now. He had their full attention.

"So who you think bodied my two lil' mans in the 60s." Sunny asked.

That's a no brainer. That had to either be Crazy Money, Sha the God, or Grecco. All three of them just came home and you could see the malice in their eyes. And don't look at C-Dollars like he's a rapper, because I think that was him on that roof with Duke, it's the same body build, and him and Looch been back to back before the whole Yong Goonz movement came about... so you see there's no telling who's doing what, you just can't tell when there's so many different factions.

Cause niggas like Thuggy Thug is a straight fucking head case. They can't control that boy. He's not riding because those niggas is saying get at the YBM crew; he's riding because he likes it. And don't let me forget about G-Pac, because I think he got more bodies then all those niggas. he's the different one, you think cause he's quiet he ain't on that Young Goonz shit, Nah, that one there keeps me on my p's and q's." Shorty-D explained with his arm wrapped in a sling.

"You talking like we ain't on these niggas level or something...fuck them niggas, when I catch any of them lames, big nigga or a worker, if they repping Young Goonz I'm leaving em' where I see em." D.B. spazzed

"Them niggas don't even live in the Rock. How you gonna see niggas that only pop up when it's time to ride on us and then disappear." Shorty-D asked, he never liked D.B. and he silently hoped that they get his ass next.

"Well I see some of them niggas every other Tuesday at that parole building...I'm tired of feeling like the mouse, in this cat and mouse game." D.B. replied, as if he figured out of the way to finally revenge Duke's death.

"25 to life is the same as catching one to the head. And that's what you gonna get fucking with Merrick Blvd at that parole slash police station." Shorty-D added.

Sunny listened to them go back and forth with the long face. He figured that one of these day's the Young Goonz was gonna come for him and his team, but he didn't think they were gonna come like that, his lil' soldiers got smoked in one of his cribs, on his block...he had no choice but to feel like he was wild easy to get. His ego was hurt and now he was ready to react off emotions.

"It's never no fun when the rabbit got the gun huh?" D.B. asked with a little too much humor for Sunny. Sunny stood up, and got up in D.B.'s face.

"What the fuck is your problem motherfucka?" Sunny asked so close to D.B.'s face that their noses almost touched.

"Young Goonz is my problem. What's yours nigga." D.B. replied after taking the toothpick out his mouth.

"So why the fuck you ain't cook nothing yet then nigga." Sunny pressed.

"Ya'll need to aim all that hostility at the motherfuckers that's killing our people." Death Row raised his voice and stepped between them.

"Look, them niggas die too, those niggas never hollered back when my young boy laid Buddah down. We shoot to kill, I don't know what ya'll doing with it." Shorty-D Boasted, not knowing that the Young Goonz did answer back, and that's why he couldn't use one of his arms.

"If I lived in Hammels, there would be more than one of them niggas dead and stinking." Sunny replied to the shot that Shorty-D threw at the rest of them.

"Ya'll still pointing fingers. And they still pointing guns. And squeezing." Death Row said as he shook his head in disgust.

P-Killa and Jiggy Jack were riding around FarRock, in a tinted up X-5 looking for Sha the God, who wasn't answering his phone or showing his face every since he of fed the YBM niggas in the 60s.

"How this shit gonna end." Jiggy Jacked asked as he drove past Gateway.

"How's what gonna end." P-Killa asked, staring out of the passenger window, "This war. What you think I'm talking about."

"The way it always end...niggas dead or in jail, nobody even remembering what the beef was about. Niggas just keep riding and riding."

"Whatever happen to the plans and the visions...so what we supposed to just devote the rest of our lives to this shit." P-Killa rolled the window down and dump the guts out of the Dutch then said, "Nah...But it's like this; we can't wave the white flag after all this blood that's been spilled. If they don't wave it, then we gotta keep riding and that's just the harsh reality of this shit."

"We smarter than this though, let's just leave the hood to these niggas and move on to bigger and better things. Not like we living out here anyway."

P-Killa laughed, "No matter where we go, there we are. Plus certain of our niggas ain't gonna wanna leave the hood."

"Well if that's the decision they make then they gonna have to deal with what comes with the life they chose."

"Yeah, but what about the niggas that's on parole. What we do, leave them to the wolves, and they weren't even home when the beef started." Remember, we didn't start this shit. I don't go out my way to look for trouble...but now it's like I gotta go all out of my way to avoid it." "Sometimes you gotta come at the people as the people... If the whole world was bad and you were good...then you would be the outcast, feel what I'm saying."

"They finally made it to Hammels projects; they circled around the hood a few times, which was looking like a ghost town. Nobody was out in the frigid cold, so they drove to Brooklyn to holla at Young Bash.

When Young Bash looked through the peephole and saw Jiggy Jack and P-Killa, he snatched the door open in a hurry, "Why you got all the lights out." Jiggy Jack asked.

"I'm hiding." Young Bash joked.

"From who nigga?" P-Killa asked.

"From the police...ya'll ain't see the news. They said the Young

Goonz is responsible for all the murders that's been happening in the Rockaway's, they had pictures of the Horseshoe dope bags, they saying when the YBM niggas put out of the WAR dope ya'll started killing up shit," said Young Bash.

"Fuck you mean ya'll...you going down too bitch." Jiggy Jack joked.

"Hell no. I ain't trying to ride...I'm trying to get rich and hide." Young Bash made a joke out of everything.

Jiggy Jack went to the computer and searched the net, trying to find something on the news about the shootings and murders.

"Where the fuck is Foe at." Young Bash asked.

"Probably in Maryland with wifey...last time I saw him we were at the strip club." P-Killa replied.

"Yo, the news said that the word WAR was written on the wall in blood. That sound like some real Sha the God shit," said Young Bash.

"We been looking for the nigga all night," Jiggy Jack said without raising his head from the computer.

"Well why the fuck ya'll come here...that crazy nigga ain't up in here."

"Here it go right here," Jiggy Jack screamed with his eyes glued to the computer.

"Oh shit, that's the Mayor, the Chief of police and the commissioner, Oh shit that's the Homo nigga Bell right there too.

They listen to 35 minutes of what the police and the media assumed what the war was about, and how they planned to bring everybody involved to justice. They were calling it a drug war one minute, and then they were calling it a gang war.

They also flashed mug shots of all the guys that was murdered in the past year.

When the news went off P-Killa said, "It ain't what they know. It's what they could prove."

Young Bash did his best slave Impression, "Ya'llz got to go...Ya'llz not welcome round here no mo."

CHAPTER TWENTY — THREE

The 30 day period was up and the under covers started purchasing drugs in Hammels projects. They were copping the dope from the YBM crew, and the crack and weed from the Young Goonz runners in the Horseshoe.

The under covers were good at playing the part of addicts, but Hammels Projects was considered a hostile environment that was getting many of media attention.

Buying the drugs was the easy part, the fear of being caught in the cross fire is what made them nervous. They couldn't wear bulletproof vest or carry their weapons, so they were vulnerable. All they had for protections was their ghost officers who kept a distance from them so they wouldn't blow their cover.

Demillio thought it would be a good idea to get the dealers to come to the undercover apartments to make the transactions. They had hidden cameras in the smoke detectors to catch the dealers dead to right.

Undercover #3158 was Hispanic lady that moved into the YBM building and started copping from the YBM crew. She convinced Ty that she was too scared of the violence to come out and cop, so he started going to her apartment to serve her. Her street name was grace and Ty knew every time she called his phone she wanted two bundles or better.

When Ty walked in Grace apartment, she had the Spanish

soap opera on the T.V. set.

"What's up baby…I need two bundles okay." Undercover # 3158 stated.

"That's wussup." Ty pulled the dope out and handed it to Grace right under the smoke detector.

"Do you think you could get me like two grams this weekend? My sister coming in town and I'm throwing a little get together for her…I'm gonna have a few friends over and I'm trying to make me a few extra dollars."

"As long as you spend the extras with me. Then I'll make it happen, just let me know a day or two in advance aight, you know its one twenty five a gram right."

"That's not a problem; because I'm gonna triple that in profit pop."

When Ty left the apartment, the drugs were sealed in an envelope with all the relevant information on it.

The YBM crew was too caught up in taking all the money that they became extremely reckless when it came to selling to the undercovers. The undercover had a hard time copping directly from the Young Goonz; in fact, they never even saw the Young Goonz that they were targeting.

So far, they collectively had over 25 subjects in the first month. Detective Bell and Detective Demillio was working hand to hand as they watched some of the footage that was caught in the undercover apartments, "This guy here is Tymeek Jones, I already flipped him against the Young Goonz. These sales you got him on might be good enough to get him on the witness stand." Bell spoke in a manner, which let Demillio know that he was now starting to see his angle.

"I don't know, the right lawyer would expose the war between the two groups then make it seem like he testifying in retaliation. It would be better if we could get these guys to flip on their own crew members. If we could get that, then we could get convictions." Demillio explained.

"Plus you know when it's time for the take down; we got ways of snagging extra fish in the drag net right." Demillio said with a wink of the eye.

"Well you know what they say. There's nothing wrong with going left for the right reason." Bell whispered.

Bell thought of something right as they were leaving his office, "Whatever you do, keep in mind that them Young Goonz got some of the best lawyers money could buy and if they get whiff of an conspiracy it'll be us at the defense table, trying to defend our conduct."

Demillio smiled, I'm what you can consider an expert witness. My answer is always the same when I'm under pressure. I can't recall, or, I could have been mistaken."

That following Friday, the Young Goonz was going, to have a sit down. It was early Thursday evening and everybody was accounted for except Foe. It's been three weeks and none of the Young Goonz had heard from him. With the war going on with the YBM crew, it wasn't a good time to be MIA.

P-Killa called Ooh Wop in Baltimore, "Hell no his ass ain't down here... he probably laid up with one of his broke ass bitches...and when you talk to him tell him I said he's playing his fucking self, not answering that damn phone when I call."

After he hung up, P-Killa figured he just got Foe into some shit with his bitch. "Fuck it; I'm trying to find my nigga." P-Killa thought. He decided to call DuPont phone next to see if Foe was in the D.

"What's good boy...tell me Foe down there with ya'll...please."

"Yeah, I was just with him last night, popping bottles. Why everything good." DuPont asked.

"Yeah now it is, son been MIA for a few weeks now so."

DuPont laughed, "You must didn't see his new bitch."

"Let me find out that nigga done went down there and fell in love." P-Killa said.

"She from New York. a Spanish stripper bitch with a crazy Nicki Minaj fat ass." DuPont screamed excitedly.

"I know this nigga didn't." P-Killa caught his self before he said what he already knew was a fact. "DuPont tell that nigga I said YGE, holla at me ASAP."

"Aight my nigga, you need to come down here and check out Bo club, the shit is off the hook." DuPont stated right before he hung up.

Foe had Priceless in the Doggy Bounce Broken Hind legs when DuPont started ringing his phone.   You wanna answer that phone or you wanna keep fucking this chocha...huh." Priceless said looking over her shoulder at Foe who couldn't even answer her question.

Her ass was slapping against Foe's six-pack so loud that he thought he was putting in more work then he actually was. Foe held her in that position for a good 20 minutes then slammed her on her back, "Yeah Papi...get rough... I ain't scared of you." Foe bent her legs up then folded em, then wore that thing out.

"Oh God. What you call this one Papi." Priceless asked as she bit on her bottom lip.

"This right here is called the Mr. Pretzel." Foe took that position from Jiggy Jack, but she didn't know it, so he was Mr. Pretzel that night. They banged out for about another hour then collapsed on top of the sweaty, sticky sheets. "Damn Pi. You a beast."

Foe looked at his phone and read the text message from DuPont (Call P-Killa YGE) YGE was the code for YOUNG GOONZ EMERGENCY. Foe jumped out of the bed butt naked, switched his Detroit's sim card to his New York sim card in and dialed P-Killa, "What happened?" Asked Foe in full Goon mode.

"Family reunion nigga. Tomorrow night at ten, the three minute location." P-Killa said with a whole lot of hostility.

"Easy tiger," said Foe with aggression.

"You know the rules nigga. Check in."

Foe laughed, "You were worried about me my nigga."

"You ain't gonna be laughing when Ooh Wop go up side your

head nigga."

"I got kidnapped. That's my story and I'm sticking to it." Foe joked.

"I know you ain't fall in love with that Spanish chick we met at the club the other night."

"I got kidnapped."

Any nigga that did over ten years in prison could relate to Foe's mind frame when it comes to women. Females could love a nigga to death, but they ain't trying to do that bid. So niggas do their time talking about, "Fuck bitches," but as soon as they bring their ass home they can't do shit without a bitch on their mind. Lil' Weezy said it best, "I wish I could fuck every girl in the world."

Foe did love Ooh Wop, but the allure of some new pussy was beyond his control. "He got kidnapped."

When he hung up with P-Killa Priceless was at the stove cooking Spanish rice and peas, fried chicken and plantains. The only thing she had on was slippers and some pink boy shorts. Foe was about to bend her ass over the kitchen sink, but the YGE was more important so he called the airport and booked a flight.

The Young Goonz held their sit down in Brooklyn at one of Dot's cribs. Everybody was in attendance and Jiggy Jack were doing the talking, "I spoke to my lawyer and he said the D.A. got something real big he's planning on doing about the violence in the Rockaway's, now I know ya'll some tough mother fuckas...but this shit got me a little worried.

I think they're cooking up a conspiracy charge or some Rico shit. There's ways around that. Stay the fuck off the phones for one. They gotta be able to link us all together in some type of criminal activity.

We officially shutting down the Horseshoe, we gonna have to get money elsewhere for the time being, cause if they catch any of us doing anything they gonna pick the jail up and drop it on our fucking heads.

They calling this shit a drug war, so if they ain't got no

drugs, they ain't got no case. Now as far as them YBM bitches, they can't fuck with the Goonies, they dropping like flies.

My concern is this, these crackers is ready to break the law to get the convictions against us. The Mayor is involved; this shit is bigger than the war now. Money is being funded for this investigation and best believe at the end of the day, they gonna give them higher mother fuckas something... I feel sorry for the fall guys cause they gonna load us up with time, just to make it seem like they did their job.

"So...No more killing." Jiggy Jack said then took a seat. Foe stood up

"When it rains it pours, and that's a fact. The law is coming, and to keep it a hundred. I don't give a fuck if they give me a hundred life sentences, as long as they don't use any of you in this room to do it."

In a situation like this they are looking for a weak link. If anybody in this room feels like they can't do life in jail for some shit they didn't do, but you know the nigga that's sitting next to you did it. And you don't love him enough to give your life for your brother then after we leave here tonight, pack everything you own, take all your money and get as far away from New York as possible. Turn your life around, shit go to church and ask God for forgiveness, but whatever you do...don't rat on the niggas that'll die for you.

I'll live, die, and kill for every nigga in this room. I heard so many stories up-north when I was doing my time, how niggas felt when one of their people walked past them as they sat next to their lawyer, then got on that witness stand and finished them. I'll rather die than to experience some shit like that."

"Real talk, " said P-Killa as he stood up and gave his piece, "Don't get what Jiggy Jack saying twisted, them YBM niggas is still riding around head hunting us. But look, the rock is so hot right now we could pull the chair from under these clowns by waiting em' out. Let's let these niggas crash into the wall looking for us. Our enemies are not to find us when they look, but as soon as they get tired of lookin...we come looking for them." P-Killa had a way of saying shit like William Wallace, straight out of the Brave heart's movie.

"Grecco being the one to stir the water all the time said, "Sound like ya'll got this whole thing figured out...but what about us that can't go out of town, fuck us. Huh."

"Sha the God finally came out of isolation but he really was in his own world, as long as he had his gun he didn't give a fuck about nothing."

"I don't need nobody to hold me down. I'm mobbing on them niggas they come my way, fuck them niggas till the sun burn out." Sha the God spoke for the first time.

"Grecco, if you don't think that we took that into consideration then you must think we ain't loyal to each other...Young Bash got three apartments in Brooklyn for ya'll," said Jiggy jack.

"I ain't going no motherfucking where...my P.O. fiending to violate me every since he found out that I'm repping Young Goonz," said Crazy Mone.

"This shit is bigger then us now, it's all type of politics going on behind close doors. They getting money to fund this investigation, the more we ride, the more money they gonna get to steal from the Government." Nitty explain.

"Ahhh shit, here we go with the conspiracy theories." Thuggy Thug joked.

"Ya'll niggas watch the Wire right, they showed ya'll how corrupt these mothafuckas is...what ya'll think, Baltimore politics is different from New York's. Ask Foe he'll tell ya'll how they doing it in B-More." Nitty tried to break it down but Thuggy Thug was on a role.

"Nigga I skip all them parts on the Wire...I only watched the gangsta shit. Marlow had me ready to leave niggas in empty apartments." Thuggy Thug said causing a few of the younger boys to laugh and give him daps.

"Art emulates reality, so if we don't stay out that shoe, ya'll gonna wish ya'll didn't skip them scenes in the Wire." Nitty added right before he gave up trying to get the shit through these niggas heads.

"Nobody saying if opportunity knocks not to answer the door with your gun in your hand...what we saying is this, don't walk out of the door looking for the opportunity," said Looch cutting his one good eye at Sha the God.

'So what I should ware my vest but don't pack my gat...that sound like some real sitting duck shit to me and I ain't with it," said Grecco.

"Me and my baby moms lives in the Horseshoe ...I'll rather get caught with it, then without it. I gotta protect my family. So fuck YBM, I ain't going no where...and fuck the police too." Chillz said without hesitation.

When money is not the issue...then everything else is in the hood, and that's just the way it is. The Young Goonz was in what you would call a loyalty verse survival situation. Either be loyal to the team that's stuck in the hood, and wait for the cops or death to come, or get then fuck out of dodge and harm's way by leaving your niggas in the hood.

The law is the strongest enemy, and ignorance to the law is not a good defense in the courtroom. Nobody's lawyer ever asked a jury to acquit his client because he didn't know that is actions could have got him put in jail.

So the only solution to the Young Goonz problem would be to end the war. How? Who the hell knows because the YBM boys were out for blood, and the Narc's had two apartment in the Horseshoe. And the Young Goonz sit down was going nowhere fast.

"I notice how every time somebody say something ya'll look at me like I'm the one that made it hot...and I ain't saying I did that shit in the 60s, but if I did, that's nothing in comparison of throwing a nigga off the roof, recording it, then putting the shit on YouTube for the world to see it. Now that's some sick shit," said Sha the God looking at P-Killa and Foe.

Foe knew what Sha the God was trying to insinuate, "Yeah them

YBM niggas is crazy, how they gonna throw one of their O.G.'s off the roof." Foe laughed trying to divert the stares off him and P-Killa.

Thuggy Thug burst out laughing, "Let's see who could top that on some horrific shit," and just like that, the seed was planted. The whole reason for the sit down went down the drain, "We should cut one of them niggas up, and leave a body part in every project in the Rock," said Crazy Mone causing Sha the God to smile for the first time in months. Jiggy Jack looked at Thuggy Thug with a look on his face that said... Thanks a fucking lot.

CHAPTER TWENTY-FOUR

Four days later was tasty Tuesday. Thuggy Thug and Smokey were parked right in front of the parole building waiting for their niggas to come out.

Rah and Bart was parked one block over just waiting on anything out of the ordinary. The Young Goonz was always ready to hold each other down, even if it meant putting their own lives on the line.

There's no honor amongst thieves...well the Young Goonz wasn't thieves, they were family. The YBM boys were there too, they were two blocks over and they were about to show the Young Goonz that they weren't playing with it at all.

Problem was laying in the back seat of a hooptie that was being driven by his partner in crime Craps. They figured that the Young Goonz would have reinforcements close by and that's who they were targeting.

The YBM crew had a few tricks up their sleeve this time around. They had the sexiest gangsta bitch from Edgemere Projects riding around the block looking for niggas parked in cars.

Her name was Widow, and rumor has it that she killed her baby's father after she caught him cheating on her. She was the only suspect in the investigation but nothing was ever proven so she never was charged with the murder.

Widow made the left turn on the block where Rah and Bart

was parked on. She slowed down and pretended to be looking for an address. When she saw two figures in a car behind tinted windows, she had to get a closer look to see if they were looking suspect. She clicked on her hazards then stepped out in her Gucci heels. The business suite she was rocking gave her a look of importance, but the tightness of the suite had her looking like Diva. Her blouse was unbuttoned down to the top of her cleavage, which had her hooters busting out of the top.

Widow purposely walked past the car the Young Goonz sat in. She stop right in front of them, giving them an up close and personally look at the fatness and roundness of her ass.

"Goddamn, that bitch look like a movie star." Bart said sounding like a youngster.

"Man, fuck that bitch. She probably a cop." Rah said and tighten his grip on the 21 shot Taurus.

"Oh shit she's coming to the car." Bart said as he tucked the 45 ACP under his leg. He rolled the window down and smiled at Widow.

"Excuse me guys, do you know where." Rah cut her right off "Nah bitch we don't know shit. Beat it."

Widow faked a shocked expression, then quickly walked to her Nissan370Z and peeled off.

Rah could care less if the bitch was police or not, because going back to jail was not an option. He and Bart were squeezing on any and everything that false move.

Widow drove back around the corner where Craps was parked. She confirmed that two young bastards were parked on the next block. She gave them the make and model of the car they were in then pulled off. Her job was done.

"Aight my nigga...tomb stones and body bags." Craps said as he started up the car.

"I ain't feeling this one, Widow could be mistaken. I don't wanna clip the wrong niggas." Problem stated.

"I was just thinking the same shit. we could wait til' everybody come out of the building and if the car move we'll know it's them."

Getting the drop on niggas that's already on point is one of the most difficult task. The risk and the balls that it demands is usually not worth it.

Today there wasn't a risk that wasn't worth it to the YBM crew, they were all in. murder on sight by every means necessary, and was time to get it in.

Problem pondered hard then said, "I got an idea, pull around the corner to D.B and them."

D.B. was driving a black Lumina with two of his shooters from Redfern Projects riding shotgun. He was just about to get out and report to his P.O. when craps pulled up.

"You went in yet." Craps asked.

"Nah...I'm going in now."

"Aight, cause it's about to go down, your boy's is ready.

D.B. smiled, "They been ready." When D.B. walked into the parole building Craps explained to the Redfern niggas what he wanted them to do.

The Young Goonz tried not to give the YBM crew these types of opportunities, but certain things are inevitable. Even though the Young Goonz was a little more calculated then the YBM crew, that didn't mean that they were more dangerous. The YBM crew was responsible for raising the murder rate in Queens. When the Young Goonz was focusing on money, before the war, the YBM crew was killing shit.

Craps bent the block that Rah and Bart was parked on. He saw that their car was parked in the middle of the block, Craps glanced at them as he drove right past them. He made it to the top of the block and instead of making the turn; he put the car in reverse. Rah peeped it instantly cause he never took his eyes off the Hooptie.

"Why the fuck that car ain't turn yet. Get on point that shit is backing up."

The Hooptie was driving in reverse real slow and already pasted two parking spaces. Bart cocked back his hammer. "You think its cops."

~ 217 ~

"I don't care who it is…If they stop let em' have it." Rah said as he cocked his hammer back. They never saw D.B. shooters bend the block behind them; they were too focused on the Hooptie.

The Lumina came speeding from the blind side. When the drop is executed properly, it has to be respected. Some of the most recognized hood legends fell victim to that good ol' drop. The hood start talking about, "Damn how that nigga let them dudes catch him slipping." What Foe always say is, "Be careful who you piss off…because some niggas won't stop until they get the drop."

The shooters from Redfern rammed the Young Goonz car from behind, then open fire on them. Rah tried stepping on the gas off impulse but the car in front of them wouldn't allow them to get away.

P-Killa always told them about defensive driving, "Never Box yourself in, and give yourself enough room to maneuver the vee." He would say.

After the Redfern boys emptied out on them, Problem hopped out of the hooptie and emptied his clip into the windshield at close range. Bart and Rah never got off a shot.

Everybody in the parole building heard the shots. The parole officers ran into the waiting area and pretty much ordered nobody to leave the building or they would automatically be violated.

Thuggy Thug and Smokey raced around the block to find Bart and Rah's hoop ride riddled with bullet holes. Rah must have tried to escape the onslaught of bullets, because he lay outside the car by the driver side door. Thuggy Thug was just about to get out of the car when he heard all the sirens closing in on them. His emotional state left him oblivious to the fact that they were at a crime scene with loaded guns on them.

"Pull the fuck off nigga." Smokey screamed breaking Thuggy Thug out his trance, as he pulled off heated. One thing about war. it's only fun when you winning.

The EMT workers pronounced Rah dead on arrival. They

were able to revive Bart after flat lining twice. The Doctors at Jamaica Hospital explained to Bart's family that he was on life support with a forty percent chance of living.

Rah's mother fainted when she heard the news of her son's death, while Bart's mother begged her God to spare her sons life. in FarRockaway, the parents of the young unconsciously wait for that call, saying that their child was murdered in the street. They see it happen to their friends, their neighbors and to strangers they see every day in passing. The parents are the real victims. I guess that's why the old Chinese lady in the movie Menace to Society told O-Dog, "I feel sorry for your mother."

Two days later Detective Demillio and Detective Bell was given strict orders to end Operation Good Neighbor.

Early that morning at exactly six a.m. Hammels Projects was raided, with over 200 hundred officers, including the five undercovers that was riding around the projects in an unmarked cars with tinted windows making identifications. They were equipped with bogus search warrants that weren't even signed by a judge.

They were running up in apartments that had nothing to do with the investigation. They had the green light to do whatever the fuck they wanted, due to the string of murders, that's been taking place in the Rockaway's.

Demillio was in charge of the take down and he was up to his old tricks. He would walk one of the subjects to an open area, tell the guy to look up then put him in the prison van after getting the conformation from the undercover officer. If the guy wasn't a subject, but he was down with the Young Goonz or YBM he would walk them down to the open area, put his walkie-talkie to his ear, then put the nigga in the van like if he was identified by the undercover. All the buy reports were forged with false information. So it was easy to make anybody fit to one of the John Doe names.

The take down rounded up 52 subjects. Ten YBM members, eight of the Young Goonz runners, Messhall, scope, Gunz, Chillz, and Scooby, Lex and T.I were also snagged up in the drag net.

Detective Bell was in a zone when they made it back to the precinct; he loosened his tie, rolled up his sleeves, and splashed some cold water on his face. The Take down was somewhat of a success. The YBM crew was caught with four guns and over fifty bundles of WAR. Ty was in deep shit, not only did he have the sales to undercover #3158 but also he was caught with two loaded guns in his mother's apartment and three bundles of WAR. Another YBM member Fat Mike was also caught with two loaded guns, and a few thousand dollars in his mother's apartment. Fat Mike made a few sales to Grace, but never inside her apartment.

Bell decided to put Fat Mike under the swinging light first. He was on his way to the bullpens to pull Fat Mike out when all hell broke loose.

The Young Goonz and the YBM crew was brawling hard in the pens They were fighting light cats and dogs, like savages. It looked like a Royal Rumble in a steel cage match.

It took the officers quite a minute to break up the rumble and to separate the two crews. Bell made sure that Fat Mike, TY, Messhall and Scooby was put in two separate pens upstairs next to the interrogation room.

Bell figured he would start with the Young Goon, because if he could flip one of them then that would cause the domino effect, and it was now or never if he was going to solve the murders. He pulled Messhall out of the pens into the interrogation room first, then began with his antics If Do you know why your here young man?"

"Yeah, my pops said my mom's got him drunk then seduced him."

"You think this is a game you little young punk...let's see

how funny you are in C-74, that's Rikers island, where they turn boys to girls." Bell said trying to lay his pressure game down on the kid.

"If you gonna charge me with something then charge me, I don't wanna hear all that bullshit early in the morning...all my friends been on the island and ain't nobody getting raped...dick head."

Bell smacked Messhall on the back of his head, grabbed him by the collar, and dragged him back to the pens. He had no better luck with Scooby. He thought Scooby was giving him the silent treatment, not knowing that he was a kid with not too many words for anybody.

When Scooby got back in the pens with Messhall, Messhall asked, "You good my nigga." Scooby looked at him with an expression that said, "Of course."

Bell knew he wasn't going to get anywhere with the Young Goonz so he focused his intention on Ty and Fat Mike. Fat Mike was already crying when Bell took him out and brought' in the dull looking room.

"You know you just threw your whole life away right."

"I was holding them for somebody...those wasn't my guns." Fat Mike cried.

"You know that's the least of your problems. The 9mm is a match for the gun that killed Buddah, so I'm charging you with first degree murder." Bell lied.

Fat Mike had a look on his face as if he was seconds away from vomiting his guts out." Oh my God, I didn't kill nobody...I never even shot a gun before, I'm only sixteen."

"Well at least your young, you should be coming home when you turn about forty years old if you get out on good behavior."

Fat Mike caught a bad case of cottonmouth as his legs shook uncontrollably under the table.

"Look I know how you feel, when I was your age I was betrayed by some guys that I thought was my friends, but this here crosses the line... to leave a murder weapon in your house, knowing that you could spend the rest of your life in jail...those are not people I would consider friends. Would you?"

"No," Fat Mike said with enough attitude to let Bell know it was time for him to make his move.

"Well if you know who killed Buddah, now would be the time to talk, because I'll make sure you won't do a day in jail...not even for the guns. Bell said, laying it on thick to scare little nigga.

"It was Pit...he killed Buddah and Ty was with him, they laugh about it every day."

One hour of questioning other people, Bell was looking for any information on the murders. He saved Ty for last because he knew he had him by the balls.

"Tymeek you're going away for a long time buddy. Bell stated in a very truthful tone.

"My lil' brother taking the weight for the two guns, so I don't know what you talking about."

"Okay, he could do that but let me show you why you getting five automatic years." Bell turned on the flat screen T.V. that was rolled into the investigation room. He pressed play on the DVD player and Ty jaw dropped when he saw himself inside of Grace's apartment, selling her dope. Bell cut the T.V. off, "That was undercover # 3158 and within the last three months you sold her over ten bundles of WAR, but that's the least of your problems. I now have two witnesses that are going to testify next week at a Grand Jury that your friend Patrick Well...Pit, Killed Buddah and you was with him, which makes you accessory to murder.

Now I'm going to cut to the chase because I have many of paper work to do...I'm a Homicide Detective, all I'm concerned with is the shooter, the district attorney play's by a different set of rules. All he's concern with is his conviction rate; he'll lock ten guys up for one murder and take them all to trial.

This is the deal, take it or leave it...it really makes me no difference Pit's going to jail for murder, I can have your name taken out of the indictment in exchange for your testimony against the

Young Goonz that killed your 13 year old friend in the front of your building that day."

"The Young Goonz didn't do that, so I." Bell cut Ty off, "Do you want the deal or not...I don't give a shit if you did it yourself, two of them bastards are going down for it, or you're going down with Patrick. You make the choice. So do we have a deal or what?" Bell asked as he stood up, giving Ty the Impression that he was about to leave.

"What about these sales." Ty asked.

"What sales," replied Bell, knowing he could make the sales disappear, which was the plan from the beginning of the investigation. Bell told Ty to sit tight as he walked back to his office.

Bell looked at his chart with all the Young Goonz it was time to pick two since there were two sets of fragments found by the crime scene unit at the YBM building.

Foe had already beat Bell at trial on murder charges, so he dint want to pick him for obvious reasons. Jiggy Jack had one of his murder charges dismissed, and C-Dollars beat him when an innocent bystander was killed on the boardwalk a few years back. Bell was drawing a blank; he eliminated all the Young Goonz that was recently released from prison, which narrowed it down, as far as the well-known guys that was prominent members of the Young Goonz organization.

Bell walked up to the board, rubbed the stubble on his chin, then grabbed D-Block's picture off the board, he removed the thumb tack, "That one," Bell was contemplating on Messhall's picture, but when his eyes landed on G-Pac's, he snatched it off the wall and said, "That's two, "

After he get the statement from Ty, he was going to try and flip D-Block and G-Pac on ratting out of the rest of the Young Goonz in exchange for their freedom to never know." Bell thought as he walked out his office back into the interrogation room, where Ty sat and waited 11 Alright, let's get down to business so I could get you out of here."

One hour later Bell went into the other interrogation where, Fat Mike sat, wiping tears from his face.

Bell brought with him a king size Snickers candy bar, a bag of Lays potato chips, and an ice cold Pepsi and a pen and a pad.

After 30 minutes of coaching Fat Mike what to say and write, Bell left the interrogation room with a full statement signed by Fat Mike implementing Pit in Buddah's murder. Bell felt that he finally got a break, three people was about to be charged with murder thanks to the, "Operation Good Neighbor," investigation. Now it was up to the district attorney to make the charges stick.

Bell walked into Demillio's office, gave him a firm hand shake, then said, "Come on. Lunch on me."

CHAPTER TWENTY-FIVE

Aday after the raid, Hammels Projects was looking like a ghost town. "The Waves." Which is the name of the FarRockaway news paper, had Hammels Projects on the front page with the words." Take Down," across the top in big bold black letters, under that read, "Special Drug unit net's 52 suspects in drug war." They put a picture on the front page of at least 20 cops surrounding a table with all the guns, drugs, money, and cell phones that was confiscated out of the various apartments that was raided by the, "No knock," warrant squad.

"Yo this shit is crazy. Most of the shit they saying ain't even true." D-Block said to Foe as he read the article in the paper aloud.

Foe was driving and wasn't surprised at how The Waves portrayed the events that took place in the Rockaways. In fact, they remixed a few of his encounters with the law, so it wasn't nothing new to him.

"I spoke to Jiggy Jack this morning; he's waiting on all them niggas to get their bails set, so he could go get them out." D-Block added changing the subject.   Foe was focus on the road with a million other thoughts on his mind, I remember the first time I went to Rikers island," said Foe.

"Here we go with one of these damn stories." D-Block thought.

"I didn't know what to expect, I was fresh to death, and the stories that I heard that niggas were getting cut for their garments if they didn't give em' up...I wasn't giving up shit, or letting a nigga cut me. I remember these two niggas pressed me on some, "Where you from shit. So I bass up on the niggas like,

"FarRock, why wussup?" one of the niggas rocked me to sleep like, "Word. My cousin from FarRock...you know Ramel," so I'm like, "I know a few ramels...what projects he live in." I never saw the other nigga creep up on me from behind, the nigga throw me in the fiend, trying to put me to sleep. I struggled up outta that shit and got it shaking with them niggas, next thing I know the whole house popped off on me, then it was like every house I went to I had to turn it up all crazy until mothafuckuz started to respect my shit. I was just trying to live, but my name was starting to ring bells around the four building (C,74) One day I went to court and bumped into my nigga Sherm The Worm from Queens-bridge projects, he told me he heard how I was turning it up and to keep keeping it official on some Queens shit."

D-Block wasn't in the mood to hear no jail war stories, so he tried to switch the subject without Foe noticing it, "We gotta stay outta the hood until many of this shit die down...wussup with a trip O.T."

"Where you think we heading my nigga." Foe stated as he switched lanes on the Belt Parkway.

One hour later, they were in Priceless upper Westside studio apartment.

D-Block was looking at Priceless wall of fame, which was full of autographed pictures that she took with celebrities. "Jasmine this is my brother D-Block—D-Block this is the reason why nobody can never find me anymore."

D-Block was caught staring at her camel toe that was protruding from the boy shorts that she had on. Priceless was so used to being naked and stared at, that she didn't even notice it, "Hello Papi," she said as she extended her hand to D-Block.

"What's good with you," D-Block said with a little smile on his face, he couldn't help but to stare at Priceless nipples poking out her white sports bra.

"Ya'll hungry Pi?"

"Na Ma Ma, we gotta get going, I just booked a flight it departs in two hours."

"Where we going Pitt

Foe smiled, "Not this time Ma Ma, I wish I could take you with me, but this is business trip." Foe lied.

"Oh. Okay."

Foe could tell that her feelings was hurt, "When I get back, I'm coming straight here." He lied again.

"How you know I'm gonna be here when you get back Pi," Priceless said with what Foe took as a sexy attitude.

"Because absence makes the chocha get wetter." Priceless melted as she felt Foe's breath caress her earlobe. "God...who is this man," she thought. "I'll be here Papi."

"I know." Foe stated as him and D-Block was leaving out of the door.

Two hours later, Foe and D-Block was at JFK Airport. They walked to the counter and gave the receptionist all the proper information for the flight that was booked online.

Foe noticed that the lady behind the counter was acting jumpy after she pushed all the information in the computer. It seemed as if she wasn't trying to hold eye contact with Foe and D-Block and they noticed it, "Fuck is wrong with this bitch." D-Block whispered back to Foe who stood behind him.

"I don't know...excuse me Mrs. Is there something wrong," Foe asked.

"No...there's no problem. Just give me a second please." She was fairly new on the job, and after witnessing the events of 9/11 every little thing made her nervous. She was an older lady of Indian descent, and pushing the help button came natural to her.

"Damn this shit ain't never take this long." D-Block whispered again. Foe was just about to say something to the receptionist when two white men walked up looking like the Men in Black with their suits on. D-Block thought they looked like the agents from the matrix.

Gentlemen...the last thing we want is to make a scene, a red flag popped up on the computer so we got to ask you guys a few question and if everything checks out okay, I promise you guys that you won't miss your flight."

Said one of the airport officers. Foe looked at D-Block and hunched his shoulders as if to say he didn't know what the hell was going on.

They were placed inside a room, one officer stayed with them while the other one left to go make some calls. They flight was scheduled to take off in another 45 minutes and Foe was watching the clock, knowing whatever the red flag was it had to be a misunderstanding.

35 minutes later the officer walked back into the room and handed Foe his plane ticket and his I.D. "Your flight will be taking off in ten minutes so if you get to the gate now you should make it." The officer turned to D-Block," as for you young man, I'm sorry to inform you that you have an outstanding warrant. I just got off the phone with a Detective from FarRockaway Queens and I was order to detain you until he gets here."

D-Block knew he didn't have any warrants, so the only thing that came to spent his mind was that somehow his name got caught up in the drug sweep, until Foe asked, "Do you know the name of the Detective that you spoke to officer."

"Yes, it was a Detective name Anthony Bell." D-Block and Foe looked at each other with the same thoughts running through their heads, "Homicide."

"I'mma call the lawyer, he'll be at the precinct in a minute."

Foe stepped outside the room and called Mike Worn, one of the Young Goonz lawyers. Foe spoke into the phone quickly giving the lawyer all the information that he needed.

Foe was just about to dial Jiggy Jack's number When Detective Bell and another officer came walking up, "One down...and the rest of you to go," was all Bell said to Foe as he walked past him, into the room where the airport police held D-Block hand cuffed.

A few minute went past and the door swung open. Bell walked out with his chest poked out and a firm grip on D-Blocks arm. The sight was rough on Foe's eyes but he didn't let D-Block see it. D-

Block winked at Foe as he passed by him. "I'm right behind you my nigga." Foe said to D-Block's back.

One hour later, the Young Goonz lawyer Mike Worn pulled up to the 100 precinct. Foe got out of the car with D-Block's wifey, they said a few words to the lawyer then got back in the car to wait and see what was going on. The thirty-minute wait seem like forever then Mike Worn came jogging down the precinct steps. The first thing Foe noticed was that D-Block wasn't with him.

D-Block's wifey started to cry, "They keeping him," she said with her eyes full of tears.

"Let's see what they said —come:" They exited the car and walked to Mike Worn.

"Look, they charging him with the murder of a 13 year old boy that occurred about two months ago. The boy name is Christopher Hayes, what I gather is this...the warrant was signed yesterday, which was the same day as the take down, that's been all over the news. It's obvious that somebody gave him up for immunity on their charges, which would give me some good tactic if thing was to go to trial."

Foe turned around and jumped in his car, peeling off fast. His mind was on some black out shit...and when Foe black out...somebody dies.

Mike Worn looked at D-Block's wifey then said, "Well I guess I'll be driving you home." Foe forgot all about shorty, he was on his bullshit.

Hammels Projects was literally one minute away from the 100 precinct. Foe jumped out his whip right in front of Shorty-D's building. It was 10:30 at night, the YBM boys thought their eyes were playing tricks on them when they saw Foe walking their way.

They knew that Foe was a dangerous nigga in them streets so as he got closer they started to spread out, and a few of them reached for their hammers.

"Why the fuck ya'll niggas scrambling for," screamed Foe with fire in his eyes.

Pit backed his hammer out, trying to show leadership since Shorty-D wasn't around, "Ain't nobody scrambling, we just ain't taking no chances over here my man."

"I ain't your fucking man." Foe spazzed, walking right past Pit without entertaining the fact that he had his little punk as gun out. Foe ran up the steps to the second floor and knocked on Shorty-D's apartment door.

Pit must have called his team because six of the YBM boys from Hammels came out of the staircase with guns out. Foe was still in blackout mode.

"Where the fuck is Shorty-D at," he asked as if he wasn't on enemy grounds. LU Monster badass, not knowing no better walked right up on Foe and said, "Nigga you wanna die." Foe snatched the little boy up by his throat so fast that the YBM boys were stuck watching the shit unfold.

It only took two smacks to the mouth to have Lil' Monster spitting out globs of blood. The YBM boys saw that shit and flipped, they pointed their guns at Foe screaming, "Let him go."

Foe span little Monster around and lifted him in the air, using his body as a shield then screamed, "Shoot mothafuckuz...shoot."

Shorty-D walked out of his apartment and told his soldiers to put their guns down. Shorty-D saw all of the blood on the floor and asked Foe, "Was that really necessary?"

"Man fuck all that, we gotta talk." Foe replied.

"Come on." Shorty-D led Foe inside his apartment. He told Foe to take a seat as he went to the back room to take the nine off his hip and stash it.

Shorty-D came back in the living room ' You know you still get that same crazy look on your face when you pissed off. I saw that look so many times when we were growing up."

"Yeah well, some things never change...but some things do." Foe said, not trying to take a trip down memory lane with Shorty-D. "Aight then what brings you all the way across hostile lines."

"They just locked D-Block up for killing your little man Chris, plus he got attempt murder charges for the rest of ya'll that got hit that night." Shorty-D was just as shocked as Foe was when he first heard the charge.

"That shit didn't have nothing to do with ya'll...so I don't know how he get knocked for that, that's crazy."

"One of the lames on your team gave Jake some false info yesterday when they got caught up in that sweep."

"Hold on...your niggas got knocked too." Shorty-D explained.

"Yeah. But my niggas don't know who cooked that lil' nigga. That day my niggas came over here and turned it up, they didn't sugar coat shit, they came over here to make a mess, which was for you not keeping your word, and making me look bad, after I told my niggas to stand down with you and your team."

"Me. what the fuck I do, I kept my word until your people came over here throwing shots at me."

"I know your man left your crib right before my nigga got hit up the block."

Foe was very careful choosing his words. Making sure he didn't Implicate him or his team in Duke's murder.

"I know how that might look, but I'm a man of my word, so I would never." Foe cut him off in mid sentence, "Fuck all that, that's spilled milk. If my nigga get indicted, I'm coming out of retirement." Foe stared directly in Shorty-Vs eyes to let him see how serious he was.

"I'm a certified G, If I find out a nigga that's under me eating cheese, he's gonna be sharing it with S.L, I just don't know what you expect me to do if I don't know who it is, and if I don't see it in black and white, then there's no proof." Shorty-D said as he stood up to look out of the window, checking on his soldiers who stood in front of his building.

"I'm not playing son...it's a rat in your house. sniff him out, or I'm exterminated the whole crib, don't say I ain't warn you...cause I'm not gonna wanna hear nothing but the BOOM from my pound. If you handle it the way I expect you to, then I'll be able to save face with my niggas as far as your name is concern.

They conversation was interrupted when one of Shorty-D soldiers banged on the door. Shorty-D screamed, "Who is it, "

"It's me, Crook, "

Shorty-D snatched the door open. "Yo...homicide just locked Pit up for killing Buddah...they read him his rights then told him what he was under arrest for." Crook said out of breath, from running from down the blvd to the crib.

Shorty-D turned to Foe and said, "I hope D-Block ain't giving it up like that. your boy still in the precinct right now. Right."

D-Block don't know who killed Buddah, so if Pit did do it...ya'll the only ones that know about it ...right." Foe had a point, "Cause if we knew it was him, he wouldn't be in jail—he'll be in the dirt...so like I was saying before we were interrupted, sniff em' out, or everybody gets it...everybody." Foe got up to leave, "Regardless to how this thing end...I want you to know that I was against this war way be-for it even started." Shorty-D explained as he walked Foe out of his apartment.

"How it started is how it started, fuck it we can't change that, so I'm gonna judge you on how it ends." Foe replied, putting on his hoodie as he walked down the stairs with Shorty-D in the front of him. 3 weeks later Ty walked out of Queens Criminal Court feeling like the rat that he became. He couldn't believe that he just testified in front of a grand jury. Even though he hated the Young Goonz he still felt fucked up about lying on D-Block and G-Pac.

The D.A. advised Ty to leave town until the trial start. "Man fuck that...I ain't going back to court for this shit." Ty thought as he walked down Queens Blvd.

If he were thinking like this before he testified then things would be looking many better for D-Block and G-Pac. Now the D.A. had enough leverage to drag the case out for three years, because there's no speedy trials in murder cases. There-for there's no statue of limintation.

It only took 2 days for the word to spread like a wild fire. D-Block and Pit was indicted for murder and it was all falling back on Shorty-D crew, which effected the whole YBM movement. The streets wasn't separating one crew from the other, they would just say, "Them YBM niggas is ratting."

The Young Goonz was promoting it hard. They were handing out sweaters that had YBM going across the top, with a picture of a block of cheese with a big bite mark in it.

Everybody that was arrested in the Operation Good Neighbors investigation was back on the streets. Some was out on bail; some came home on probation, while most of the fiends got outpatient drug programs. The YBM reputation was so tarnished that motherfuckers were saying that they snitched on the whole projects, and that's why the hood was raided and the Young Goonz ran with it.

CHAPTER TWENTY-SIX

The Young Goonz was back in the Horseshoe. None of the crews from Hammels Projects had dope on the streets; everything was pretty much at a stand still.

Thuggy Thug, G-Pac and Nitty, and Crazy Mone were standing in front of 84-12 kicking it. "Yo that shit is crazy how they put that body on D-Block. "Nitty said as he crushed the Cush inside the Dutch Master.

"Yeah, that's fucked up. If I catch anyone of them rat bastards I'm popping they fucking heads off." Crazy Mone said, looking toward the YBM building.

"If ya'll would have fell back like niggas told ya'll to, then he wouldn't be locked up for that shit." G-Pac stated.

"I do what I wanna do...not what a nigga tell me to do." Crazy Mone responded to G-Pac's comment, and meant every word he said.

"Regardless to what, them bitch made niggas is fucking with the fuzz." Thuggy Thug said in his best Impersonation of a west coast nigga.

"Man I ain't trying to be at war with no rats. That's a major no no... even if we win we lose. Niggas need to dead this beef now, because the cops are involved." Nitty explained.

"Dead the beef...I ain't deading shit, if anything, shit about to get more violent...word to Buddah." Crazy Mone spazzed.

"If anybody holding, dip off now. Here come the D's." Nitty said, "Detective Bell came cruising through the Horseshoe with his window rolled down. It was many other people outside but Bell focused his attention on the Young Goonz.

He saw something that sparked his interest, but he maintained his composure. Bell drove past 84-12, swung around the back of the building, called for backup then swung back around the front. He was driving at a moderate speed, trying not to alarm anyone.

Bell came to a slow stop, at the front of 84-12 where the Young Goonz was hanging out, "Hey...what you guys out here doing, planning the next murder."

Thuggy Thug laughed, then said, "Murder...nah we chilling...nonviolence is the way. it disarms the opponent." The rest of the Young Goonz laughed at Thuggy Thug quoting Martin Luther King.

"Wait wait...I got a better one, this one is even funnier." Bell said, getting out of his unmarked car. He pulled his gun out of the holster, pointed at G-Pac, and screamed, "Freeze. Move and I'll blow your fucking head off. The Young Goonz didn't know if Bell was joking or not until they saw all the backup cars come speeding to the building from all different directions.

Bell put the cuffs on G-Pac and tried to read him his rights, but was cut off by G-Pac, "Let me guess. I'm under arrest for murder right."

"You could bet your ass on that buddy," replied Bell.

G-Pac was relieved somewhat, to find out that he was charged with a murder that he didn't commit, rather than one he did do. Now that he and D-Block was both arraigned on the indictment, the D.A was obligated to turn over the Rosario material, which included Ty's statement with his named redacted out.

D-Block mailed the statement to Jiggy Jack and that's when it was confirmed on the streets that the YBM crew was no good. Jiggy Jack had some shirts made up; this time he put the whole statement on it.

Young Goonz

The statement explained how whoever wrote it was standing in the front of 85-02 with his friends, and how D-Block and G-Pac came around the corning shooting. It seemed as if the whole FarRock was wearing the shirts. On the back of the shirt had a picture of the rat Master Splinter wearing a YBM hoodie, with a gun in his hand.

Death Row was furious. It wasn't a good time to be repping YBM, his hate for Young Goonz grew even stronger. Yeah, somebody in Shorty-D crew was ratting, but the way the Young Goonz painted the picture, Death Row mines well have told himself.

Things were getting even worst for Shorty-D when Pit sent Fat Mike's redacted statement to all the O.G's. Death Row didn't want the statement to get in the Young Goonz hands, so he had to go out of his way and personal; visit Pit on Rikers. He assured Pit that he would get him the best lawyer money could buy, and that whoever ratted on him wouldn't make it to trial.

After the visit ended Death Row made an O.G. call, that they were holding there next get together in Hammels big park, where they were going to have a face-to-face talk with the Young Goonz. Death Row set the time for three o' clock in the evening the next day.

So there they were about fifty mothafuckers in the park. The tension was thick as shit. On the front line for the YBM crew was Death Row, D.B. Shorty-D, Sunny, Problem, Craps, Gilette, Fat's, Face.

On the front line for the Young Goonz was P-Killa, Thuggy Thug, Foe, Loc, Crazy Mone, Sha the God, Jiggy Jack, Messhall, C-Dollars, and Smokey.

"The Young black mices...is on the set." Thuggy Thug joked to the two crews, who only stood about three feet apart, facing each other. The Young Goonz laughed...The YBM didn't.

Death Row cocked his head to the side making a hood gesture, as if to say, "You got that one."

"We ain't here for all of that. We came here for a solution."

"Not for nothing, but I ain't comfortable conversation with you dudes, everybody that got caught up in the sweep is in this park right now... that means one of you niggas Stink, and probably wired for sound, so we just hear to listen not talk," said Foe.

"Ya'll niggas got some real wild Imaginations, yeah there's a rat in this park, but I doubt if he's in this mothafucka wearing a wire, but fuck it, if that's how you feel then check it...we gonna find out who's ratting and get him to recant his story. We know y'all didn't spill the boy Chris' blood and even if y'all did we don't condone snitching, that's against the code and it will be handled." Explained Death Row.

"The same way ya'll handled S.L...yeah aight, my niggas is trying to come home now." C-Dollars said, indirectly letting the YBM know what they already knew.

"Yeah. ya'll niggas too slow." Thuggy Thug said with a smirk on his face.

Face didn't entertain Thuggy Thug; it wasn't a good time not to humble yourself if you were YBM.

"Fuck S.L, everything would have panned out in due time...but thanks for savin us the hassle." Face said sarcastically.

"We wasting time and we giving the police a show." P-Killa said, pointing at the nine cop cars that surrounded the big park.

"Ya'll niggas jumped out of the window with a hole in your parachutes, shit get a lil' thick. And niggas start eating cheese, so I don't see the purpose in this until my niggas come home/nothings gonna change...in fact, shit is gonna get more drastic. Trust me ya'll ain't seen nothing yet, and I ain't talking cocky, I'm just being honest." P-Killa threatened.

"Worst for who, not us, cause we with whatever." D.B. spoke out of pure recklessness.

"Don't respond to that. They listening." Thuggy Thug joked, pointing at the police.

"Let me cut straight to it, we gonna find out who told and get that person to recant, but it's gonna be hard to focus on that when we gotta be ducking bullets." Sunny said.

"It just gives us a few days and all this shit will be taken care of." Shorty-D requested.

"Shut your fat mouth. You don't have a voice in this, you the one breeding mice nigga." Chillz said to Shorty-D, disrespecting him with no regards to his status.

"You ain't gonna talk to me any ol' way, I ain't no rat. I'll leave you right here in this park nigga," said Shorty-D.

"Bet he won't be the only one getting left in this mothafucka." Smokey barked, ready for action.

"Chill out, cause if you kill my nigga your niggas gonna rat on you." Messhall joked. Causing a few laughs.

"You better keep that one good hand in sight be for I get a lil' jumpy." Sha the God said, due to Shorty-D's hands going in and out of his pockets.

"This what we gonna do. When I heard about this come together I knew nobody was gonna admit to talking to the law in front of everybody, so what lima do is this. Everybody in here is getting one of these cards. This is my niggas private investigator, if you talked to the pigs, all you gotta do is call this number and let this guy know that the pigs pressured you into giving a false statement." Jiggy Jack walked around getting the cards snatched out of his hands by the YBM crewmembers.

"So where do we go from here...the call's gonna be made, but until then should we put this beef on Ice or leave it on the grill." Sunny asked.

"Ya'll got 72 hours to make the call or else." P-Killa let his words lingering in the air.

Problem and Foe caught eye contact and it was like two waves crashing into each other, mentally.

Jiggy Jack didn't want things to come to an end on a negative note, so he said, "We didn't start this, and ya'll know it...all we asked is niggas keep it official and get that call made, we about money...and ain't nobody eating off this shit we doing but them." Jiggy Jack pointed to the cops and continued to speak.

That same night, Foe decided it was time to go spend some quality time with Ooh Wop in Maryland. He had many of shit on his mind, and she was the only person in the world that knew how to clear his head when he was in that zone. Yeah, Foe had a hand full of females that he was intimate with, but none of them had his heart like she did.

Of course, that wasn't good enough for her. She would always say, "Fuck them bitches...you can't trust none of them but me." He knew she was right, but sometimes it ain't about trust, sometimes he was just trying to get a nut. When he felt like loving, then he would give it to the one that deserved it...and that was Ooh Wop.

"What's going through that head of yours?" She asked.

"Life." Foe simply replied.

"What about life."

"It's like, every time you think you got it all figured out, you realize that you don't."

"Maybe life is just to be lived...not understood."

"You know the one thing I can't understand to save my life.

"What's that handsome?" Ooh Wop asked, wrapping her arms around Foe.

"I can't understand why yo ass can't cook." Foe joked. Ooh Wop picked up one of the couch pillows and playful hit Foe with it. Foe wrestled it out her hand, tucked it behind is head and pulled her on top of him.

Ooh Wop stared into Foe's eyes and thought, "Why can't you leave the streets and them foul ass bitches alone and stay here with me until we grow old and grey." She didn't want to say it to him, knowing he would say something to piss her off.

So she kept it to herself and enjoyed being in the arms of the only man she ever loved. Foe met Ooh Wop after the fugitive squad chased him out off Baltimore city back in the days when he was running from a body in New York. Which stemmed from a situation that occurred where else but FarRockaway. Ooh Wop held him down like steel for the 3 years he spent on Rikers. Foe eventually beat the case, but had to do a few more years when he was found guilty of a gun charge.

Ooh Wop tried to stay faithful, but there's only so much loneliness a person can take. She met a lame nigga, and confused a good feeling with love, but Foe was very understanding, so when things took a turn for the worst with her, Foe did what any real nigga would do...he held her down, the same way she held him down when he was in the joint.

The love that he had for her was 10 times stronger than the disappointment. So there they were...together. Like she said, "Life is to be lived... not understood.

Shorty-D was under extreme pressure. he was about to lose his O.G. status which meant he would lose his power and possibly his life. He called all of his soldiers that were caught in the drug sweep to his crib. One day had already flown by, and now he was down to his last 48 hours to sniff out of the rat.

"All I ever did was show ya'll love and loyalty...now it's my head on the chopping block and ya'll niggas, rather one of ya'll niggas is just gonna let it go down like that...fuck it, off with Shorty-D's head, as long as it ain't mine. Is that how you feel."

They all started talking at the same time, saying, "It wasn't me," and swearing on all type of dead relatives.

"I don't give a fuck who told...just call that fucking number and recant your story...I put that on my gangsta, won't shit happen to you." Shorty-D was in between spazzing and pleading with his crew, which only made him look desperate.

"I bailed ya'll out of jail because I love ya'll, and this the thanks I get...Don't do it for D-Block and G-Pac, fuck them niggas...do it for me."

Ty was sitting there with the straight face, but the shit was eating him up. He knew if he made the call he would have to do the time for the sales and the guns, and from what the D.A. told him at the Grand Jury, he might even do some time for perjury, plus everybody would know that it was him that ate the cheese.

Ty sat there thinking what would happen if he didn't make the call. Eventually he would have to get on the witness stand and lie. He even thought about what would happen if he disappeared, just run from it all. He figured that he would have an outstanding warrant, plus it would be obvious that it was him that told, not to mention all the bullshit Short-D would go through, being ousted out of the YBM. Ty didn't know what the hell to do, but he did know one thing...he shouldn't never had talked to the police.

The second day passed and Ty still didn't make the call. He had until three o'clock and it was already ten o'clock in the morning.

The good news for the Young Goonz was that Bart came out of his coma and he was talking. He wasn't able to walk, and he had a shit bag that was making him feel like the stuff that was in it.

Young Bash, Messhall, Thugy Thug, and Smokey was all at Jamaica Hospital trying to lift Bart's spirit, but all Bart wanted to know was how many YBM niggas died behind what happened to him and Rah.

Young Bash tried explaining everything that transpired since then, with the drug sweep in the hood, and how D-Block and G-Pac got knocked for a body they didn't do. Then he told him about the meeting with the YBM crew in the big park, but Bart asked the same question again, "How many of them niggas died after me and Rah got hit."

The silence in the room answered Bart's question. "Ya'll niggas ain't gotta ride for me and Rah...when I heal up niggas gonna burn for this shit...matter fact, fuck ya'll niggas, fuck out my face." Bart pushed the help button, the nurse walked in, "Is there a problem?" she asked.

"Yes, I'm ready for my bath. My guest was just leaving." Bart replied. The guilty feeling that the Young Goonz left the hospital with, even made Young Bash want to dust off his hammer and lay a few motherfuckers down.

"Stop at Modells." Young Bash demanded from the back seat. Thuggy Thug was driving. When they got to five towns, he made the turn into the shopping area and pulled up in front of Modells. They all was still having visions of Bart laid up in that bed, less than a hundred pounds when Young Bash jumped out of the car.

Young Bash came out of Modells moments later with a big Modells bag in his hand. He jumped back in the car and they headed to the Rock.

"What's in the bag," Thuggy Thug asked.

Young Bash emptied the contents of the bag on the back seat. Gloves and winter face wraps fell out. Thuggy Thug smiled, then screamed, "That's what the fuck I'm talking bout...Killa Bash is back...nigga, I said Killa motherfucking Bash is back."

CHAPTER TWENTY-SEVEN

D-Block was in the intake bullpens in G.R.V.C. better known as the Beacon on Rikers Island. He had his back to the wall, with his bags of property by his side. Three dudes were on the gate talking to some other dudes, who was in the pens across from the one they were in. One of the dudes that was in the pen with D-Block kept looking back, as if the conversation was about him.

D-Block was on point, thanks to the many stories Foe told him about jail, and how to pick up on the vibe. He actually felt like he's been in this position before, due to them stories that he really didn't want to hear at the time.

D-Block was smoking a Newport when the three dudes walked up to him.

"Yo son, let me get a light." The shortest dude in the trio asked.

D-Block took one last pull off the Port, dropped it on the floor, stepped on it, and then said, "I don't smoke."

One of the other clowns laughed then said, "You a funny nigga...where from."

"I'm from where asking to many questions could get you smoked." D-Block replied.

Somebody from across the pen screamed, "What's all the talking about, that's one of the Young Goon niggas, pop that nigga face off."

D-Block reacted off impulse, he pushed off the wall and stalled on the closest nigga to him, dropping him with a hard hook to the jaw.

The other two dudes rushed D-Block at the same time, and the shit was on and popping. D-Block was holding his own with the two dudes, but when the nigga that was dropped got up and jumped in, they hemmed D-Block up. It wasn't a pretty sight once he hit the floor. They put all types of hands and feet on D-Block's head until the C.O.'s came and broke the shit up.

D-Block had to be helped to his feet, but when he got up the first thing he said was, "Young Goonz in the building...I'm built for this shit...D-Block, remember the name."

If a man were judged in times of adversity, then D-Block would be considered one of the greats.

He was escorted to the clinic and treated for minor scrapes and bruises. He was then escorted back to intake to get his property. After that, he was escorted to where he was to be housed. As soon as he entered 9A, he saw the clowns that were in the other pen telling niggas to pop off on him. He knew that they were YBM, but he didn't know what projects they were from.

The C.O. told D-Block that he had a visit, and if he wanted to make it down there before he get stuck in the count, then he better hurry it u p .

Ten minutes later D-Block walked in the visiting room. Jiggy jack and D-Block's wifey sat at the table as he approached them. The first thing they noticed was D-Block's busted lip and swollen eye.

"You should see how the 3 niggas look that jumped me." D-Block joked. Jiggy Jack smiled, but his wifey didn't.

"Them rat niggas didn't call the Private investigator, so it look like ya'll gonna have to ride this thing on out...G-Pac said he was at the Hospital with his son when that shit went down, his son had an asthma attack and he had to sign all type of paper work. I sent the Private investigator to the Hospital to check into his alibi. If that shit checks out G-Pac gonna get out soon, and since that's the same witness that nigga credibility will be shot." Jiggy Jack explained.

"That's wussup...stay on top of all that...I'mma hold it down in here, G-Pac in C-95, so I'm for dolo in this bitch, them YBM niggas is deep in this mother fucka."

That reminded D-Block's wifey, "Oh yeah, I spoke to Foe last night, and his crazy ass put me on a mission."

"A mission for what?" D-Block asked.

She looked around for the C.O.'s, when she saw that none of them was looking, she dug inside her panties, pulled out a little black balloon and passed it to D-Block.

"What the hell is this?" D-Block asked, snatching it out of her hand quickly.

"That nigga had me go to, rather made me go to Rite Aid and get two scalpels, number 11's, wrapped the shit's in black tape and put em' in the balloon...that nigga crazy, who thinks of shit like that."

"Tell him I said touchdown."

When D-Block got back to 9A, it was a little bit after count time on Rikers, so everybody was still locked in their cells.

"Dead man walking," was screamed out as he walked up the gallery. When D-Block locked in his cell, he dug the loony out and bursted it open. The two scalpels gleamed in his hand. He rapped a towel around his neck, laid on his bed and waited for his cell to open.

"Always be ready. So you won't have to get ready." Foe's voice lingered in D-Block's head from a conversation they had a year ago.

Shorty-D was walking around his apartment with a shotgun in one hand, and a glass of Jack Daniels in the other. None of the O.G's was returning his calls and he couldn't trust nobody in his crew, because he wasn't sure who was ratting. "I don't need none...of...you disloyal...bitches." Shorty-D said aloud to himself in a drunken slur, feeling the effects of the whiskey.

He peeped out of the window holding the shotgun up like the famous Malcolm X picture.

Shorty-D felt betrayed by everybody he ever loved within the YBM family.

The money that he stacked from selling the WAR was looking real low, due to the fact that he bailed all his soldiers out, the same niggas that left him to the wolves.

The last O.G that was out of the YBM crew was O.G. Gangsta and it was Shorty-D who put the bullet in his head. They had all came to the conclusion that once you are selected as an official O.G. of the Young Black Mafia...Death is the only way out.

Some might say that they were taking the whole, "Mafia," thing too far, but truth be told, there's no way they could allow somebody who was no longer affiliated to walk around with all that information. Shit that could take down the whole team.

"I just gotta think...them niggas not killing me, fuck that...how the fuck am I gonna get out this shit." Shorty-D continued to ramble to himself aloud.

He pondered on what to do for about an hour, sitting in the dark drawing a blank. So he did the only thing that made any sense to him, he picked up his phone and made a call.

It was four o' clock in the morning when the ringing phone woke him out of his sleep. The caller I.D. on his phone told him exactly who was calling. He started to ignore it, but something in his gut told him to answer it.

"What do we possibly have to talk about."

"They gonna kill me." Shorty-D sobbed.

"You drunk nigga...ain't nobody thinking about you.'

"Not your people, my people...I need your help."

"And why should I help you.

"Cause I've always kept it tall, and now it's like I don't have nobody I can trust to turn too." Shorty-D said. The liquor had him telling the truth. And you think you can trust me.

"I know I can...plus I'm not coming at you empty handed."

"You think I need your money."

"I ain't talking bout money...I got something with more value to you then money."

"Stay where you at, I'mma send somebody to pick you up in the morning."

"Don't do me like that my nigga...I ain't stupid. If it ain't you I'm squeezing on everybody."

"Aight I'll be there in a few hours."

"Good looking my nigga, I owe you my life."

"I don't want your life...but yeah, you do owe me big time and I want mine up front...be ready when I get there."

" Aight I'll be ready...one." The phone call ended about a half hour after it began.

"Baby is everything okay." Ooh Wop asked."

"Everything's cool...go back to sleep." Foe replied, kissing her on her forehead.

Foe couldn't go back to sleep after Shorty-D's called, so he started his early morning workout. By the time he finished his sets, he had it all figured out. If dudes from the hood used their brains for good instead of evil...the things they would be able to accomplish would be unlimited.

One month later. "I change my mind...take me home please." Young Bash joked.

"Stop playing nigga, get ready. Soon as this nigga come out that build-ing, knock his fucking head off. Foe said.

Young Bash couldn't help his self. He was a jokester. He was just trying to keep his nerves from jumping out of his body. He didn't put in no work in a long time so he had the jitters the way he did when he went on his first line up mission.

"How you know this the building my nigga." Young Bash asked.

"Trust me; this is the right building...stop looking for a way out." Foe joked.

The heat kind of died down in FarRock after the raid. The last murder that went down was S.L.'s, which was months ago at this time. Foe felt absolutely no pressure parked in the back of Edgemere Projects, Laying on niggas in the Astro van that was Identical to the vans that fix the elevators in the projects.

"It's one thirty, too many people is outside right now." Young Bash complained.

"If you ready to leave...then get out and go...I'm staying." Foe replied.

"You must be crazy if you think I'm gonna get out this ugly ass van and walked through Compton."

Foe laughed, "Yo, you heard what happened with D-Block."

"Nah...what happened."

"The bird ass YBM niggas ran up in his cell...I heard it was blood and feathers all over the cell by the time the C.O.'s got there. One nigga was cut so bad, that he had to get reconstructed surgery to his face. Them scalpels ain't no fucking joke." Foe laughed.

"Where he at now."

"O.B.C.C, in the box. The Ill shit about that is his aunt is a Captain in that building, so he good.

"We got action." Young Bash stated, jacking a bullet in the chamber of the Smith & Wesson.

Craps walked out of his building without a worry in the world. "Damn the nigga Problem ain't with em. His baby moms is, and she's pushing a stroller," said Young Bash.

Foe pulled the ski mask over his face, and then said, "So." As he slid out of the Astro van. Young Bash had no choice but to follow.

Craps was talking shit to his baby moms when he saw something moving toward him real fast, from the corner of his eye. Craps turned his head to see two mask men running toward him with guns in their hands. He didn't think twice, he took off running, trying to put as much space as possible between him and his family that he could.

Young Bash was on his ass though, but that's when the adrenaline caused him to fumble. Young Bash slipped and fell, his gun slid out of his hand and up under a park car... Craps leaped on the opportunity, he turned around and ran to the car where the gun was. He bent down to reach for it.

Young Bash was slow getting up as he saw Craps reaching under the car to get his gun. That's when Foe came running up on Craps, he kicked him to the ground, looked Craps right in his eyes, pointed the Ruger at his head and screamed through the ski mask, "Tell Leeky, I said what up ."... BOOOM BOOOM BOOOM.

Craps baby mother saw the whole situation unfold in a

matter of seconds. She left her baby stroller to the side and ran toward Craps, who at this time was lying on the ground lifeless.

She started to scream, "NOOOO."

Foe and Young Bash was running straight her ways on their way to where the Astro van was parked. Young Bash had fetched his gun from under the car when Foe was airing Craps out. Young Bash turned the gun to the side as Craps baby mother tried to past him, "WHACK," Young Bash smacked her so hard in her mouth with the gun that she literally did a monkey back flip and landed flat on her face.

What Young Bash did next was to extreme, even for Foe who had done many of wild shit in the past. Young Bash ran up to Craps baby stroller and kicked it so hard that it flipped in mid air three times before it landed upside down.

Foe jumped in the back of the van as Young Bash got behind the wheel, put on a yellow hard hat, then pulled off. "You fucked that whole package up. How the fuck you fall nigga."

"Shut up...I'm rusty." Which was half joke and half truth. Young Bash merged off the highway 20 minutes later singing, "Hello Brooklyn, "

"You know you going to hell for that shit you did...right," Foe said, still visualizing the baby stroller being kicked with so much force.

Young Bash laughed, "Now you don't have to worry about being lonely down there..., plus they say, God protects babies and fools, so I'm good."

Foe shook his head then said, "Think about what you just said my nigga."

CHAPTER TWENTY-EIGHT

"**M**ONSTERS**,**" was what got printed on the front page of
the Waves. The story was edited with enough to bring
tears to the eyes of the local tenants. The story also
made the front page of all major Newspapers.

It seemed as if every cop in America was in FarRockaway
Queens. FarRock never saw police actively like this before. When
the hood get's this much media the big boys have to step in.

Hammels, The 60s, Edgemere, 40's, Redfern Projects, and side
blocks literally had about 50 beat walkers in them. They were in
buildings throughout the whole FarRock checking people I.D.'s and
asking them who was they going to see in that particular building.

If a shot went off in Hammels, the backup squads would raid
every project and side block, simultaneously. Plus they would be
doing checkpoints just in case somebody would try to flee the scene.

They knocked down every YBM and Young Goonz apartment or
house door that they knew of. The neighbors were so tired of the
shootings that they said fuck it and started supplying the cops with
whatever information that they overheard through hood politics.
The heat was unbearable, motherfuckers had to pack they shit and
leave.

Death Row had a hard time trying to get Problem to go out of
town with him. Problem was at the point where he was ready to kill
niggas mothers.

The Young Goonz murdered his right hand man / child hood

friend, broke his baby mother's jaw, which was wired shut now, cracked everything that surround her right eye socket, plus knocked her front two teeth out

Craps son, who was Problems God son, suffered from a concussion and three broken ribs. Problem never cried when it came to losing his niggas but this was different. He, Craps, and Leeky was inseparable when they were growing up. And now they were both gone...he cried like a baby.

It was the pain, the hurt, and the lost that caused his emotional breakdown. What drove him down the dark road even further was the fact that Death Row was right, it was just too hot to strike back. He would have to leave The Rock like everybody else, but he promised his fallen comrades that he would be back with a vengeance the moment the heat die's down.

The Young Goonz was spread out in so many different locations out of town that it would be Impossible to pen point them all at one time.

When the money is right and you're always planning for the rainy days to come, the storm feels like nothing but a sun shower.

Bottles were popping and bitches were popping up pregnant everywhere they went. It's always hot to be the boy's from New York, as far as the females were concerned.

Three months had already passed since the tragedy that shocked the conscience of everybody but the Young Goonz. G-Pac was in Queens Criminal Court at his alibi hearing. His lawyer Bret Snider had everything laid out nice and simple.

First thing that Snider did was play the 911 call with G-Pac's voice on it, requesting an ambulance for his son. Next Snider called in an expert witness, who testified that the voice on the 911 tape was indeed that of G-Pac's. He compared it to phone conversations that him and G-Pac had over the phone that he recorded. The next witness he called was the Nurse that cared for G-Pac's son; she produced evidence that G-Pac signed all the medical paper work dealing with the child's health insurance, so forth and so on.

The district attorney David Chong had no choice but to grant Bret Snider's motion to dismiss, because G-Pac could not have been at the scene of the crime.

Detective Bell stormed out of the courtroom in disgust, knowing that he fucked up big time.

Bret Snider drove G-Pac straight to JFK airport and put him on a flight to Atlanta, where he met up with Looch and C-Dollars. All the Young Goonz called to congratulate G-Pac.

D-Block's aunt had one of her C.O. friends that were always willing to do the Captain a favor, pass D-Block a phone so he could find out of the details and pass it along to his lawyer.

"Don't worry about shit my nigga, the D.A. gonna have to be real thirsty to take you trial...you just gonna have to lay up for a few, but your lawyer gonna eat that case." G-Pac explained to D-Block.

"I ain't worried my G...I'm just patiently waiting...get wasted. And fuck a bitch with a fat ass for me my G." D-Block said.

After the phone call ended D-Block past the C.O., her phone back and said, "Good lookin, when I get out of here I'mma take you out and show you some young grown man shit."

"Boy, sit your lil' young, bad ass down somewhere," she said, knowing she was at least twice D-Block's age.

D-Block lay in his bed for about 20 minutes, just zoning out, thinking about what Foe told him, "When you in that box for 23 hours a day, you will get to know yourself mentally. All you got is your thoughts, and if your thoughts ain't right...a nigga bound to lose his mother fucking mind."

D-Block stood up, walked to his cell gate and screamed out, "ALL YA'LL YBM NIGGAS COULD SUCK MY DICK...YOUNG GOONZ ON THE SET LIKE WHOA."

All the YBM niggas that heard him started wilding out, screaming fuck the Young Goonz, and how they were gonna cut D-Block when they catch him in the court pens.

D-Block laughed, and listened to how he made all them

lames entertain him with their threats.

Nine months later. The courtroom was jammed pack. D-Block sat at the defense table with the well-respected Mike Worn. This was the third day of trial and everybody was anxious to see who the D.A Chong would call to the witness stand. Within the last three days, Chong called several witnesses to the stand and called Detective Bell, the crime scene investigator, and the Coroner.

So far, the D.A. whole case was based on the violence that's been taking place in the Rockaways. The jury consisted of 12 people that lived in every other part of Queens except FarRockaway, in fact, they were all from the suburbs.

Chong was painting a picture that somehow if they convinced D-Block FarRockaway would be a safer place to live. Foe was dressed in a casual shirt and tie with Ooh wop at his side. P-Killa, Jiggy Jack, and C-Dollars all wore matching Armani suits. The Young Goonz cleaned up nice for the trial. They looked like young black businessmen, instead of street thugs.

All of D-Block's family was also present in the courtroom. For some strange reason, when your 19 years old running around the mean streets of FarRockaway you look like you actually been living a hard life. But when your 19 years old, sitting on trial for murder you look your age, maybe even younger.

There was a buzz in the courtroom; it was time for Chong to call his witness. "We're ready your Honor," said David Chong Assistant District Attorney for the County of Queens.

The bailiff voice boomed through the courtroom, "The people of the state of New York call Tymeek Jones to the witness stand."

Only in movies, the spectators start acting out when the witness is called to the stand. in the real life experience, the defendant sit there and call the nigga all type of bitches, and bitch ass niggas...under their breath though.

Young Goonz

Ty walked into the courtroom with the toughest face Foe ever seen in his life, and his ditty bop was hard enough to hear Tupac's song, "Ambition of a rider." As his theme music, as he walked pass D-Block Ice grilling him. The nerve of this prick," D-Block thought, without showing any emotions on his face.

"Raise your right hand...do you swear to tell the truth, nothing but the truth, so help you God," asked the bailiff.

"I do,"

David Chong stood up and walked to the witness stand where Ty sat. "Were you currently a member of the Young Black Mafia?"

"Yes...I was."

"Now when you say, 'You was', does that mean that your no longer apart of, or affiliated with the YBM organization?"

"Yes, I'm no longer affiliated."

"And how long has it's been since you left the YBM crew?

"It's been about a year now.

"And why was it that you decided to leave the YBM crew a year ago Mr. Jones?"

"I left for two reasons.

"Well just tell the jury the first reason you left the YBM crew.

"The first reason was I didn't wanna get killed."

"And what was the other reason you left the YBM crew Mr. Jones?"

"Because my friend Christopher was killed for being a member of the YBM crew."

"When you said you left because you didn't want to get killed. Can you explain why would you be in fair for your life?"

"We were in a war with the Young Goonz, and they already killed many of YBM members."

"Objection your honor...that statement is speculation and totally not relevant in this trial...and I asked that it be stricken from the record." Mike Worn barked.

"Objection sustained...members of the jury; you are to disregard the witnesses last statement," said the judge.

"Like they didn't hear the shit already." D-Block thought, but still with the poker face.

"Was the YBM crew at war with the Young Goonz? Chong asked.

"Yes we were."

"Your honor I would like this photo to be marked as exhibit A," said Chong Chong handed the photo to the bailiff and asked him to please hand it to the witness.

"Examining that photo Mr. Jones can you explain to the jury what's depicted in those photos."

"This is a picture of the front entrance of my old building 85-02."

"Thank you...let's go back a year ago...is this the building that your friend Christopher was killed in front of?"

"Yes."

"Can you tell us if Christopher was a member of the Young Black Mafia?" "No he was not, he was only 13 years old."

"Lying motherfucka," D-Block thought.

"Can you tell the jury where your friend Christopher was, and where you were when he was shot and killed."

"I was like standing right here next to this black gate." Ty point to the area in the picture as he spoke.

"Did you see who shot and killed your friend Christopher?"

"Yes I did."

"And is that person here today in this court room Mr. Jones?"

"Yes."

"Can you point to that person and indicate an article of clothing that that person is wearing."

"It was him. He's wearing the white shirt and black tie." Ty said pointing at D-Block.

"Let the record reflect that the witness has identified the defendant," said the lady Judge that look like she was born with an attitude.

"Okay, can you tell the jury how well do you know the defendant."

"I knew him all my life; we were in the same class in grade school."

"And how close was the defendant when he started shooting."

"Maybe about 10 or 15 feet."

"So what you're saying Mr. Jones is that you were able to get a real good look at the defendant."   "Yup...it was him."

"Do you know how this war started between the Young Goonz and the YBM crew?"

"Objection." Mike Worn screamed as he jumped to his feet.

"My client is not on trial for the war between two street crews; my client is on trial for an isolated incident."

"I'll allow it. Overruled, you may answer the question Mr. Jones," said the judge who was Pro Prosecution.

"Yeah, I know why the war started...The Young Goonz killed five YBM members in one day."

"Mistrial...I'm moving for a mistrial," screamed Mike Worn, over the loud outburst in the courtroom.

"Ladies and gentlemen of the jury, at this time I'm going to ask you to step in to the jury room for a quick recess...please don't talk about the case, it's not until all the evidence is heard that you are allowed to formulate opinions," said the judge.

D-Block watched the Jurors facial expressions as they exited the courtroom. And the look on their faces told it all. The five murders got so much media, that they had to hear about it. They just looked shock that this case had ties with that blood bath.

The jury was all out and Mike Worn made his oral argument he stated that the inflammatory remarks stated by the witness, tainted the jury's mind, and that his client would not be able to get a fair trial, which is guaranteed by the U.S. Constitution.

D.A. Chong argued that although the error was improper, a curative instruction given by you your honor, would be more than enough to suffice any prejudice caused to the defendant, therefore no mistrial is warranted."

The judge being as foul as she could be, agreed with Chong to have the testimony stricken from the record, and to pretty much tell the jury to pay no attention to the five murders that was mentioned...but they already heard, so the seeds been planted... "Welcome to Queens supreme Court."

The jury was ushered back into the courtroom. The judge instructed them, then told the D.A. "Your witness Mr. Chong."

David Chong stood up, walked toward the jury box, turn his head and look at Ty, "I only have one last question...are you sure that it was the defendant that was doing the shooting?"

"I'm 100 percent sure," said Ty with the straightest face a liar could ever muster up.

"No further questions your honor." Chong stated as he took his seat at the prosecution's table. Ty cut his eye at D- Block who was staring daggers and all type of hollow heads in his face from across the courtroom.

CHAPTER TWENTY-NINE

"Are you ready for your cross examination Mr. Worn?" the judge asked.

"Yes your honor." Mike Worn was known for his excellent cross-examination tactics, which he was praised for in Queens County.

"Mr. Jones, you testified on direct that you witnessed my client shoot and kill your Young Black Mafia friend...is that correct?"

"Yeah, that's what I saw."

"Do you remember writing a statement to a Detective Anthony Bell about the details of the shooting?"

"Yeah."

"And isn't it true that this statement was written by you some months after the shooting occurred?"

"Yeah." "Can you explain the time lapse from the, time that you claim you saw my client do the shooting, to the time you made the statement."

"Well. I guess it's never too late to do the right thing."

"So basically you here today as a good citizen for the community?"

Ty didn't know how to respond to the question, so he sat there looking stupid Mr. Jones it's not a trick question. Yes or no?"

"I'm not saying that I'm a saint, but I have changed...so yeah, I guess you can say that I'm here for the community."

"So what your saying is, you're not testifying due to the fact that the D.A. offered you Immunity in exchange for your testimony here today."

"Yeah, I got immunity."

"Okay let's speak about what caused you to testify here today. Were you involved in a long term drug operation where you sold drugs to an undercover officer for several months?"

"Yeah, that's true."

"And isn't it also true that the day you was arrested for selling to undercover #3158, you cut a deal where if you wrote a statement on my client for a murder charge then you wouldn't do any time for your drugs sells. Objection your honor...totally improper," said David Chong.

"Mr. Worn please ask your questions in a proper manner, take this as a warning...there will be none of that in my Court room." The Judge said.

"She ain't say all that shit when the D.A. was doing his bullshit." D-Block thought.

"Mr. Jones is it true that on the morning of the take down your mothers.

Ty squirmed in his seat and said, "Yes." At this point, the jury was appalled at pretty much everything that came out of Tymeek Jones mouth.

Mike Worn felt that it was time to put the nail in the coffin. "When you wrote this statement, were you clear when you stated that you saw two shooters on that day, my client and G'shawn West?"

"Yes, that's what I wrote in my statement."

"Well is your statement accurate Mr. Jones?"

"Yeah, it's accurate."

Mike Worn turned to the jury then asked Ty without looking at him, "So wouldn't that make your testimony here today inaccurate?"

"No...I don't see how."

"Well didn't you testify earlier today under oath, that you

saw my client shoot and kill your friend Christopher?" Mike Worn asked in a voice just below yelling, the way they do it on T.V.

"Yeah, I said that but..."

"And isn't it true that G'shawn West couldn't be at the scene of the crime because he was at a Hospital with his son who was suffering from an asthma attack?"

"Objection your honor my witness is not aware of the underline facts of G'shawn West case." Chong explained.

"Ladies and gentlemen of the jury, a stipulation will be read into the record concerning the details of that case after defense counsel rest his case." Explained the judge.

Mike Worn turned to face the jury and without looking in Ty's direction he asked, "How many shooters did you see that night."

"Two, it was two of them."

"So if there were two shooters Mr. Jones, how do you know which one of them killed your friend."

"I..." Ty was stuck on stupid.

"No further questions your honor," said mike Worn.

Ty testimony was a train wreck, but the jury still didn't look at D-Block any different. They didn't live in the hood, so for them to get a visual of certain details, was truly impossible. Most of them hated the hood, and the animals that live in it.

"Any other witnesses Mr. Chong?" The Judge asked.

"No your honor, at this time the prosecution rest."

Now it was time for Mike Worn to present his case, and poke holes in the D.A.'s case.

D-Block turned to look at Foe, knowing it was him that worked with Mike Worn to put together his defense, and present it to the jury.

The Judge banged her gavel then said, "Mr. Worn ...your witness please."

The bailiff voiced again boomed through the courtroom. "The Defense calls to the witness stand, Mrs. Sabrina Barnes. After Brina was sworn in, Mike Worn stood up and began to present his case...that he felt confident about, "Good morning Mrs.

Barnes...can you tell the jury where you reside at."

"Yes...I live in Hammels Projects in FarRockaway Queens, building number 85-02."

"Do you recall the shooting that left a 13 year old kid dead in the front of your building?"

"Yes...I remember the incident like it was yesterday...it was sad."

"Did you hear the gun shots?"

"Yes...they woke me out of my sleep; my window is right above the building's entrance."

"Okay. Let me bring you back a few hours on that same day, when you made it home for work that day. Mrs. Barnes, did you witness an altercation on your way in your building that day."

"Yes I did. one of the young boys that live in my building hit the Jamaican van driver in the face with a bottle, causing the van man to bleed all over his clothes."

"Okay, so what if anything did you do."

"Well I know the older guy's that he hangs out with, so I grabbed him, and took him up the stairs to them."

"Mrs. Barnes, do you know the name of the crew that the young boy hang's with."

"Yes, they call themselves the YBM crew."

"Okay, what did you do when you took him upstairs?"

"I spoke to Davonn about the incident."

"And why did you speak to Davonn in particular about the incident?"

"Because he's like the leader of all of them."

"Can you tell me what Devonn street name is?"

"Everybody calls him Shorty-D."

Mike Worn turned to the judge and said " no further questions your honor."

David Chong stood up and said, "I only have one question your honor...

"Mrs. Barnes did you see who was doing the shooting on that night?"

Young Goonz

"No Sir."

"Nothing further...you can step down Mrs. Barnes."

D-Block had been on Rikers for about a year now so he noticed how fat Brina ass looked in her skirt.

You would think that a dude that's facing 25 to life in prison would have a whole lot on his mind except pussy. A nigga could be being strapped into the electric chair and he might be thinking to himself, "Well I guess I won't be getting no more pussy."

The bailiff screamed, "The Defense now calls his next witness...Devonn Mergen."

Everybody that sat in the audience thought their ears were playing tricks on them when they heard Shorty-D's name, but the eyes don't lie. Shorty-D walked into the courtroom wearing his arm brace.

Even P-Killa was shocked. Foe looked at him and winked, then turned to D-Block and gave him a nice little nod.

This was the first time anybody saw Shorty-D in 10 months. Somebody started a rumor that the YBM crew killed him, then through his body in the bay with the fishes.

Foe had plugged Shorty-D in with some of his niggas in Baltimore, and they set him up with somewhere low to lay his head, and a block to get money on.

"Mr. Mergen can you explain who you were and what did you represent about a year ago." Norn asked.

"Yeah no doubt...my name was Shorty-D and I was one of the four O.G.'s that ran the YBM crew in the Rockaways, better known as the Young Black Mafia."

"And where did you live during this time Mr. Mergen?

"85-02 Rockaway Beach Blvd."

"Do you know a young lady by the name of Sabrina Barnes that also lives in your old building 85-02?"

"Yeah, I know Brina for a long time now."

"Do you remember speaking to Mrs. Barnes the day of the shooting?"

"Yes I do."

"And do you remember what the conversation was about."

"Yeah, one of my soldiers had busted the man upside his head with a bottle, so she brought him to me so I could handle the situation.

The jury didn't like Shorty-D's vibe, but they were indirectly fascinated by his aura of confidence.

"What did you do after that?"

"I barked on the lil...I mean, I scold the boy in front of Brina, but to tell you the truth...I didn't give a shit."

"Watch your language in my court room Sir...you've been warned, said the judge, who wouldn't have any problem with holding Shorty-D in contempt, and locking his ass up.

"Oh my bad."

"I notice that your arm is in a sling...can you explain to the jury how that came about." Mike Worn continued with his questioning.

"The night Chris got killed, I got shot too...I only have 35 percent usage in this arm."

"Let's back up a second...can you tell the jury what you and your soldiers were doing right before you guys were shot." Mike Worn had a certain tone with him that made the jury interested in the witness answer.

"We were hanging out in front of the building, like any other night, drinking and bullshitting...oh I'm sorry your honor lady." Shorty-D's Ignorance of the English language was somewhat entertained to the jurors that only heard this kind of slang on B.E.T. "Like I was saying, we were chilling ... then this Jamaican man with bandages all over his face walked up on us, and started screaming about somebody cutting up his face. I told the man to leave, and that's when two other guys came from around the corner with Jamaican flags wrapped around their faces shooting at us."

"Mr. Mergen did you see the guy's that was shooting faces."

"Didn't I say they had flags wrapped around their faces."

"Mr. Mergen do you know Tymeek Jones." Mike worn asked after taking a sip of his bottled water.

"Yeah he was one of my soldiers."

"Was Mr. Jones there the night of the shooting?"

"Yeah he was there but he must have been the first one to duck, because he didn't get shot like the rest of us."

"Well Mr. Jones testified that it was the defendant that shot you and your soldiers."

"Wouldn't you lie to if you was facing all the time that Tymeek is facing."

"Just answer the questions Mr. Mergen, you not here to ask any questions. The Judge said to Shorty-D.

"Do you know the defendant Mr. Mergen?" Mike Worn asked.

"Yeah I know him...and to be honest, I really don't like him, but nobody deserves to go to jail for something they didn't do. I'm a gangsta, not a liar."

"Mr. Mergen, are you still leading the Young Black Mafia in Hammels Projects?"

"Nah...you can't live that life with one arm. Shorty-D joked, causing a few jurrors to chuckle.

"No further questions your honor," said Mike Worn.

The longer Shorty-D stayed on the stand, the worst it would have gotten on the D.A. chances of getting the conviction. Shorty-D wasn't what you would call a character witness, but his arrogance and way of life made him very believable.

David Chong stood up and said, "I have no questions for this witness your honor." Now it was time for the closing arguments, which was the most important part of a trial. This was the last chance Mike Worn and David Chong would have to convince the jury that D-Block was innocent or guilty.

Mike Worn started his argument by thanking the jury for their time and their patience. He went on to highlight the fact that there was no physical evidence connecting his client to the shooting.

He spoke about the D.A.'s only witness, which was a criminal that were caught in a long-term drug operation, and was caught with two loaded guns and thousands of dollars.

Worn went on to highlight the testimony given by Sabrina Barnes, that there was an altercation where a Jamaican man was assaulted by the YBM crew, hours before the shooting.

He ended his arguments telling the jury that they should take Tymeek's testimony with a grain of salt that he was so desperate to wiggle out of his wrong doings that he picked two individuals that had absolutely nothing to do with the shooting. Mike Worn had the stipulation read to the jury about the details of G-Pac's case that was ultimately dismissed by a judge at what is called an alibi hearing, attacking Ty's credibility.

He asked the jury to look at the facts and the lack of evidence when they make their decision, and if they were to do so, then there could only be one just verdict...which would be not guilty.

David Chong knew didn't have much to work with. He even felt D-Block was innocent, but he had a job to do. Chong figured the only way he could get a conviction was to play on the conscience of the jury, because the case was weak. He tried to somehow make them feel like a not guilty verdict would be like condoning the violence in the Rockaway's, but a guilty verdict would be sending a strong message to the Rockaway's, that they wouldn't get a fair trial in Queens Criminal court, when it came to solving the murders that was rapidly rising in the area.

After about a hour of charging the jury with the law, the judge gave them the case to deliberate. The jury room is where racism, Ignorance, boredom, and who gives a fuck, all goes down.

Some of the jurors believed he did it, and some didn't. The rest of them just wanted to go the hell home. The thing about the verdict is it has to be unanimous, everybody has to agree on one verdict, guilty or not guilty, and if they couldn't then it will be a mistrial.

D-Block was back in the bullpens doing push up's, trying to keep his nerves down. If you never waited for your verdict on a murder trial, then you'll never understand the feeling that somebody that did experienced.

That's a feeling that can't be verbalized in words. All of the young Goonz, and D-Block's family left the courtroom to have lunch on Queens blvd.

They talked about the case, what looked good and what didn't, and what jurors they liked or didn't like.

The first day of deliberations came and went with out of the jury reaching a verdict. On the second day, the jury wanted to have some of the testimony read back to them from Tymeek Jones and Shorty-D, but they still wasn't able to reach an unanimous verdict.

That night, Foe had mixed emotions. He and Ooh Wop were at the Q-Motor inn, smoking haze and sipping on some iced cold Nuvo. Foe knew from experience that two to three days of deliberations, meant that somebody was in there fighting for you and somebody wasn't.

If the majority of the jury members felt that you were guilty, then they would be in there trying to sway the rest of them to vote guilty.

Foe was laid back on the bed, in another world. Ooh Wop tried to bring him back to earth with that sugar mouth of hers, but he was far too gone. He never even noticed his cell phone ringing.

Somebody left him a text message, but he didn't notice that either. Ooh Wop picked up the phone and read the message aloud to Foe, (Any enemy of my friend...is an enemy of mine...C. C B.) The caller I.D. said Bandana Skeen.

Skeen was a nigga from Hammels Projects that Foe had mad love for. He wasn't affiliated with the Young Goonz, he had his own team in the middle of the projects, but Loyalty is an understatement to describe the bond that Skeen and Foe shared.

Foe didn't understand why Skeen would send him I a message like that out of the blue, and he damn sure couldn't figure out what CCB stood for. It was one o' clock in the morning, he was mentally drained, so as soon as Ooh Wop read the message, it went in one ear and out of the other.

Skeen was getting money in the Bronx, so Foe said

something to Ooh Wop in the sense of, "My nigga Skeen probably looking for a good connect on some dope." Which really didn't fit the message that was read to him, but hey, he had many on his mind with the trial, and possibly a verdict in the morning?

CHAPTER THIRTY

T he next morning, the courtroom was packed to capacity, as usual. D-block sat at the Defense table, looking tired of waking up four o' clock in the morning for the past week to start another long day of trial.

The Jury was in the jury room making progress. Four hours later, they sent the note to the judge. D-Block was escorted from the bullpens, back into the courtroom, for the reading of the note, which was procedure.

"I've just received a note at 1:45p.m saying that, "We the jury, has reached a verdict," said the lady Judge, who couldn't wait to have a drink inside of her chambers.

Mike Worn whispered in D-Blocks ear, "No matter what the verdict is ...try not to make any outburst."

D-Block didn't respond, he just stared at the juror's door, waiting for them to enter the courtroom for the last time. Everybody in the courtroom was on pins and needles, lost in their own thoughts when the back door of the court room flew open and banged hard against the wall.

The shit scared everybody, even Foe jumped. David thong's counterpart Phil Anderson ran into the courtroom in a frenzy, he walked to the prosecution table and whispered something into Chong's ear.

Chong's eyes got as wide as cartoon characters as he shot straight out of his seat, "Your Honor, the people needs a recess at this time," said Chong.

Mike Worn jumped out of his seat, "Absolutely not...there's no legal reason to stop a jury from rendering its verdict, so whatever Mr. Chong is trying to accomplish is unconstitutional." Worn objected.

"I'm afraid Mr. Worn is right...in my 23 years on the bench, I never stop a jury from returning its verdict Mr. Chong," said the judge. "Maybe if your request was made during deliberations, we could have had a hearing on whatever the matter is. But at this point, there's no way that I could intervene in a case like this."

Chong was furious, so out of desperation he screamed, "Tymeek Jones was murdered last night in the Bronx. And I feel that there should be a thorough investigation to see if his murder is in any way connected to the testimony he save here in this court room your Honor."

Nobody in the courtroom could believe their ears. Somebody smoked the nigga Ty that fast.

D-Block was pissed off, "Why the fuck would these niggas do some dumb shit like this while I'm still on trial," he thought as he turned around to look at Foe.

Foe gave D-Block a look that said, "It wasn't me," Foe mind went straight to G-Pac, who has been talking about killing Ty rat ass every since he took the stand.

Mike Worn jumped up, "Your Honor, My client and this case have absolutely nothing to do with Mr. Jones unfortunate death, and the verdict must be read without being tainted with this new information."

The Judge didn't believe for second that Ty's murder didn't have any thing to do with him testifying in her courtroom, but after hearing all the details of the case, she couldn't be sure If he was killed by the Young Goonz or the YBM crew.

"I'm sorry Mr. Chong, but Mr. Worn is right...bring in the jury," said the judge, as she gave D-Block a cold stare that said, "Boy you better pray they find you not guilty."

"D-Block was relieved that the jury wouldn't hear about Ty getting cooked." Thank you, sweet Jesus," was all he could think to himself as the jurors walked through the door.

Young Goonz

"Ooh Wop, being Foe's second brain, pulled his I-Phone off of his hip and scrolled down his text messages and showed Foe Skeen's message. He still didn't get it, or why she was showing him that shit at a time like this.

Ooh Wop used her thumb to cover the first part of the message, so all Foe could see was CCB. The trial had Foe's brain off balance, so he looked at her confused.

Ooh Wop whispered in his ear, "C C B... Click Clack Boom, "That's when it hit him like a ton of bricks, as he read the whole message from Bandana Skeen (Any enemy of my friend...is an enemy of mine. CC B) The D.A. said he was killed in the Bronx, and that's where Skeen was getting money at...small world. Foe deleted the message, and then put the phone back on his hip.

"Ladies and Gentlemen of the jury, have you reached your verdict?" The Judge asked.

"Yes your Honor, we have," said the Foreperson.

"Hand it to the bailiff please."

The bailiff took the verdict sheet, past it to the judge, waited for her to read it to herself then passed it back to the foreperson.

"I am now going to ask the defendant to rise and face the jury." The Judge cleared her throat, and then continued, "For the charge of murder in the second degree, how do you find the defendant?"

"We, the people of the jury find the defendant..."

To be continued....

Tears of a Hustler 5
"The Spades"
&
The Teflon Queen pt 2
Coming soon!

Now Available

Good2GoFilms Present:

BLACK BARBIE THE MOVIE STARRING SILK
WHITE
ORDER NOW FROM WWW.GOOD2GOFILMS.COM
$7.99

NO WAY OUT THE MOVIE
STARRING SILK WHITE

Good2go Publishing Order Form

Last
Name _____

First
Name _____ M.I. _____

Addres   Apt./Un
s _____ it _____

Cit   ZIP
y _____ State ____ Code _____

                                   E-
Phone ( ) _____ Mail _____

Method   of
payment   ❑   ❑   ❑
                Check   VISA   MasterCard

Credit   Exp.
Card # _____ Date _____

Name as it appears on
card _____

Signature _____

Item Name	Price	Qty.	Amount
TEARS OF A HUSTLER (AUTHOR SILK WHITE)	13.95		
TEARS OF A HUSTLER PT 2 (AUTHOR SILK WHITE)	13.95		
TEARS OF A HUSTLER PT 3 (AUTHOR SILK WHITE)	13.95		
TEARS OF A HUSTLER PT 4 (AUTHOR SILK WHITE)	13.95		
NEVER BE THE SAME (AUTHOR SILK WHITE)	13.95		
THE TEFLON QUEEN (AUTHOR SILK WHITE)	13.95		
MARRIED TO DA STREETS (AUTHOR SILK WHITE)	13.95		
HE LOVES ME, HE LOVES YOU NOT (AUTHOR MYCHEA)	13.95		
Subtotal			
Tax			

Shipping (FREE) U.S. MEDIA MAIL	
Total	

MAKE CHECK PAYABLE:

GOOD2GO PUBLISHING
7311 W GLASS LANE
LAVEEN, AZ 85339

CPSIA information can be obtained
at www.ICGtesting.com
Printed in the USA
LVOW10s0912081017
551661LV00010B/399/P